NIGHT COMES DOWN

A C.T. FERGUSON CRIME NOVEL

THE C.T. FERGUSON MYSTERIES
BOOK 13

TOM FOWLER

WideningGyreMedia

Editing by Chase Nottingham

Cover Design by 100Covers

Published by Widening Gyre Media

Paperback ISBN: 978-1-953603-50-0

For Lisa and Isabel, who always keep things bright.

CHAPTER 1

MY PHONE VIBRATED on my nightstand again.

I grumbled and picked the blasted thing up long enough to silence it. This would only buy me a minute or two, tops. My wife Gloria—and it felt awesome to think of her as my wife—muttered something incoherent. Sure enough, another call came in. It was T.J., just like it had been the previous few times. "I know how to use the alarm feature, you know."

"You're late," my secretary said.

"A perk of being the boss is you're always on time."

"It's after nine-thirty. You're almost always here by nine."

"I'm jetlagged."

"You've been using that excuse since you got back from your honeymoon."

"I'm well aware," I said.

"It was two months ago," she pointed out.

"The doctor says I'm particularly sensitive to long flights."

"Bring a note, then. I'll see you soon." She broke the connection.

"Dammit." T.J. was right. I'd made a habit of showing up at irregular times since Gloria and I returned from Hawaii.

Jetlag served as a convenient—and accurate—excuse the first two days. Since then, however, I simply struggled to find motivation. I was happier than I'd ever been personally, and the cynical part of me wondered if this would have some deleterious effect on my professional life.

So far, it had. I would make this trade again a thousand times over, of course, but I needed to get back into the swing of things with my job.

I drank a cup of coffee, left one on Gloria's nightstand, threw clothes on, and kissed my sleepy wife goodbye. The drive to the office was quick, a perk of leaving after rush hour ended. T.J.'s yellow Mustang sat at one end of the lot, and I parked my black Audi S4 sedan beside it. We occupied the second floor above a car repair shop. It wasn't the most glamorous location, but Manny—the owner—was a good guy, and he didn't seem to mind some of the more interesting aspects of my job.

I opened the outer door. Another lay ahead, and it took customers into the body shop. Off to the side was a set of metal stairs. I climbed them and opened our second-story door. T.J. looked up when I walked in. She was twenty and pretty but not so much people would stop and gape at her. Her long blonde hair was tied into its usual high ponytail, and the ribbon matched her red shirt. T.J. stood five-nine, and she looked tall even sitting behind her desk.

I stopped and took in the place. She'd put a small Christmas tree near the coffee maker and even decorated it with colorful lights and glass balls. A streamer made of small Santa cut-outs hung from one side of the office to the other. Garland encircled the main door and the one to the restroom. "Someone's been busy on a Monday morning," I said as I slung my bag off my shoulder.

"One of us needs to be. No doctor's note?"

"My dog ate it."

"You don't have a dog," she said.

"You should work for a detective agency," I said. She fixed me with a neutral expression. "I know . . . I haven't exactly rushed back into things."

"That's an understatement, boss. You've pretty much been loafing."

I prepared another cup of coffee. "Don't apply for any jobs in the diplomatic arena."

"I sent you the financials for the last couple months. We're still in the green."

"Even with me paying all your salary?" For the first six months of her tenure, my friend Melinda's foundation covered half of T.J.'s wages. They'd gotten her out of a bad situation and trained her, and then I took a chance on her— one which paid off very well.

"You could even afford to give me a raise," she said with an artificially sweet smile.

"If you're nice," I said, "maybe Santa will leave a little something extra in your stocking this year." T.J. deserved a bonus. I'd figure out a way to get her one. With Christmas about two weeks away, I still had time to do the math.

"A big case would be nice. You seem like you need a little motivation. It would definitely help the bottom line before the end of the year."

"Great. Go out and find us one."

She pointed toward the entry. "Your name's on the door. I think it means you need to do all the searching."

I scanned the spreadsheets T.J. sent me. While Gloria and I spent two weeks in paradise and a few more days recovering from the flight back, T.J. worked some small cases. Before I left, I told her to make sure it was something she could do from her desk. She'd picked up a lot from me since she started, and I had to admit she made a better student than I did a teacher. "Maybe we'll get lucky in the next few days. It's almost Christmas, after all."

"Here's hoping," T.J. said.

"You're thinking of your bonus." She bobbed her head, and I made a tsking motion with my two forefingers. "Not in the spirit of the season."

"What can I say? I guess commercialism finally got me."

"Don't feel bad," I said. "You and everyone else."

———

I left work a little early to head home and change. Gloria reminded me we were due to attend some event the mayor was putting on. Considering he rushed our marriage application and performed the ceremony himself, I felt a tiny sense of obligation even if I didn't like the man. I met him on a case a couple years ago when he was just a rich business owner. He didn't leave a good impression then, and he'd done little to improve my initial assessment in the intervening time.

Gloria used to organize fundraisers for his charitable endeavors, so she enjoyed a different—and better—relationship with Vincent Davenport. I arrived at my Federal Hill rowhouse to find Gloria half-dressed in the bedroom. When I gave her a lascivious wink, she smiled and shook her head. "Later. We need to get nicer clothes on."

"Can't we be late?"

"No. Davenport wants to do more work with my company. Non-political stuff . . . I told him I wasn't interested in campaign dinners. It'll look bad if we show up late with our hair in disarray."

"It would mostly be yours," I pointed out. "I keep mine cut pretty short exactly for situations like this."

"Uh-huh." Gloria looked at the collection of dresses she kept at my house. I didn't have nearly the closet space she enjoyed at her much larger home in the tony Brooklandville area of Baltimore County. Still, she selected a sharp royal blue number. I doffed my sweater and jeans for a black Tommy Hilfiger suit and chose a tie to go with her dress. A few minutes later, I was ready, which meant the waiting would begin.

Gloria needed to adjust her makeup, fix her hair, check her appearance a hundred times, and only then could we leave. "You look great," I told her on several occasions. It didn't seem to matter. The dress came down to her knees and fit her well with its neckline high enough to be professional but just low enough to be interesting. "When does this thing start?"

"Six," she said as she fluttered between stations.

I glanced at my watch. Five-twenty. "Where is it?"

"The headquarters of his bakery."

We had plenty of time to get there so long as Gloria finished reasonably soon. "I'm heading downstairs," I said. After about ten minutes, she joined me on the first level. We got our coats on. I shrugged into my usual Ralph Lauren number, and Gloria opted for a waist-length faux fur.

"We'll take my car," she said. "I'll drive there. You can get us home." Her red Mercedes AMG coupe sat beside my S4 on the parking pad behind the house. In case the color, speed, and sound of the car didn't communicate its rocket-like nature loudly enough, the sleek shape of it drove the point home. I loved getting behind the wheel every chance I could. Gloria didn't drive much slower than I would have. We breezed into Canton, found parking nearby, and walked up to the D&S headquarters. Davenport—along with his former partner—built a single location into a regional baking empire.

The crowd gathered in a large conference room. I'd sat in smaller lecture halls in college. A Christmas tree occupied much of the right side of the stage, and various holiday decorations abounded. This evening's talk would probably be as boring as most of what I endured during my Loyola University days. At the appointed hour, a tall, slender black man I didn't recognize took the stage. He wore a suit I would be proud to own. The gentleman introduced himself as Albert Everett, the COO of D&S. He made a few opening remarks and then introduced the mayor to an impressive round of applause. I offered a golf clap to keep up appearances.

The lights flickered as Davenport took the stage. He was an age peer of my parents. A little gray intruded on his dark hair, and he wore glasses. They were the only obvious concessions to age. Davenport moved like a man who exercised regularly, and he flashed a ready smile as he grabbed the mike. "I guess I need to remind Albert to pay the electric bill." Everett spread his hands as the audience laughed.

"Thank you for coming tonight, everyone. I don't get down here a lot anymore. Being the mayor takes up most of my time." A fresh round of applause rang out. I declined to join in this one. As a non-voter, I felt it my duty to avoid clapping for any politician more than once. "I put D and S into a blind trust once I got elected, and I'd like to thank the leadership team for keeping the company moving.

"Every holiday season, I do a lot of reflecting. Many people do. I'm coming up on the halfway mark of my first term as mayor, and I'd like to think I've done a good job so far." This drew another ovation. I groaned. The mention of a first term implied a second. Gloria clapped enough for both of us. "This doesn't have anything to do with why we're here today, though. I can make a political speech anywhere. Seriously, as the mayor, they can't stop me." I rolled my eyes as polite chuckles greeted Davenport's alleged joke.

"Twenty years ago, I thought I'd taken D and S as far as I could. I'd bought out my old partner, and the company was doing well. I thought we had another gear or two in us, but I didn't have the ability to unlock it. One man did. Dale Willett was a product line manager back then. He came to me with an idea for some major process improvements. They came with some serious budget requests. I liked his ideas, so I greenlit everything.

"We still use the Willett method today. Other businesses talk about stuff like Lean Six Sigma. We had our own back then, and it was all thanks to Dale Willett. Now, you might be wondering where he is. The truth is, I'm not sure. He left the company a couple years after we adopted his process improvements. I tried to invite him today but never heard back. Dale . . . wherever you are . . . thanks for what you did for this company. I hope we have another twenty years of success. By then, maybe I can retire."

Davenport left the stage to more applause. Albert Everett took the mike again and invited everyone to a reception on the production floor. "We'll even let you take some bread home," he added to a round of moderate laughter.

"Are we staying for this?" I asked my wife.

She shook her head. "I just wanted to come for the speech. Let's go somewhere else. We're all dressed up."

"For now." She grinned as we stood. The lights flickered a couple more times. Everett made another joke about the electric bill, but he looked confused as he walked off the stage. "Maybe you can help the mayor raise enough funds to pay BGE."

Gloria smiled, and we walked out of the venue hand-in-hand.

After driving to Fells Point for dinner, Gloria and I walked the streets. A chill had settled in since the sun went down a few hours before. The wind off the harbor made it worse, but we lingered nearby to enjoy the view and browse the shops. All featured varying levels of Christmas decorations. Employees in the more crowded venues needed an injection of holiday cheer. I bought my cousin Rich a record from the Sound Garden. He hated when I called him a hipster for listening to his music on vinyl, so I made a mental note to write a comment into his card.

We stopped into the Daily Grind for coffee. Yielding to the late hour, Gloria ordered decaf. I made no such concessions. Caffeine could be enjoyed at any time. Besides, as an experienced coffee drinker, I had no trouble falling asleep shortly after downing a mug. Gloria smirked as I sipped my latte. "Pretty late to be having that at your age, isn't it?"

"Thirty-two is still part of my prime years," I said. My birthday passed with a moderate amount of fanfare nine days before. This wasn't a milestone, but it was the first time I really got to celebrate the earth making it around the sun another time since I turned thirty. The prior year, I marked thirty-one in a rehab hospital after getting shot. Zero out of ten; would not recommend.

"You're lucky to have a much younger wife," Gloria said as she linked her free arm with mine.

"Enjoy your twenties while you can. If my mental math is right—and it basically always is—you've got about half a year until you join me in being over the hill."

"You'll always be a little farther down the other side."

I was about to reply when the city got dark.

Street lights and traffic signals worked one instant and

were off the next. People stopped in their tracks to gaze about. In Fells Point, restaurants and shops gave off enough illumination to keep the sidewalks lit. Every place we could see still had power. "I think your buddy Davenport needs to worry about the city paying its electric bill," I said.

"Weird." Gloria looked around. "Traffic lights are out as far as I can see. This is no isolated incident."

At the intersection ahead of us, a city surveillance camera sat atop a pole. Normally, each gave off a blue light from the top. Nothing. I frowned. The closed-circuit system should have been separate from the lighting. "This *is* weird," I said. "Camera's off, too." I pulled Gloria toward a tavern with a rooftop deck. We climbed the stairs and stepped out onto the sparsely-crowded balcony area.

It gave us a much better view of the city, and everything looked darker than normal. Less populated areas of Baltimore wouldn't enjoy the benefit of stores and eateries to keep the sidewalks lit. They'd be dark. The more immediate problem was traffic signals. People in Maryland were bad enough drivers when the red, yellow, and green bulbs worked. Cops would need to direct traffic at a bunch of intersections. I called Rich, a lieutenant in the Baltimore police's homicide division, and it went right to voicemail. His evening must've gotten much worse in the last few minutes.

"Let's go home," Gloria said.

I agreed, and we picked up her car from a nearby garage. The trip proved a little adventurous but not awful. Other drivers seemed to get the seriousness of what happened, and we didn't pass any accidents on the way back to Federal Hill. We went into the house. "I hope things are back to normal tomorrow," I said as we shrugged out of our coats.

"What if they're not?" my wife asked.

"No idea," I said, "but it'll probably be chaos."

CHAPTER 2

I TRIED CALLING Rich a few more times and finally got through. "Little busy," he said when he picked up. I couldn't remember the last time I heard him out of breath.

"Gloria and I were in Fells Point when the lights went out. It seemed pretty widespread."

"It is. The whole city is affected. No street lights, no traffic signals, no cameras. There could be other systems down, too. We just don't know yet."

"Holy shit," I said.

"Yeah. It's all hands on deck at this point. We need to direct traffic at the busiest intersections. There are hundreds of those. Some areas are going to be pretty dark, so there's a concern about crime going up. We need to beef up the police presence there. Plus, all the other shit already on my plate."

"Anybody know what happened?"

"If they do," Rich said, "it hasn't made its way down to me yet. Shit like this is above my pay grade. I guess the commissioner's involved, but it's going to be a lot of city workers figuring it out."

I thought about the sequence of events. The lights flickered at D&S, but it was a private company. The sun went down early in December. Dusk settled in before five o'clock, and in areas without a lot of ambient illumination, it could be quite dark by seven or eight . . . which was around the time everything went off. I didn't know how the city set up its systems. A lot of them were probably older, poorly designed years ago, and upgraded over time without really being replaced.

In an ideal world, traffic signals, streetlights, and CCTV cameras would all be controlled separately. If I were in charge of the network, I would've insisted on segmenting them off with a robust firewall or two restricting all but the most necessary traffic among them and an intrusion prevention system to keep malicious actors at bay. I also would've ensured redundancy. It would make management easier, and it would also leave the city less vulnerable in case the plague of malware reared its ugly head. "Rich, has anyone thought about ransomware?"

He snorted. "I haven't heard anything about it. Wouldn't surprise me. It's been on the rise for a while, right?"

"Right," I said, "and it's been successful on the city's networks before."

"You'd think they would've learned from the experience," my cousin said. "Look, I have a lot of shit to handle. We all do. This is going to be hell until it gets straightened out. If I get a chance to talk to someone higher up, I'll mention the idea of ransomware, but I don't know what kind of response I'll get. Some of these old cops can barely turn their laptops on without calling the help desk. Gotta go." He broke the connection.

I never envied Rich his job. Policing was difficult and thankless, and working as a homicide lieutenant probably ramped up both factors. Tonight, however, I felt sorry for him. If no one knew what happened, it meant no one worked on a fix. Daylight tomorrow would bring at least some respite, but the city would be in the soup again when night came down.

As I changed out of my good clothes, I hoped the whole mess got resolved quickly.

———

Gloria wanted me to stay in, but I ventured outside.

Power remained on at our house and others I could see. A short walk showed the lights still on at neighborhood eateries. Whatever issue plagued the city, it hadn't filtered down to the rest of the electric grid. Yet. I didn't want to think about how dreadful the security would be there. Industrial systems tended to be more vulnerable than most people thought. Stop signs governed the intersections nearby, but a few blocks away, police would be directing traffic and trying to avoid a spate of accidents.

I walked back inside, and Gloria hugged me. "How is it out there?"

"Pretty normal around here," I said. "Darker than it usually is, but not much else. We're lucky. This is a good area. Plenty of light sources."

We sat on the couch and turned on the local news. "A mysterious outage has city officials scrambling for answers," the male anchor announced. "Power remains on for almost all customers. However, all traffic and street lights in the city are out. We've checked in with the surrounding areas, and their services have not been interrupted."

It was probably prudent for the broadcast to leave out the CCTV details. Things would be bad enough without people realizing they might be able to get away with petty crimes normally seen by the electric eyes. Other areas remaining unaffected reinforced my original idea. Some sort of malware ran amok in the city's systems. Most of these attacks happened because someone opened an attachment or file they shouldn't have. Baltimore's IT staff would be pulling some serious overtime between tracking down the root cause and bringing everything back online.

"We've reached out to Mayor Vincent Davenport," the female anchor said. "So far, his office has not returned our requests for comment. No city officials are talking about the problem at the moment."

"Let's hope this means they're all working on a resolution, Jane," her partner at the desk said.

"We have reporters on the scene throughout Baltimore. There is an increased police presence and not just for directing traffic. Our team coverage begins with . . . "

Gloria turned the volume down. "You must have a theory. This seems right up your alley."

"Some kind of virus." I shrugged. "Usually triggered by an insider who didn't mean to do anything wrong."

"Nevertheless, it could be malicious?" she asked.

"Sure. Wouldn't be the first time the city has drawn this kind of fire."

"They might need your help."

I waved a hand. "They have plenty of people on the payroll who can fix this."

"Maybe they don't. I know you've never liked Davenport, but I also know you love Baltimore. Your sense of duty is going to take over at some point. You won't be able to sit idly by." Concern knitted her brows.

"No one's asked for my help yet," I said.

"What if they do?"

"First of all, I'd be surprised. But if they were in a bad

spot and needed a hand, I'm sure I'd answer the call." I paused. "I'd be certain to rub Davenport's face in it, too."

Gloria grinned. "Of course you would."

"He'd get over it. I don't think any of this is going to be necessary. IT departments are better at finding and eliminating malware today. It might take a little while, but they'll get things running again. Whatever idiot opened the cat picture with the virus attached will get a stern talking-to, and everything will go back to normal until the next time it happens."

"Pretty cynical outlook," Gloria said.

"It's pretty much how these things go down." I shrugged.

"Let's hope it goes better this time."

"Yes," I said. "Let's hope."

———

My phone vibrating on my nightstand roused me from a deep sleep yet again.

My bleary eyes focused on the windows first. Still dark outside. This meant it was too early for T.J. to chide me for not coming in yet. The screen showed BPD Captain Leon Sharpe as the caller and the time as 3:54 AM. I couldn't summon many reasons for him to be phoning, but none of them were good. I hoped nothing happened to Rich. He might have listed me as his next of kin. "Leon, it's not even four," I mumbled.

"I know how to tell time, thanks." His booming voice didn't even betray a hint of weariness. "Can you come down here?"

"What's going on? Is Rich all right?"

"He's fine," Sharpe said. "He mentioned your idea to me, and I ran it up the chain. Let's just say it has some legs."

"Me and my big mouth," I said.

"We want you to consult on this, and the city will pay your rate."

I yawned. "Consulting hours are available on the fifth Friday of the month from noon until twelve-oh-five."

"I'm serious," he said. While Sharpe never sounded like he was kidding, I couldn't recall hearing more gravitas in his voice. "The mayor asked for you personally."

"Are you trying to get me to say no?"

"You're the one who floated the malware idea. I think it took a little while for it to catch on, but I can tell you we're on board. You're good at this sort of stuff."

"I'm sure the city already employs people who can take care of this."

"Not my area," Sharpe said. "I don't do HR for the mayor. He asked for you. I presume you're going to say yes." His tone indicated the captain might pick me up and snap me in two if I declined. He could probably do it, and I didn't care to find out.

"All right," I said. "I'm in. Make sure there's coffee."

"There will be. Come to City Hall as soon as you can." Sharpe ended the call. I set my phone down and sighed. Gloria stirred beside me.

"Looks like I need to save the city after all," I whispered.

"Mmm." Her sleepy eyes fluttered. "They called you?"

"Sharpe did, yeah. I'm headed to City Hall. Your buddy asked for me personally. I'm sure it felt like passing a kidney stone. Part of me wants to go just to see him look like he's in pain."

"You're doing the right thing," Gloria said. She stretched and snuggled a pillow under her head. "Let me know how it goes . . . and please be careful. It might be pretty crazy out there."

"It's four AM," I said. "I'll be all right." I brushed my teeth and changed into a hoodie and jeans. If I were going to assume the role of a well-paid IT consultant, I needed to look the part. I could always fake the general malaise and frustration with client management's stupidity. "I'm off to save Baltimore," I told Gloria. "You can take me for my cape fitting when I get home."

She smiled and went back to sleep. We heroes led difficult lives.

CHAPTER 3

I PARKED in a garage near City Hall. The walk to the building was short but felt longer because it was the middle of the damn night. I checked in with the guard downstairs, told him why I was here, and he directed me to a room on the third floor. Normally, I would take the stairs on such a short jaunt, but this morning, I rode the elevator. I'd only been inside the building a couple times—and not for years—so I followed my nose and the scent of coffee when I stepped off.

Several people sat huddled around a large conference table which could accommodate at least twenty. Vincent Davenport occupied the head. Of course he would. The police commissioner, a burly half-Asian man named David Ngo, sat to his right, and Leon Sharpe dominated the poor seat beside his boss. Ngo wasn't a small man, but he looked average next to the captain. A few other people I'd never seen before were on the opposite side. A short black fellow with glasses huddled over a laptop. He blew out a deep breath and looked relieved as I walked in. He must have been the IT staffer.

I eschewed sitting down and poured myself a disposable cup of coffee. Powdered creamer was the only option, so I used it and hoped for the best. The result turned out to be exactly as mediocre as I expected. I slid onto a chair beside Leon Sharpe. The commissioner—whom I'd never formally met—frowned at me. "Can we get going?" I said. "I'd like to save the city before lunch."

"We don't need the attitude," Ngo said.

"Yet you do need the expertise. Consider the snark a bonus you don't have to pay for."

Davenport held up a hand. "Mister Ferguson, thanks for coming in. I know we haven't always seen eye to eye. I'm going to speak for everyone when I say I appreciate any insights you can offer us with this problem." Ngo's face suggested he'd recently chugged an entire bottle of lemon juice, but he didn't object.

"I presume we have an IT guy here," I said. "Honestly, I figured the city could sort this out without bringing in a handsome and expensive consultant."

"No offense to Charlie there, but we've had a lot of brain drain in the IT department recently. Bunch of guys have left, including some of our most senior staff. It's a problem, which means this attack comes at basically the worst possible time."

"I'm a programmer by trade," Charlie said, pushing his glasses up on his nose. "Been working as a software support engineer and forensic guy. Today, I'm trying to be the malware expert."

"We're all here to resolve the issue," Davenport said. "This is our top priority until it's resolved. The press already knows a little bit about what's going on. All comments and requests should be handled through my PR office." Bad publicity would be pretty far down on the list of worries if we didn't get the whole mess resolved soon. Leave it to Davenport to mention the media angle. "Charlie, can you tell us what you know so far?"

"We're screwed." He spread his hands. "Everything affected is on different parts of the network. I think it had to start as different attack vectors. It would be hard for someone to move laterally and turn everything off."

"But not impossible," I said.

Charlie shook his head. "Technically not, no, but I think it's unlikely. The CCTV system uses totally different credentials, for one thing."

"What about admin accounts?"

"No indications of someone using one to do this kind of damage. I've checked the logs, too." He plugged his laptop into a projector, and we could all see his desktop on the large white screen. "I've been looking at a high level, in any case. Let's drill down into something we know is affected. I'm going to check on the traffic signals."

We watched as Charlie opened a remote window to connect to another computer. When he tried, the login attempt failed, and the normal Windows desktop changed from medium blue to black. A large white skull and red lock filled the screen. A message followed a few seconds later.

Baltimore is hacked. Things will only get worse. It's time to pay in more ways than one. If you want access back, pay us in Bitcoin to a wallet we will send to the robber baron mayor's inbox. We'll tell you how much later. Stew on this for a while and realize we're being nice right now. When night comes down on your city, we may not be so generous. You have twenty-four hours to think about it before we cause more chaos.

"This is new," Charlie said. No one responded. They didn't need to.

———

"Ransomware," I said.

"Shit." Charlie took his glasses off and rubbed his nose. "I know we got hit by something a while back. It'll be tough, but we might be able to recover from this."

"I want to know who's doing it," Ngo said.

"Most ransomware attacks come from nation-state actors," I said. "Sometimes, it might be a hacktivist group."

"What countries would want to cripple our city?"

I shrugged. "Outside my area of expertise. We may not know their motivations other than the unrest they've already caused. I think we should focus smaller. Any groups have a grudge against Baltimore?"

"Why would they?" Davenport asked.

"Well, they might not like you." He frowned, but I continued. "It actually could be something as simple as a personality conflict. Also, police tactics are coming under fire all across the country." Ngo scowled. "I haven't heard of any incidents recently, but you never know what's going to make a story and get people riled up."

"I run a tight ship," the commissioner said.

"But you haven't been here very long," I pointed out, "and the men who held the job before you made their share of mistakes. It might not be something recent."

"You sound like you've been a hacker."

"I have." Ngo narrowed his eyes at me. "The details aren't important, but I've seen how these groups work from the inside."

"I have a concern," Charlie said. "So far, they've taken down systems on three different segments. How the hell do we keep them from causing more damage?"

"We have to assume your network is compromised," I said. "Most security is predicated on keeping people out. We do a much worse job at containing them if they manage to pull off a breach."

"I'm open to suggestions here."

"Change all admin passwords. Something strong and complex. Remotely logoff any privileged users. Send out-of-band communications about what's going on and how to re-authenticate."

"All right." Charlie nodded as he typed a note. "I'll also check with our firewall team . . . what's left of them, anyway. We should be able to do something to make sure everything stays segmented. If we can keep whatever this is from spreading, we can contain it here and worry about cleaning up just what's down so far."

"Which is still a lot," a man on the other side of the table said. Based on his sharp sweater and pressed chinos at this ungodly hour, I pegged him as some kind of accountant. Why he'd been invited was not the mystery the mayor summoned me to solve, however.

"All right," Davenport said, "let's start there. If we can isolate this ransomware, it'll be a lot easier to clean up."

"Sir, we can't pay the ransom," Ngo offered. "I know they haven't told us how much yet, but we can't enable these bastards."

I hoped the mayor would agree. Instead, he said, "Let's see how this all unfolds, David. We need to keep all our options on the table, even if some of them are distasteful."

Ngo replied with a semi-polite, "Yes, sir." It was more than Davenport deserved in the moment.

————

"Wow, Ferguson. I haven't heard your voice in a while. Four years?"

"Sounds right." I'd excused myself from the meeting to call Ai Deng. During my thirty-nine months in Hong Kong, she was my closest friend in the hacker group we worked with. Deng was petite, pretty, and very smart. She also remained far more plugged in to the global scene than I did. While we'd chatted online a few times since I left Hong Kong, this marked our first real conversation since the Chinese police kicked the door in and accelerated the timeline for my return to the States.

"How are you?"

"Married . . . if you can believe it."

A light chuckle filled the line. "I'm not sure I can. You never seemed the type. I knew I wasn't the only girl you took to bed while you were here."

"I'm a one-woman man now, Deng," I said. "Besides, I'm not calling to catch up. This is about something happening right now."

"What's going on?"

"Baltimore got hit by a ransomware attack. It's . . . not too bad all things considered. I don't want it to get worse."

"If you want to fly me out there for a consult," she said, "I'm a first-class girl all the way."

I smiled. "I'll make sure the city bean counters know. I was wondering if you'd heard anything about some kind of activity recently. Especially from our former friends, but not limited to them."

"Most of those guys aren't my friends anymore."

"Mine, either," I said. "You're the only one I've stayed in any sort of contact with, but I know you're a lot more into what happens over there than I am. Our local police commissioner wants to think some other country is coming after us, but I don't see it. I think it's more likely to be a bunch of people with some powerful software and a grudge."

"We don't hear much about Baltimore," she said. "No offense to your city, but you're not exactly New York, LA, DC, Chicago . . . do I need to go on?"

"No. I get it. We're pretty provincial here, so a lot of people would be offended by what you said even if it's true. Can you keep an ear to the ground? See if you can pick up anything? I'd love to know who we're up against and what we might be looking at in terms of capability and motivation."

"For you, Ferguson? I'll find out."

"Be careful," I said even though I knew she would. Deng was a woman operating in a field dominated by antisocial men, most of whom objectified her every chance they got. She'd done well for herself. "If you find something, let me know as soon as you can. We're trying to contain this, and the city's staff is pretty depleted."

"I'm on it. Good to talk to you again."

"You, too." I ended the call and returned to the conference room. "I have a colleague overseas," I told the assembled people. "She hasn't heard anything about a group coming after us, but she's going to see what she can find out."

"How do we know she's not behind it all?" Ngo said.

"Because she has principles," I said. "It's why we didn't fit in with most of the people we worked with."

Ngo thrust a finger at me. "I've got my eye on you."

"It's your time, but it's the city's money. I think there are better uses for it."

Before the commissioner could respond, Sharpe broke in. "Thanks for asking around, C.T."

"Sure," I said. "Now, let's see just how badly we're screwed."

CHAPTER 4

"I THINK we're screwed pretty bad," Charlie said, keeping his voice down.

He and I huddled around his laptop at one end of the conference table. Conversations continued about twenty feet away, but I tuned them out. "It's not just the traffic signals being down. People see it, and it's the obvious result. This attack knocked out the resources those systems run on."

"You think it might have been an inside job?"

He paled but eventually bobbed his head. "We can't rule it out."

"Someone could've fingerprinted your network and learned all this," I said. "If they did it over a long enough period of time, their scans could blend in with the normal noise on a network."

"Low and slow," Charlie said.

"Exactly. Hard to detect. You have another way to check the logs?"

He pondered my question for a moment. "I think so. I have access to a dashboard someone created. We can probably get in there . . . if it's not already owned, too." Charlie opened a browser and authenticated. A busy webpage filled his screen. "Not my design," he added.

"I should hope not."

"Bosses like to have all their info in one place." He pointed to the mess on display. "Things like this are the result." A few clicks later, Charlie entered credentials again, and a site called *Baltimore City Security Incident and Event Management* came up. "I'm in. This still seems to be working."

"All right," I said. "We can't count on this remaining up forever. If you can export what we find somewhere else, I would." He nodded. "Attacks like these don't come out of the blue. There's a lot of research and recon before any malicious packets arrive."

"Which should appear in the logs," Charlie said.

"Right. You want to find extra scanning activity, lots of traffic at odd hours, increases in failed logins, a high volume of password changes, lateral movement by accounts you wouldn't expect . . . factors like those." His head bobbed fractionally as he worked. "The mayor said you've lost a lot of IT folks recently. Insiders would speed the recon up. Any of them likely to hand over a network diagram to a bunch of hackers?"

"Can't think of any. We need to check out one of the computers. See what's really going on."

"If it really is ransomware, there are a few popular strains in the wild. We'll have something to go on."

"I need my lab computer," he said. "Has forensic analysis tools on it, and it's isolated from the network in case something bad happens."

"Let's go," I said.

We left the conference room and rode the elevator to the basement. Charlie used his badge to enter a data center—he insisted I wait outside, and I appreciated his dedication to security protocol—and retrieved a hard drive. We then walked down the hall to an office. Computers, spare parts, and other equipment littered the area. Six desks were spaced out in the large room, but only two held enough clutter to indicate someone used them. The rest got converted into a fairly disorganized storage system. "I'm here," he said, and he dropped into an uncomfortable-looking chair. A tower PC and laptop sat on the desk, along with a keyboard, mouse, three monitors, and enough detritus to open a spare parts shop.

I hunted for a nicer seat, found something which didn't look too repellent, and wheeled it to Charlie's station. He connected the drive he took from the data center to a reader plugged into the desktop model. A good forensic technician never worked off the original. It got preserved as evidence once a bit-by-bit copy finished. Charlie started the process. "Looks like it'll run for about an hour," he announced despite the fact I could see the timer. "I'd like to have some idea what we're up against."

"All the ransomware out there encrypts data," I said. "Unless you have a quantum computer hiding down here, the sun will swallow the earth before we crack their crypto. The really pernicious ones also encipher your backups and make it so you can't restore your way out of the problem."

"I'll have to check on those." He opened a browser and consulted some good websites for information. "Just want to know what the common protocols and attack vectors are. Whether or not we can use our backups, I don't want this shit to spread anywhere else on the network."

"Might be hard to contain. Even if we've isolated the affected areas, one email attachment to the wrong employee in another division will most likely screw us even worse."

"We can't block email attachments," Charlie said.

"You *can*," I said. "Whether you should from a business perspective isn't a question an outsider like me can answer."

He grunted and looked at some more websites. "Seems unusual we haven't gotten a ransom demand yet."

"There's supposed to be something in the mayor's inbox eventually. Either way, I hope it doesn't mean there's more damage to come."

"You think it might?"

"I think we need to prepare for the possibility this is going to be a lot bigger than it currently is. It might be an opening volley. Proof of concept. Now, the attackers are learning what worked and what might not have, and they'll come back with something bigger. The systems which are down now are inconvenient, but the city can still operate and do most things. If someone really wanted to throw a wrench in the works, there are much higher-value targets."

"You're scaring me now," Charlie said.

"Good. It's a pretty frightening proposition."

"I'm going to check on something in the data center." He locked his PC before standing. "Wait here." During my first case, Rich's failure to secure his computer while I sat nearby gave me a way into the BPD's network I still enjoyed to this day. Charlie wouldn't be so careless. I appreciated the caution. If more employees behaved in a similar manner, the city might have a chance to get through this mess with a minimum of damage.

I nosed around the area while I waited for my host to return. The empty desks held stacks of supplies for printers, copiers, and similar office machines. There was plenty of shelving to hold everything, but the *animal, vegetable, mineral* organization system currently in use introduced a ton of inefficiency. I wondered how Charlie could work here every day and not yearn to fix it. No one would tell me I had OCD, but I couldn't walk by such a disaster and not try to bring some order to the chaos. I discovered a box of granola bars which were due to expire soon. I grabbed a couple, opened one, and downed it pretty quickly.

"We might be royally screwed," Charlie said as he walked back in a moment later. "Backup server is inaccessible. I might be able to get to specific records, but I'm not counting on it."

"This is going to get worse before it gets better," I said, "and we haven't even considered the inevitable demand. Someone needs to tell the mayor and the bean counters." I pointed at Charlie and dropped my thumb onto my forefinger. "I nominate you."

———

I was still sitting with Charlie when my phone buzzed. Gloria called. I stepped away from his desk to answer. "It's early for you. Seven-twenty."

"Early for you, too," she said with an alluring sleepy husk to her voice. "Everything all right?"

"With me? Yes. With the city? Definitely not."

"Is this still related to the lights going out?"

"And the traffic signals," I said, "and the CCTV system. Yeah." I walked a little farther away and lowered my voice. "We suspect it's a ransomware attack."

"Oh, my gosh." Gloria's voice sounded more awake now. "Are you there to help them get rid of it?"

"I think my role is still fluid. The police commissioner doesn't seem to want me here. As long as Davenport thinks I can add value, I'm good. The city has apparently lost a lot of IT workers over the last couple months. They're running a skeleton crew, so this is happening at the worst possible time."

"Sounds like you might be a while."

"Probably," I said. "I don't know how long. I'm happy to consult and do what I can, but I'm not an incident responder, and I'm not some lab guy who's spent the last decade reverse engineering malware. At some point, the city might need a person with more specialized expertise than I can bring to the table." *Argue for your limitations, and sure enough, they're yours,* I thought. Richard Bach's wisdom played in my head often during my recovery from getting shot. This marked the first time I applied it to something technological. While I took computer science and even earned a master's degree in it, I remained largely self-taught at the darker side of the profession.

"I'm sure you'll have a breakthrough," Gloria said. "There's no one more qualified to help the city." I smiled. A little more wind filled my sails. "I don't know a lot about ransomware, but this seems pretty light for an attack so far . . . right?"

"It is. Makes me think it's going to get worse soon. Even with a full crew, I doubt the workers could lock everything down in time, especially if the malware is already active and waiting." I wondered if Charlie kicked off any thorough scans. Most programs were easy enough to evade for a cunning adversary, but the city's antivirus suite could pick off the low-hanging fruit.

"Maybe we should go to my house for a while, then."

"I think it's a good idea," I admitted. Gloria lived in the county, so any problems plaguing the city wouldn't bother us there. "You go when you're ready, and I'll meet you there whenever I'm able to get away."

"All right," my wife said. "Be careful, C.T. I love you."

"Love you, too." I ended the call and returned to Charlie's desk. He remained hard at work. His screen showed a Remote Desktop connection which allowed him to manage a server. "Did you run any kind of malware scan?"

He nodded without taking his eyes from the monitor. "One of the first things I did. Ran it on everything I could think of and could still connect to."

"Nothing yet?"

"Nada."

"Damn. I was hoping we'd be able to pick off something."

"It'd be nice," he said. "All the same . . . I'm not surprised. Our software is signature-based."

The application he described compared what it found to known malware identifiers in code. This quality made them easy to evade. Clever programmers could change enough about their software to keep the functionality and evade the scanner. "It was probably a long shot, but it was necessary."

"Yeah." He turned to face me now, and weariness tugged at his face. "I don't think we have much cause for optimism. Unless someone had a very narrow agenda, this is going to get worse, and probably soon."

I wished I could have said something to counter what he said, but I couldn't.

———

A short while later, Charlie's desk phone rang. "It's never good news when someone calls me on this thing," he muttered before picking up. "All right . . . we'll be back up there as soon as we can." He hung up. "We're being summoned back to the conference room. There's been some kind of development."

"It can't be positive," I said as I stood. We walked back to

the elevator, rode it to the third floor, and returned to the
conference room. The same people who were there before
occupied the same chairs. I moved over one just to be
different.

Davenport cleared his throat once Charlie and I sat.
"We've gotten a ransom demand. It came attached to my
email like the first note promised."

"And you opened it?" I asked, spreading my hands.

"The message ensured me there was no malware."

"Jesus Christ. There's a lot here I can't fix."

"I disconnected my computer after opening the PDF,
Mister Ferguson. I'm not willing to trust an attacker so
blindly. We printed the document and scanned it so I can
display it here." He picked up the remote and turned the
projector back on. A multi-page note filled the screen.

Robber Baron Davenport,

*Belated congratulations on your victory. You might be the
perfect man to lead Baltimore. Both you and the city are
outdated, deceitful, and corrupt.*

*By now, you've noticed a few of your systems are offline.
Your staff is probably trying to regain access. It's futile. We've
locked everything out. Those systems are dead in the water
and will remain so.*

*We'll take more down, too. You've gotten off easy so far,
and you don't deserve to. Unless you pay us 20 million in the
cryptocurrency of your choice, things will only get worse. The
lights are off right now. We're going easy on you. This won't be
the case much longer.*

*We'll send another message with the crypto wallet ID you
can use for payment. You're a hidebound prick, so I'm sure
your money and the city's is tied up in banks, stocks, and other
old-school investments. You'll need some time to liquidate*

things. We're not unreasonable. Look for another email later today.

We're sure you're probably wondering why. Because you've spent your life making money off of other people, you're probably finding a way to make this about yourself. You're a small part of the reason. The BPD and how it treats people have contributed a lot more to our anger. If you want us to go away for good, you'll need to make some major changes in addition to paying a lot of money. If you don't, things will get a lot worse than what you're currently facing.

The message ended without a signature or other form of attribution. My first instinct was someone totally uninvolved tried to profit off the situation. The ransomware angle made the news. Anyone could know about it.

The police commissioner gave voice to my speculation. "How do we know this isn't some crank who happened to watch the news or read a paper?"

"Can I see the printout?" I said.

"I'm not sure what good it'll do," Davenport said. He grabbed a stapled set of papers from the small desk beside the table and slid them down. The top billowed as they glided down the table. "At the advice of my secretary, I printed the email header, too . . . whatever it is."

"Your secretary needs a raise." Charlie got up and sat next to me. I moved the papers so we could both look at them. "A ProtonMail address . . . they won't give up whoever it is." I focused on the timestamps and sender information in the header. "Look here." Davenport came around. I pointed at the passage in question. "It first went into a queue eight hours ago. Whoever wrote it probably wanted it to hit your inbox at a certain time. You can see here how it bounced around a few sending servers. All designed to make it harder to trace the source."

"Could you do it?" the mayor asked.

"ProtonMail will stonewall us," I said. "Security and privacy are what they sell. They're overseas, and they don't give up their client data."

"What do we do, then?"

"Keep working. Make it harder for them to knock anything else offline."

"We have to do more." Davenport walked back to the head of the table, took his seat, and pounded on the polished wood. "We have to."

CHAPTER 5

DAVENPORT SLUMPED IN THE CHAIR. For the first time since I arrived, he looked tired. To accentuate this, he took off his glasses and rubbed the bridge of his nose. "Sir, the city has the money," the accountant said. "It'll basically drain the emergency coffers. We won't have much wiggle room on anything until the next fiscal year."

"Which is ten months away," the mayor said. He shook his head. "Too risky. It sounds like we're low on funds there already." The bean counter confirmed this with a single nod. "No. I don't think we can take the risk. One natural disaster or major event, and we're in dire straits."

"We shouldn't pay these assholes, anyway," Commissioner Ngo said.

"I agree," I added. He glared at me, and his glower communicated exactly what he thought of us being *simpatico* on the point.

"What's the alternative, then?" Davenport slipped his glasses back on. "We merely sit by and let them take system after system offline until we're crippled?" Charlie started to say something, but Davenport stopped him with an upraised hand. "Don't tell me you can protect everything before they strike again. I won't believe it."

"I wasn't going to, sir," Charlie said. "By this time, most workers are in the office. I don't think we've sent out any communications yet."

"We haven't."

"We should. People need to know what's going on. They've heard it on the news or read about it online already. We also need to remind all workers of best practices when it comes to email. Don't open messages from people you've never heard of. Don't open attachments."

"We could block attachments," I said. "It's technologically feasible. It would be inconvenient. Your employees would need an alternative for sharing files, along with any external folks."

"SharePoint's a possibility," Charlie said. "We use it internally already. It would take some work to configure it for anyone not on our network, but we could do it."

"How long?" Davenport wanted to know.

"With our current staffing levels?" He shrugged. "At least a day. Probably more. The solution itself isn't hard to setup. We just need a lot of information first."

"I'll think about it." Davenport sighed. "I know what you all are going to say, but it would be easier if we simply paid the ransom."

"We don't know they'll actually release our systems and leave us alone," Ngo said. He jerked his thumb at me. "What if we hacked them back?"

"It's risky," I said. "We'd need to be a hundred percent sure on our attribution, and they're going to do everything they can to make it difficult."

"You're the consultant. Work out the details."

"And you're the police commissioner. Stop arresting people on bullshit charges."

Ngo's glare returned. "Listen here, you prick—"

"Gentlemen," Davenport broke in. "I appreciate the spirited discussion. Mister Ferguson, I understand the bind we're in when it comes to identifying who's responsible. I also understand sweeping policy changes in the police department wouldn't happen immediately and may not be enough to satisfy our adversaries. This is why I think we should pay them. Maybe it doesn't get them off our backs completely, but it buys us time, and it turns our lights and cameras back on."

"Sir, we agreed the city would be in a bad way if we drained the coffers," the accountant said, reminding everyone he still used his share of oxygen in the room.

"I could pay it myself." Davenport picked up the receiver of a phone on the table and pressed a few buttons. "Get my accountant on the line . . . now." He waited a few seconds. "Louis, the shit's really hit the fan. You've heard what's happening? . . . They want twenty million . . . I know I don't have it sitting in a goddamn account. This is why I'm calling you. How soon could you liquidate it? . . . Do it faster. I don't care if it costs me a couple percent . . . Yes, I know how much I'll have left after this. No one's going to cry for me. Make it happen, and let me know when it's done." He hung up.

"It's a mistake no matter whose money we use," I said. "What if they take the nine-one-one system down next? Or the power grid? Where does it stop? You can't just sell off assets every time they knock over a network."

"He's right, sir," Ngo said. "You can't give in to these jackals."

"Let's at least have the option," Davenport said. "Even if we don't use it, it's available if we need it."

I couldn't find fault with his logic. While I liked the idea of a bunch of criminals bleeding Vincent Davenport dry, I didn't want to see the effects on the city. They might escalate their attacks regardless whether anyone paid this particular ransom. Charlie leaned closer to me and whispered. "I'm going to send the email I talked about. I'll also encourage people to make sure they have paper backups of critical data."

"I hope it's in time to make a difference," I said. I didn't think it would be. Again, I got the feeling things would get worse before they improved, and I wished I could shake it.

———

Charlie drafted the email, and I suggested a couple small fixes. I added a mention of physical backups. Even if none of the city's computers came with DVD drives anymore, users could still copy their important data to a flash drive. Charlie confirmed Baltimore issued them for this purpose. "I guess people will start the mad hunt through their desk drawers," I said as he sent the message to all city employees and contractors.

"Whatever. If it helps, so much the better. Sometimes, little mitigations make a big difference in the end."

"I've been wondering about the disaster recovery plan."

Charlie snorted. "I think you and I are it."

"Seriously?"

"I don't want to keep going to this well," he said, "but we're really understaffed. The guys who put the plan together are pretty much gone. I'm trying to stick to it as much as I can."

"I need to know about using the cloud specifically," I said. "They're not on-premises resources, so they shouldn't get caught up in whatever else might happen. It's a good backup solution . . . at least for servers."

He nodded. "It is . . . or it would be if we'd started it weeks ago. We have some components in the cloud, sure, but we're not using it for DR."

"You could start. Get more capacity. Upload your standard server build and spin up new machines as you need to."

"I don't know." Charlie frowned. "My boss should be in the loop on this."

I waved a hand. "Better to beg forgiveness than ask permission . . . especially in times like these. I'm sure the bill is a lot less than twenty million."

"True." Charlie logged in to the city's cloud provider. "I'll get started. This isn't going to be an immediate solution, you know. If bad shit happens for the rest of the day, we're probably going to be caught with our pants down as far as those systems go."

The door opened, and a face I didn't want to see walked in. FBI Supervisory Special Agent Jason Hess led a couple of studious-looking women in pantsuits into the room. Hess was in his early forties, and his blond hair had grown a little more gray since the last time I saw him. Davenport frowned when the new retinue entered the conference room. Ngo and Sharpe shook their heads and looked down. "Good morning, everyone," Hess said. He introduced himself for those who didn't know who he was.

"What the hell are you doing here?" Davenport said. "We didn't call the FBI."

"You should have," Hess said. "We can help a lot more than any consultant." His eyes found me, lingered for a moment, and moved on. "My understanding is you're woefully short-staffed in the IT department."

"We're handling it."

"Mm-hmm. So far, you've lost street lights, traffic signals, and CCTV. I can imagine your resources are already pretty strained. Especially the police."

"Piss off," Ngo said. "We don't need the feds coming in here and taking over."

"I'm not trying to take over," Hess said. "We'll be here to help your efforts. My people don't know your network, so a lot of the work there will still fall on you, but we can fortify your defenses. We can monitor what's going on and learn who's responsible." The two women with Hess—both recent college graduates by my guess— remained silent and let him do the talking. They were probably the techies.

"Let me guess," Davenport said, "it's an offer I can't refuse because it's somehow illegal to say no to the FBI."

Hess shrugged. "You have a choice, Mister Mayor. At least for now. Have you gotten a ransom demand?"

"We have."

"Don't pay it."

"We're leaving all our options open," Davenport said.

"I can't discourage you strongly enough."

"Working with you is also an option, right?" Hess confirmed this with a nod. "Then, so is paying whoever did this. When I said all options, I meant it. If you want to work with us, those are the terms. You're a means to an end. You and your crew aren't in charge."

"Understood." Hess said. "I'd like to introduce you all to Amanda and Lynn." The former was a blonde with long hair, and the latter a redhead. Their pantsuits—differentiated only by color—suggested they shopped in the same store. "They're from our cybercrime team. Consider them a resource, too . . . a means to an end, if you prefer."

"Very well," Davenport said. "They can sit with our computer folks. Charlie, take these two ladies downstairs."

"Will do," Charlie said. He led Amanda and Lynn out.

Each grabbed a rolling laptop bag from outside the door, and their wheels buzzed along the linoleum all the way to the elevators.

Hess looked across the table at me. "Can I have a word in private?"

"This should be good," I muttered, but I got up and went with him. We moved about fifty feet down the hallway.

"What are you doing here?" Hess demanded.

"The mayor called me in. I'm consulting."

"I know about Hong Kong."

"I should hope so," I said. "It's a major city."

He rolled his eyes. "I'm sure you understood what I meant. Any idea who's behind this?"

"No. And if you're insinuating it's someone I know, I doubt it. Not really the style we used back then."

"I'd like you to stand down," Hess said.

"And I'd like you to jump in the harbor."

"You could be interfering with an investigation."

"Now, you want to investigate," I said. "I brought you evidence a couple years ago, and you sat on it. If I'd waited for you, the man who killed my sister a decade before would still be out there."

"You got your guy," Hess said. "I'm glad you did."

"I'll bet. You stuck your thumb up your ass, and I caught a murderer who probably would have killed again. You want me to stand down?" I scoffed. "Fuck off. I'll probably figure this out before you and the Techie Twins do."

"Don't go rogue," Hess said, pointing his finger toward my chest. "If we get a lead, the FBI is going to respond. If you're in the way, I can't guarantee your safety."

"As soon as you file a hundred pages of paperwork and beg Quantico," I said, "you'll respond. I like my odds."

Hess shook his head. "We're on the same side . . . mostly. I don't want to arrest you."

"So don't. I'll catch the hackers, you can haul them off to jail, and we both win. Cool?" He didn't say anything. "Okay. Good talk."

"Remember what I told you," Hess said as I walked away. "We don't need you going rogue."

I ignored him and returned to the conference room.

———

Everyone eyed me up as I took my seat again. "You staying?" Leon Sharpe said.

"Hess can't throw me out," I said. "I'm here as long as the mayor wants me to be."

"You have some history with the FBI I should know about, Mister Ferguson?" Davenport asked.

I shook my head. "Just Hess. I built a case a couple years ago and took it to him. He . . . didn't do anything with it."

"Murder case?" Commissioner Ngo said.

"Doesn't matter. It's taken care of. Turns out I didn't need the feds after all."

Charlie returned a moment later. He dropped onto the chair, sighed, and logged in to his laptop again. "I set them up with domain admin accounts," he said.

"Wow," I said. No one else at the table seemed to know what this meant.

"They're feds." He shrugged.

"I guess I'm just not a fan of handing untrusted outsiders the keys to the kingdom. They might be very capable, but one wrong click, and your network is in trouble."

"It's already in trouble," Charlie said, "and it's getting worse. I think we just lost another segment."

"Which one?" the mayor demanded.

"It's a specialized one. Major case files."

"Jesus Christ!" Ngo roared. "If we've lost access to those, we're screwed. Investigations will stop. Court cases will be affected. This is huge."

I wheeled closer to Charlie's seat. "Does it look the same as the others?"

"I think so. I'm going to try and remote in to one of the servers there." He opened a remote desktop window and made the connection. Rather than the normal Windows Server login, we saw a black screen with the message sent to Davenport earlier written in bright red. "I can try the other two, but I think we'll get the same result." He did, and he was right.

"Still don't want me to pay?" Davenport said.

"We need access to all our work." Ngo slapped the table-top. "I don't want to give in to these bastards. Too many cities and hospitals have. No one should pay them a cent."

"People cough up the money because they see it as the least bad choice," I said. "Not everyone can recover from a ransomware attack. I'm not sure the city can . . . at least not easily."

"Good thing we have a high-priced consultant who doesn't need the feds on the job, then," the commissioner said.

His barb hit home. I felt like I hadn't done much yet. Sure, I'd offered some advice to Charlie, and I probably knew more about malware than just about anyone currently drawing a paycheck from Baltimore. Still, the feeling I could be doing more nagged at me. "You got another laptop?" I asked Charlie.

"You want him logging in?" he said to Davenport.

"Get him whatever he needs."

"I'll take some champagne, too. Or at least a good break-fast sandwich."

Charlie snorted and stood. "Gimme a couple minutes." He left the room, returning shortly with a computer under his arm. It was old enough to still have a disc drive built in to one side. "I'll get you logged in with our domain admin account." I tried to watch what he typed, but his fingers were fast, and I didn't catch all the keystrokes. "You know how to use Windows?"

"Better than a lot of people who work for Microsoft," I said. Thankfully, a network diagram resided on the desk-top, so I opened it. It contained a massive drawing. I also found a list of networks, IP address ranges, and servers . . . all of which would be useful. After a few minutes, I found a semi-recent snapshot of the major case data. It resided on a different part of the network than where Charlie looked earlier. To make sure it stayed safe from the enemy, I copied the files to a local device. "Looks like there was a backup about a week ago. It'll take a little time, but we can spin up a cloud server and restore the data there."

"It's a week old," Ngo said.

"You can have something backdated seven days or noth-ing. I don't want to tell you how to do your job, but this really is an easy choice."

Sharpe leaned in and whispered something to his boss. After a moment of consultation, Ngo sighed and said, "Fine. Do it. It's better than nothing."

Charlie logged in to the city's cloud service account, and I started the process. "We may not have the same luck else-where," I said. "I know data seven days old is less than ideal. This whole mess is still going to get worse before it gets better."

"I don't care what you all tell me," Davenport said, "I'm leaving the option of paying these pricks on the table."

"I still don't think you should."

The mayor rubbed his temples. "Let's see how much worse it gets."

CHAPTER 6

CHARLIE AND I KEPT WORKING. Despite our efforts, no other opportunities to stem the tide made themselves obvious. With a small staff and not a lot of leadership, we were in a reactive mode. "We need to get further ahead of this," I said as I watched the rather boring progress bar of a cloud server creation.

"How?" Charlie asked as he typed.

"Block attachments. Put more restrictive firewall rules in place."

"We'd break our normal operations."

"It would be an inconvenience," I admitted. "In trade, we'd have better odds of not losing more functionality. Look, the mayor has bigger fish to fry here. I don't want him coughing up millions of dollars, and I think you feel the same." Charlie nodded. "We should just do it, then."

He sighed. "Let me try to get a few things setup first. I'll need to go over the SharePoint architecture for starters. We can ignore external parties for now, but we can't break something like document sharing among city employees."

"All right."

Voices rose from the hallway as footsteps stomped closer.

"Stand down, officer," someone said, and it sounded like Rich. My suspicion got confirmed a couple seconds later when my cousin barged into the conference room. "Sorry for breaking in, everyone." He nodded at Ngo and Davenport. "Sir. Mister Mayor." His eyes found me and blinked a few times, but he continued as I reasoned he would. "We've lost access to major case files. Officers and detectives are already stretched thin by having to do so much traffic work. Whatever cases we manage to work are dead in the water without our data."

"I'm working on it," I said.

"You're consulting on this?" Rich asked.

"The mayor has agreed to pay my usurious fees. Expertise like mine doesn't come cheap." I tapped the side of my head.

Rich rolled his eyes. "How are you working on it?"

"I found a backup from seven days ago. At the moment, we're standing up a new server in the cloud, and when it's ready, I'll restore the data there. You'll need to map to it, but I can tell you how."

"A week old?" Rich groaned. "I'm sure many of those cases saw a lot of progress."

"Hopefully," I said, "your cops put good notes on paper. Besides, a week is better than nothing . . . as I've already pointed out to your boss." Ngo pursed his lips but didn't say anything.

"I guess we'll take it as a stopgap," Rich said. "Do you think you'll be able to get more recent stuff back?"

"Don't know. Based on how things look at the moment, I'm not optimistic."

"While I'm here, what's the plan for dealing with this? We got hit a while back but nothing this bad. A lot of my guys are wondering."

"We're keeping all our options on the table, Lieutenant," Ngo said. "There's your answer."

Rich frowned. "Does all our options include paying the attackers?"

"I'm keeping it open, yes," Davenport said. "No one seems to agree with me, but my first duty is to the city, not the ideals of law enforcement or sticking it to the criminals. If things get a lot worse, we might be forced to meet their demands."

"I would advise against it, Mister Mayor," Rich said.

"Mm. You and everyone else I've talked to today. I hope I don't have to, but events of the last several hours aren't exactly trending in the right direction. You want to make sure it doesn't happen? Catch whoever's responsible and get our access back."

"We're doing our best out there."

"So are we," Davenport said.

Rich glanced at me again and left. I wondered what he thought of yours truly working as a consultant for the city. Hell, it seemed weird to me. I normally worked for people who felt they didn't get a fair shake from the system. Here I sat in the employ of the system itself. If we got a break later today, I would stand under a hot shower for a few extra minutes.

———

I got the new server online. Following the city's official documentation proved tedious. It was poorly written, steps were out of order, and the whole thing seemed like it had been organized by a goat with a dartboard. Despite these challenges, I was able to begin the restoration process. The police major crimes case data would be seven days old, but I hoped the cops could work off their paper notes to fill in the gaps. Those who weren't stuck directing traffic at major intersections, at least.

Leon Sharpe's phone rang, and he excused himself to answer it in the hallway. A moment later, he reappeared in the doorway and pointed a beefy finger at me. "You. Come with me."

"Little busy saving the day here, Leon."

"Charlie can finish whatever it is. We're taking a ride."

Considering the ease with which Captain Sharpe could have picked me up, pressed me over his head, and carried me out of the building like a barbell, refusing seemed pointless. "All right. Meet you in the lobby." He nodded and left. I brought Charlie up to speed on my server progress.

"What's the captain want?" he asked.

"No idea. This seems pretty self-sufficient for now."

He nodded. "I'll take care of it when it's ready."

"All right," I said. "Your documentation sucks, by the way. See you later."

"Thanks for your help," Charlie said.

I left the conference room and hustled down the stairs to find Leon Sharpe waiting. "Let's go," he barked, and he walked to an SUV. He and I climbed in the back, and a uniformed officer led us away from the curb.

"Where are we going?" I asked.

"Central Booking."

"Is there something there specific you need my genius for?"

"Can you keep a secret?"

"As well as anyone else."

"Meaning what?" Sharpe said.

"Meaning if someone kidnaps me and wants to take a power drill to my kneecap, I'm spilling the beans."

He shrugged his brawny shoulders. "I think we have one of the hackers in a holding cell. You're going to help me talk to him."

"Must be an idiot to get caught so quickly and for something which should be anonymous."

"You'd think so," Sharpe said. "Apparently, this clown got pretty lit last night. Made a drunk post or two on his Instagram. Someone saw it and reported it. Wasn't hard to track him down from there."

"Wow. Idiot isn't a strong enough word."

"Whatever you want to call him, I'll take a break in the case . . . especially so early. This asshole will be looking at a string of charges. More if we want to involve the feds. I think he'll tell us what we need to know."

I remained skeptical. The person might have some insight into what the team did and what tools they used, but I doubted we'd get much else. Five minutes in an interrogation room wouldn't compel him to give up the decryption key. He probably didn't know them, anyway. A proper hacking group would have generated the key randomly and stored it securely. If no one knew it, no one could be forced to tell it.

The ride to Central Booking took a lot longer thanks to the lack of traffic signals. Cops did the best they could, and Sharpe's SUV didn't get any special privileges. The driver pulled the vehicle into a nearby lot. Sharpe and I climbed out. He flashed his badge to the desk sergeant, announced I was with him, and we headed back inside the gloomy facility.

The walls were gray. They matched the floors, and the cell bars were in the same color family. Central Booking was a lifeless and soul-sucking place. I'd occupied a cell here a couple years ago. While I'd rate it well above the Chinese prison, it still ranked as a building I didn't care to come back to. Leon Sharpe stomped ahead, ignoring a few barbs from prisoners. I followed him through a few doors deeper into Central Booking.

We came to an area with four rooms. Two officers stood watch. Both straightened their posture when Sharpe approached. "Where's the hacker?"

"Room three, sir," one of them said. I followed the captain inside. The door clicked shut behind us. A white guy so slender a stiff breeze would capsize him sat cuffed to the desk. His blond hair was thin and wispy. It made him look older. I placed him in his mid-twenties. A tattoo peeked out from the left sleeve of his shirt. His eyes were narrowed, red, and unfocused.

Sharpe turned a chair around and dropped onto it. I remained standing. The prisoner tried to meet the massive man's gaze and turned away. "You know why you're here?" Sharpe said.

"Drunk and disorderly," the guy said in a mousy voice. "I heard the officers say it when they brought me in. Can I go now? I'll pay the fine." Even a few feet away, I could smell the booze on his breath.

"You're looking at a lot more than a hit to your wallet. What's your name?"

"My friends call me Cold Frost."

"You see any of your fucking friends in this room?"

"No."

"Give me your real name," Sharpe said.

"Clarence," the captive said.

"All right, Clarence. Here's what's going to happen. You posted a drunk photo, and you claimed to be working with hackers who are currently a pain in my ass. You're going to tell me everything I want to know."

"Who's he?" Clarence pointed at me.

"I'm the only guy who can keep the captain from

piledriving you onto the floor," I said. Sharpe smirked. "The more of his time you waste, the less control I have of this situation."

"Time to talk, Clarence," Sharpe said. "Who are you working with?"

"It's . . . kind of a loose group. We sort of came together recently."

"How touching. This group have a name?"

"APT double zero."

"Advanced persistent threat," I added when Sharpe's response consisted of a puzzled expression. "It's common for groups with APT and a number to be associated with nations like Russia or China."

Clarence put his hands up. "Not us. We're all Americans. I guess our leader just liked the name."

"Who is he?" Sharpe wanted to know.

"Factor Zero."

"All you assholes have such stupid names?"

"They're common in the community," I said. I didn't recognize either of the ones mentioned so far. My job meant I didn't remain as active as I'd been in the past. Still, I felt sure I would have heard of a major operator. Either these two were new on the scene, adopted fresh handles for the current operation, or they were mediocre. I kind of hoped for the trifecta.

"I get a lawyer, right?" Clarence asked.

"You can have one," Sharpe said. "Once an attorney gets involved, though, you can't really talk to me anymore. I don't like lawyers, Clarence. I'd be willing to make a deal with you so long as you're speaking for yourself."

"How do I know you're not going to try to put the squeeze on me?"

"Oh, I'll definitely try to squeeze you. But I'll do it worse if some expensive prick in a fancy suit does your talking for you." He shrugged. "It's your call."

I felt torn on this one. Part of me believed accused criminals had the right to a competent attorney—either their own or via the public defender's office. Another part of me wanted Sharpe to fit Clarence for thumbscrews and give them a few good turns. The hacker shook his head and sighed. "Fine. We can talk for now." He held up a hand as best he could with the cuffs on. "If I think you're overstepping, I'm shutting this down and asking for a lawyer."

"I understand," Sharpe said. "If you cooperate with us and tell us what we want to know, I'll recommend the state's attorney go easy on you. If you want this leniency, I have a specific request in mind."

"What is it?"

"You give us the scoop on the operation and the people. Then, you call your little band of hacker friends, tell them what happened, and recommend someone to take your place."

"Who?" Clarence said.

"Let me handle the personnel angle," Sharpe said. "It'll be someone capable, but they'll be a plant." He glared and jabbed a finger at the slender Clarence. "If you tip them off, I'll break you in half over my knee and deliver the pieces of your corpse in person. You follow me?"

Clarence's voice shook when he answered. "Yeah . . . I get you, man."

"Good. Wait here." Sharpe looked at me and jerked his head toward the door. We left the room. Rich approached.

"I came as soon as I could, Captain."

"You're just in time," Sharpe said. He confirmed one of the rooms was empty, and we all walked into it. Sharpe closed the door. None of us sat. "Rich, the guy in room three is one of the hackers responsible. I told him we'll go easy on him in exchange for a favor."

Rich crossed his arms. "What's the favor?"

"He's going to tell them he's out but recommend a replacement."

"Who?"

Sharpe bobbed his large head at me. "You."

CHAPTER 7

A BEVY OF objections rushed to my mind. In a truly eloquent moment, I said, "What?"

Sharpe's gaze didn't waver. "I want to send you undercover with these pricks."

"Leon, I'm not sure this is a good idea."

"I agree," Rich added. "C.T. isn't a trained officer."

"Your reason would rank about five hundredth on my list," I said.

"I think it's the right fit," Sharpe said. "Would you rather I send a cop?"

"God, no. Your people probably don't have the skills they would need. Besides, if we're dealing with seasoned criminals, they'll smell a cop right away."

Sharpe spread his hands and offered a humorless smile. "Now, you see why it needs to be you."

"Even if I agree to this," I said, "there's no way your boss will want to send me."

"Let me worry about the commissioner," Sharpe said. "Follow me." We left the interrogation room and walked out of the area. Sharpe opened another door. The basic table and uncomfortable chairs were gone, replaced by a round conference model and padded office seats. He picked up the phone in the center and pushed some keys. "Get me the mayor's conference room." We all sat. My stomach clenched and not only with hunger. Sharpe spoke again a moment later. "I have Rich and C.T. Ferguson here with me. Putting you on speaker."

"What is it, Captain?" Ngo asked.

"I have an idea. We've arrested one of the hackers after he made a drunken social media post. I think he's willing to play ball in exchange for a lighter sentence."

"What kind of ball are we playing?"

"The kind where we send a ringer in," Sharpe said. "Someone who could keep up with the hackers but be working for us to gather info and help us bring the whole ring down."

"Who'd you have in mind?" Davenport asked.

"I want to send C.T. in."

"Absolutely not," the commissioner said. "I'm not putting a civilian in the middle of an operation."

"First of all," I said, "everyone on this call is a civilian. You're not a goddamn admiral. Second, I'm not some buffoon off the streets. I've been doing this job for years, I can take care of myself in a fight, and I've worked with hacking groups before."

"Great. We're going to send a criminal in with the criminals. How do you think this is going to end, Leon?"

I answered for Sharpe. "With your hacking group in handcuffs. You can think what you want of me and what I've done before. I don't give a shit. I'm more qualified than anyone in your police department."

"We have forensic guys. Good with computers."

"What's going to happen when a cop gets made?"

Silence filled the line. "We'll take it under advisement,

Captain Sharpe," Davenport said. "It sounds like Mister Ferguson is willing to do it if we think it's worthwhile."

"I get time and a half for hazard pay," I said. "Plus the same rate for overtime."

"We're not paying you triple for anything," Ngo said.

"Two hundred and twenty-five percent. Don't they teach math when you major in criminal justice?"

"Listen here, you smug prick—"

"Like I said," Davenport broke in, "we'll consider it. There are perks and drawbacks we'll need to consider. Captain Sharpe, you should be part of the conversation."

"I'll head back over shortly," he said and hung up.

"A little heads-up would've been nice," I said. "You really sprang this one on me, Leon."

"Gotta keep you expensive consultants on your toes."

He had a point.

———

T.J. called as we climbed back into Sharpe's limo. I declined it and then sent a short text. *Working. Talk soon.* She replied with a thumbs-up emoji. I rolled possibilities for this under-cover assignment through my head. The commissioner was right—I wasn't a cop. While this didn't hamper me 99.7 percent of the time, it could be a problem if I provided enough intel on the hackers for the police or feds to raid their location. I would be another civilian caught breaking the law, and while it could all be sorted out after the fact, I didn't relish the idea of getting tossed to the ground and cuffed.

"Having second thoughts?" Sharpe asked as we waited for an officer to send us forward at an intersection. Thankfully, it was a short drive.

"No. Just wondering what happens if I provide enough info for you to kick the door in."

"You'd be arrested. Same thing happens to undercover cops, too. We need to keep up appearances."

"Sure," I said, "but I don't have the secret decoder ring to get me out of the handcuffs as soon as you haul the real criminals off."

"I'd make sure you were protected," he said.

"All right." I nodded. "Good enough for me."

The driver curbed the black Yukon in front of City Hall, and we got out. Sharpe and I took the stairs to the third floor. "I want to make a couple calls," I said. He walked into the conference room, and I headed farther down the corridor. I tried Gloria first. Background noise on the line suggested she was driving.

"I'm headed to my house," she confirmed when I asked. "How are things with you?"

"Interesting. The cops found one of the hackers. Guy was an idiot and made a drunk Instagram post. Anyway, there's a chance I might be going undercover in their group."

"Isn't that dangerous?"

"I can't imagine they're armed vigilantes," I said. "I can probably duck a keyboard if someone tosses one at me."

"I'm serious," she said. "They might want to send you in with the wolves, but you're still a civilian."

"I know. Sharpe said he would make sure I was protected if they kick the door in." I flashed back to the Chinese police raiding our compound in Hong Kong. The loud thunk of boots blasting the room open still stuck with me.

"It sounds like you're not going to be joining me," Gloria said.

"I don't know. The commissioner's against the idea, and Davenport is trying to keep everyone happy. I'm in a holding pattern right now. I want to drive home and make sure my go bag has everything I'd need." I always kept it ready in case I was forced to beat a hasty retreat, but I could swap in different supplies if I knew I'd be a rogue agent.

"Be careful . . . and please keep me posted."

"I will," I said. "Might need a rain check on the cape fitting. You're the wife of a hero. You have to get used to these things."

Gloria chuckled. "Good to know. I'll see you when you're not saving the city. Love you."

"Love you, too."

I popped back into the conference room. Charlie remained hard at work at one end of the table, and everyone else huddled at the other. I dropped onto the seat beside him. "Anything new?"

He shook his head. "I still think we're going to struggle with this."

"I agree," I said, lowering my voice. "I'm just a consultant, but you work for the city. They might listen to you over me. Get an actual incident response company in here. Someone who does this shit for a living. It'll cost money, but it's worth it to have the expertise, especially if the city is short-staffed. I might be moving on to . . . a different way of going after the problem."

"What's your double-oh number?"

I grinned. "Nothing so dramatic, I hope. In your research, look at No More Ransom. They have a bunch of decryption tools. If this attack used some popular software, you might be able to undo it."

"All right." We bumped fists. "If I don't see you again before all this wraps up, thanks for your help."

"You got it."

"You're leaving?" Ngo asked as I headed for the door.

"I don't want to miss the chance to bill my expensive breakfast to the city," I said.

He scoffed. I left.

————

I stopped by the office on my way home. It took a little longer than usual, but with rush hour over, cops directing traffic at the intersections had an easier time of things. A few more busy mornings and afternoons, however, might leave commuters in open revolt. I opened the door to find T.J. at her desk drinking coffee. With plenty more waiting in the pot, I helped myself to a cup before plopping down in my chair and blowing out a deep breath.

"You look tired," my secretary said.

"I was up before four. Been going pretty much ever since."

"That's a concern at your age."

"Ha ha," I said. "Have you seen or read the news since last night?"

"Yeah. Some kind of malware attack against the city."

"It's pretty bad already. The attackers picked a couple of major public-facing systems."

"Sounds like you think it might get worse," T.J. said.

I nodded. "I do. The city is short-staffed in the IT area. They asked me to consult. I'm happy to do it, but they need more than me, and they need some specialized skills. In the meantime, one of the hackers got hammered and took to Instagram. He's sitting in Central Booking. Leon Sharpe wants me to go undercover."

T.J. frowned. "Sounds dangerous."

"It probably will be," I said. "Gloria is going to get me fitted for a cape when this whole mess is behind us."

"If you're going to be embedded somewhere, I want to help."

"I appreciate it. I'm not even sure it's going to happen yet. The police commissioner would rather toss me off the Bromo Seltzer tower than agree to send me in there, I think. The mayor could overrule him, but he's trying to keep the peace right now." I shrugged. "I guess we'll see. I'm going to make sure my go bag is current and ready in case I get the green light . . . no pun intended with the traffic signals down."

"If you go spy on the hackers," T.J. said, "are you going to be able to talk to me? I don't want you to be alone in there."

"We'll figure it out. I have a couple burner phones. I'll text you from one of them when I get back to my house. Store the number as something no one would think to trace back to me or your job. We can also use an app like Signal. Just make sure messages delete once they're read."

"You think the mayor will sign off on it?"

"Yeah. Ultimately, I think Sharpe wears his boss down because they don't have a better option, and Davenport approves it under a united front." I raised my mug in mock salute. "To politics."

"All right. I'll keep things running in the meantime."

"You did a great job while Gloria and I were honeymooning," I said.

"And I've picked up some of your slack since you came back and coasted," T.J. pointed out.

"I think my coasting days are over." I downed my java and stood. "I'll keep you in the loop as best I can. Might be at odd hours. If I do this, I don't know how many chances I'll have to send messages."

"I understand." T.J. got up and hugged me. "Times like these, I worry about you."

"You stopped not-so-secretly rooting for my demise?"

She grinned. "I still call dibs on your car."

"Of course you do," I said.

———

I noticed the tail pretty quickly.

A dark-colored sedan turned onto Eastern Avenue just after I did. Other vehicles came and went, but this car stayed behind me. If I changed lanes, the other driver mirrored the movement a few seconds later. I would never be called the most observant person in the world, so whoever glued himself to my rear bumper wasn't very good at it. I wondered who it could be. Other than the brand-new consulting gig, my docket was free of cases. No one should have cause to follow me.

In the past, I used shenanigans at a traffic light to lose people glued to my bumper. With the BPD directing cars at major intersections, my usual tactic was off the table. I kept an occasional eye on the rearview mirror as I drove toward Federal Hill. The sedan remained behind me. When I turned down the alley running behind the group of rowhouses, my pursuer continued down Riverside Avenue.

The parking pad was empty. My Audi S4 looked lonely without Gloria's Mercedes rocket beside it. I walked inside and headed upstairs. Opening blinds as little as possible, I looked out at the street. The sedan's headlights winked out It sat on the opposite side of the road about three houses farther along. The driver offered no indication he noticed me.

I checked the 9MM on my hip and exited via the back door. My house was the last in the group, and leaving the alley via the far end would leave me exposed. I took the long way. It added an extra loop and a few minutes, but it would be worth it. Parts of Federal Hill were known for pubs and eateries—and, of course, the Cross Street Market—but a lot of it was residential. My street counted as one such area.

It meant not a lot of people would be around in the middle of a weekday. I walked down the sidewalk approaching the mystery car from the rear. The driver alternated between looking at my house and straight ahead—to his left or directly in front of him. Thanks to my circuitous route, I was on his right. He might see me in the passenger's door mirror as I got closer, so I slowed my pace. When his head turned toward my home, I quickened my strides again.

I held the gun in my right hand and tapped on the window. He jumped and turned in surprise. His hand reached under his jacket. I rapped the glass again and shook my head. He relaxed and glowered at me. "Unlock the door," I said.

It took a few seconds, but he did. I climbed inside.

CHAPTER 8

THE GUY LOOKED to be of average height and build. He was around my age with blond hair, a mustache, and stubble on his chin indicating trouble growing a beard. I sympathized. "Why are you following me?"

"Orders," he said.

"Whose?"

"I'm FBI."

"Let's see a badge." I waved my pistol enough for him to pay attention to it. "Slowly."

The fellow reached inside his jacket and took out a wallet. A gun also peeked out from within, but he didn't try to grab it. He showed me a federal badge and a laminated card identifying him as Special Agent Patrick Zellhoefer. "Irish and German?" He nodded. I rubbed my chin. "Explains it."

"Yeah," he said with a sheepish grin. "Every time I try to grow a goatee, it looks patchy."

I holstered my gun. "Who put you onto me?"

"Hess ordered it."

I suspected this as soon as I saw the FBI badge. Hess clearly didn't trust me after I went around him and found the man who'd murdered my sister years ago. "Let me guess . . . he thinks I'm going to go rogue."

"He does," Zellhoefer said.

"Look, I know you're just doing what your boss told you to. He thinks I'm some wild card, and I think he's a glorified pencil pusher who would rather sit on his hands than risk getting them dirty. We're not going to agree very often."

"He's not what you make him out to be."

"Doesn't matter," I said. "You could write a ballad and sing my praises, and he won't believe you. The reality is he and I both want to see the city's problems resolved."

"Are you going to stand down?"

"Not a chance."

"Sounds like you'll be seeing more of me, then."

I sighed. "All right, in which case let me give you a piece of advice, then. They offer some kind of strategic driving class at Quantico?"

"Yeah," he said.

"Take it. Go again if you already did. I'm not the best at this, and I made you pretty much right away. If you were following someone dangerous, this could have ended poorly for you."

"I see what you mean."

"Can I trust you with a piece of information?" I asked.

"Depends what it is."

I figured he'd give me the diplomatic answer. Zellhoefer was young. Probably new on the job. The Baltimore Field Office may have been one of his first couple assignments. I hoped he didn't grow too attached to Hess. "All right, I'll take a chance on you. The police arrested one of the attackers after he went on Instagram three sheets to the wind." I held up a hand to hold off his question. "The cops and the mayor are debating sending me undercover with the hackers. I . . . have experience in this area, and I could be an effective plant for the city. Obviously, this all goes to shit if you and your Fedmobile are following me every-where I go."

"What am I supposed to do, then?" he said.

"You have a choice. You can tell Hess about our plan, which means he'll want to get involved and probably screw it up somehow. Or you can say nothing. Act like you're keeping tabs on me. Drink coffee and catch up on your comic book reading for all I care."

His head bobbed slowly. "I'll think about it."

"Good," I said. "I presume you'll see Hess later today?"

"Yes."

"Great. Tell him if he wants to talk to me, he can pick up a fucking phone next time." I got out of Zellhoefer's car and walked back across the street.

After I dealt with the young FBI agent, I made some overdue lunch. It felt like a soup and grilled cheese day, so I indulged. The yawns started soon after, and I walked upstairs to take a nap. The city could manage without me for a while. Some-time later, my phone buzzed, and a pounding came from downstairs. I checked my phone. Rich called twice. I picked up this time. "What?"

"Let us in. Sharpe and I are at the back door."

"Fine." I rubbed my eyes, got back to my feet, and opened up for them.

"You have someone sitting on your house," Rich said.

"I know." I said. "He's FBI. I spotted him when I left. We had a nice chat." I looked out my kitchen window. Rich's blue Camaro sat next to my S4. It looked a lot less official than

Leon Sharpe's Yukon with city plates. "What brings you two here?"

"I've been talking with the mayor and commissioner," Sharpe said. "I think I've worn them down. They're willing to send you in among the hackers."

I blew out a deep breath. We all sat at my kitchen table. Sharpe's massive frame made the space feel crowded. I'd been on board with this idea. Now, with the reality of it happening staring me in the face, I hoped I could deliver. I hadn't been embedded with a group of keyboard warriors since the Chinese government gave me a hard boot from Hong Kong. Four years was a long time. My skills remained up to par, but I didn't seek new and innovative methods to knock over systems the way I used to.

"You having second thoughts?" Rich asked.

I shook my head. "Just a little apprehension. I don't know this group, their methods, or their ultimate agenda. We can presume it's more than turning the lights off, but how much more?"

"I can try to send a cop in," Sharpe said. "We have a few who have taken some cybercrime training."

"They won't know a lot of the technical how-to," I said. "I'm sure they're good at their jobs, but what they learned doesn't fit what you'd want them to do. They're blue teamers. You need a red teamer."

"You're concerned what they might ask you to do?"

"I am. Look at what they've done already. Those aren't major systems in the grand scheme of things, but the city is feeling the effects. What if they make me take something really important down?"

"Could you find a way to undo it?" Sharpe said.

"Maybe." I shrugged. "Probably. Could I do it while the

enemy is watching me, though?" I paused. "Anyone else want coffee?" They both nodded, so I got up to make a pot.

"Cops who go undercover face similar problems," Rich said. "There's always the concern you'll be asked to do something which is a bridge too far."

"Or ordered to," Sharpe added.

"I wouldn't be pulling a trigger," I said as I set the machine to brew a half carafe. "The effects of what they want to do could be a lot farther reaching. We don't know how closely this group monitors everyone. Could I even get a warning out?"

"If you don't want to do it, we'll understand."

"No. I'm your best shot."

Sharpe nodded. "All right. Here's how it'll work. The city will put you up in a safehouse. We should probably get you in there today. You still have your other car?"

"Yeah." In addition to the S4, I owned a Chevy Caprice Classic from the late 'eighties. It was a few different shades of blue, but it blended in a lot better than my S4. The chop shop owner I acquired it from even made a few improvements.

"Use it," the captain said.

"You still have your disguise from Frederick?" Rich said.

"It's all upstairs." A few months ago, I worked a case about an hour away. It marked my first time doing anything approaching going undercover, and I changed my appearance so no one could easily compare me to the handsome private investigator who sometimes received glowing coverage in the *Baltimore Sun*.

"Good. Unless you plastered your picture everywhere during your hacker days, it should work for you. You still have an alias?"

I nodded. "Not as active as it once was, but people plugged into the scene will know it."

"If they know you by reputation," Sharpe said, "it's bound to help."

"I guess." The coffee maker beeped. I prepared three mugs. Both Rich and Sharpe took theirs black. As a man of refined taste, I opted for some creamer. "I'd want to know more about the organization before I go in. There's some research I can do here, but we should talk to Clarence again. Is he still going to recommend me as his replacement?"

"If he knows what's good for him."

"All right. This is going to be hazard pay, Leon. I wasn't kidding. Time and a half."

"We'll do it," he said.

"Put it in writing and send it to T.J. I'm not starting until I've heard she has a copy of the contract."

"You don't trust me?"

"I don't trust your boss or the mayor," I said. "They'd both leave me to the wolves as long as the city's name stayed clean."

"All right. I'll have my secretary send it over."

"Good."

Sharpe set his mug down. "Let's go talk to Clarence."

I drained the rest of my coffee. "Yes. Let's."

———

Rich accompanied Sharpe and me, and we met Clarence in the same room as before. Sharpe stopped to get something on the way in, but he kept it in his pocket. Clarence's eyes looked brighter and clearer, and the smell of alcohol coming off him was gone. He must've gotten a shower and drunk a bunch of water. "Oh, man. I was hoping I wouldn't need to see you again. Who's the new guy?"

"Lieutenant Ferguson," Rich said, "Homicide."

"Homicide?" Clarence blanched. "We . . . I didn't kill anybody."

"Yet. It's a matter of time until the lack of street lights or traffic signals leads to a fatality." Clarence swallowed hard. Rich smirked. "Not why we're here now, though."

"Why, then?"

"You said you'd recommend someone to take your place," Sharpe said. He leaned closer to Clarence when he spoke. The proximity of a large, imposing man with a voice to match probably worked very well.

"I can't exactly pick up the phone in here." Clarence gestured to the spartan room. "No one's let me make a call."

Sharpe took a mobile from his pocket and set it on the table. It was a basic Android smartphone. Several generations old. The kind a hacker could root easily and unlock all the functions the manufacturer never intended the public to have. "How about a text?" He held up a finger and then used it to point to me. "He's going to supervise you. If you do anything besides send a message, I've authorized him to break this phone and cram it up your ass sideways."

Clarence looked between us, then inclined his head. "Fine. Who am I recommending as my replacement?"

"Me," I said. "Tell them you've lined up Foxtrot. Like the dance, but the ohs are zeroes." Rich snickered. "What? I was young. I thought it was cool."

"You're Foxtrot?" Clarence said. "I've heard of you."

"I hope the rest of your friends have, too." I tapped Clarence's cell and pushed it closer to his cuffed hands. "I can sign an autograph for you later. Ten bucks if you want a picture, too. Now, send the message."

"Right." He picked up the phone and slid the screen up to expose a physical keyboard. I liked these models back in the day. Over time, I've warmed up to the onscreen keypad, but it took a while. Clarence opened Noize, a secure messaging app popular with people who didn't want the government snooping on them. I would need to install it on my burner. He found a contact identified as Frank Zebulon. Factor Zero.

I got popped. Sorry. Shouldn't have made a drunk post. The cops don't know shit. You're still good. They're super dumb when it comes to this stuff.

No reply came after a moment. Clarence continued. *The cops want to hang a lot on me, so I don't think I'm getting out of here anytime soon. I want to recommend Foxtrot to replace me. We probably should've reached out to him at the beginning. He's local and knows the city better than I do. He might be able to help you pick better targets.*

We waited. A couple minutes later, Clarence's phone dinged. He opened the app.

Fine. I didn't know he was still active, but if he can find us, he's in. You're out. I don't want to see you again.

"He sounds like a real charmer," I said. "Where are they holed up?"

Clarence shrugged. "I don't know."

"What do you mean you don't know?" Sharpe roared. Clarence cowered. "You were with them. I swear, if you're trying to screw me . . ."

"I'm not." He raised his hands as much as the cuffs and table would allow. "Look, I'm pretty good, but I like the booze. I've had half a load tied on since I've been here. I'm not from Baltimore. I don't think I could tell you where they were if you gave me a map."

"You're not exactly helping your cause," Rich said.

"I wish I knew. I can tell you Factor doesn't want to stay in the same place for long. He's talked about changing locations every couple days."

"He probably figured something would happen," I said. "Kind of like your post." Clarence frowned. "Maybe you can still help. If I can find your asshole friends, what am I going to be walking into?"

"Factor Zero's a control freak," Clarence said. "Even if he's heard of you, he'll probably want you to prove yourself."

"Not a problem. How many other people?"

"Four or five. Oh, and there's an armed guard. Remember how I said he's a control freak? He said the guard is there to shoot anyone who doesn't do what they're supposed to."

"You can still say no," Sharpe told me.

I shook my head. "I'm in, Leon. Let's try to find these pricks."

CHAPTER 9

AS WE LEFT CENTRAL BOOKING, my phone vibrated in my pocket. Ai Deng called using a secure app. I held a finger up and walked away from Rich and Sharpe to take it. "Hello, Deng."

"Ferguson, you really landed in it."

"What do you mean?"

"I asked around about the people who are going after your city," she said. "APT Double Zero. They've made something of a name for themselves among those of us in the know. You aware who the leader is?"

"Someone named Factor Zero. Sounds like he's a lot of fun at parties."

She snorted. "He's a chaos agent. Hacking is just how he brings it about."

I didn't like her term or what it meant for the immediate future of Baltimore. "You think he has something bigger in mind?"

"Probably," she said. "I know who a couple others in the group are, too. Not people I've worked with . . . or would want to. I'm choosy there."

"Like who?"

"You ever hear of Iceman?"

"Sure," I said. "Val Kilmer played him in *Top Gun*. He was kind of a dick to Maverick."

"He's not a top-flight operator," Deng said, "but he's good. I'm a little surprised you haven't heard of him."

"I try to keep up, but I'm a married man with a fairly stable day job."

"Married, huh?"

"I told you, yes."

"Right," Deng said. "Congratulations. Anyway, some people pick more original handles than others. He's of a similar mindset to his leader. Wants to tear down the power and the establishment with it."

"And he thinks knocking over a few systems in a medium-sized American city is the way to do it? Doesn't really fit. There are better targets than Baltimore. One of them is forty miles away."

"I'm telling you what I know. You're the detective. You'll need to make it all work."

"All right. I appreciate the insight."

"These guys are dangerous, Ferguson. Some kind of unrest seems to follow them."

"Define unrest," I said.

"I think you know what I mean. There's always some sort of violence."

With the police needing to spend part of their force directing traffic, any form of unrest would be harder for the city to answer without help. "We've been operating under the theory things would get worse before they improved."

"Sounds like one of yours," Deng said. "It's kind of in your wheelhouse."

I grinned. "I guess I haven't changed a lot in four-plus years."

"You haven't, and you're not wrong. I'm sure whatever they've done so far is inconvenient, especially if your city is short-staffed. They'd better get a handle on things now while they can."

"I've given them some resources to try," I said. "Guess I'd better tell them the urgency involved."

"I think you'd better. Good luck, Ferguson."

"Thanks, Deng." She broke the connection. I joined Rich and Sharpe in the SUV.

"Friend of yours?" the captain asked.

I nodded. "A person who has some familiarity with a few of the people we're up against."

"And?"

"It's not good. You guys need outside expertise to keep a handle on things. I told Charlie. Make sure you run it up the chain."

"I will," Sharpe said. "We're going to drive back to City Hall. You might want to get started on figuring out where these guys are holing up."

"Can I borrow Rich?"

"Happy to help," he said before Sharpe could answer.

———

At City Hall, we climbed into Rich's blue Camaro and drove to my office. He correctly chose the V8 model but paired it with an automatic transmission. The car's lack of a third pedal earned Rich some mockery every occasion I rode in it. I backed off this time. The stop-and-go pace caused by traffic signals remaining down made an automatic the wiser choice under these circumstances.

He drove to my office, and we walked in to find T.J. eating an overstuffed sandwich for lunch. "There's one for you, too," she said around a mouthful of food. "In the fridge."

"Thanks. I might eat it later."

"Dibs if you don't," Rich said. "I haven't had anything since early this morning."

"Take it, then." I stood behind T.J. "Let's pull up the hacker's post from this morning." Rich grabbed a foil-wrapped package from the small refrigerator. "He says he doesn't know where his friends are holed up."

"You believe him?" she asked.

I shrugged. "Either way, he's not telling us. He says he isn't from around here and doesn't know the city well. It's plausible."

"How are we going to find the hideout, then?"

"We'll look at what's around him in his post. Houses. Street signs. Pubs. Whatever. The guy in charge is supposed to be something of a control freak, so it's likely our friend didn't wander too far."

"All right." T.J. queued it up. She and Rich chewed in stereo on either side of my head. At least the tuna salad crammed between the overworked pieces of wheat bread smelled good. She played the video. Clarence staggered around, slurred his words, and admitted to having a role in the hacking operation which disrupted services in Baltimore. If he went to trial, he was sunk.

I didn't care about legalities, however. We needed action-able intelligence.

"I don't see any street signs," T.J. said when the forty-five-second clip ended.

"Me either," I said. "Either he was careful not to film them . . . unlikely with him being drunk . . . or he remained on one stretch of road. It's not a long video, and he's not exactly setting a good pace."

"I'm surprised he remained standing the whole time," Rich added.

"For the price of that sandwich," I told him, "I expect some piercing insights." He took another bite and offered a faux serious thumbs-up. T.J. chuckled. I shook my head as she played the video again.

"There are some houses behind him," my secretary said. She paused the playback. "It's hard to see the numbers with the street lights out. We could brighten things up."

"House numbers don't matter much without the street name," I said.

"He's right," Rich said. "Let's see if we can spot anything else." T.J. resumed the clip. Clarence stumbled across a road. A cross street loomed behind him, but the camera angle didn't reveal any signs. "There." Rich pointed at the screen. "Over his right shoulder. He comes close to a building. Looks like a bar."

T.J. paused and zoomed in. Though the letters became less distinct, the larger size helped. "The Cardinal Tavern," I said. "I don't think I know it."

"I've been there once," Rich said. "Good place."

"Where is it?"

"Brewers Hill. Clinton Street, I think."

"Clinton and Hudson," T.J. confirmed with a quick web search. "It's well-reviewed."

"Let's hold off on the celebratory dinner until we actually have something to celebrate," I said. "There are a lot of places they could be using."

"You think they tried to be legit and rented a place?" Rich said.

"Not if they're going to be moving every couple days. I think they're probably squatting in places they know are abandoned. Recently so . . . the power would need to be on."

Rich balled up the foil wrapper from his sandwich. "Couldn't they just steal it?"

"Probably," I said. "It's not the best play. The city doesn't manage electricity. BGE does. A private company with its own security team and fraud investigators. Maybe our hackers are better than their guys, but when you increase exposure, you increase risk, too."

"I can run a real estate and rental search," T.J. said. "That script you gave me should work."

"Good idea."

"Do I want to know?" Rich said.

I shrugged. "It scrapes and compiles listings. Nothing illegal about it."

T.J. ran the script, and it returned a lot of results. "I can't filter by neighborhood names," she said, "but I can plug in the surrounding streets." She got a hit on Clinton, across the road and about four houses south of the Cardinal Tavern. "This could be promising. Insurance agent retired suddenly. It happened after the first of the month. Power is likely on through the end."

"Especially if whoever manages the place wants to show it," I said. "I think we should start there. Let's see if there are any other good fits, but I want to check this one out tonight."

"What are you going to do?"

"What else? Break in and join the team."

"You sure it's safe?" T.J. said.

"It's probably not," I said, "but we need to find these assholes before they set up shop somewhere else."

———

"You seem to love that disguise," Gloria said as we lay in her king bed.

"It served me well in Frederick."

"Joey was right, you know. It does make you look a bit like a failed rock singer."

"Don't be cruel," I said. She rolled her eyes at my Elvis joke and gave me a light slap on the shoulder. My friend Joey Trovato actually said I resembled someone who failed an audition for Aerosmith. The woman who handled these things for him couldn't get rid of us fast enough. "I just need to look enough like someone else to fool these guys. I've never associated my hacker alias to my real identity. If I walk in there as me, they might make the connection. I know my picture has been in the paper a couple times even though I try to avoid it."

"I get it," my wife said. "I'll miss you."

"I'll miss you, too. Hopefully, I won't be gone very long."

"It sounds dangerous." She snuggled closer and draped her leg atop mine. "Most of your cases do, but from everything you said, these guys aren't messing around."

"They might want to sow some kind of unrest," I said, "but at the end of the day, they're sitting at keyboards. I think I'll be able to hold my own."

Gloria grabbed my wrist and looked at my watch. "I don't think you need to leave just yet." She wriggled her way completely on top and kissed me.

"You're probably right."

Later, I did need to go, and I threw my clothes back on. Gloria remained in bed. "I don't know how often I'll be able to talk to you," I said. "It sounds like the boss runs a tight ship. "You have my burner number."

She nodded. "I'll check in with Rich, too."

"Good. I might get to talk to him and Sharpe at the safehouse. We may need to arrange some cloak-and-dagger stuff to make it work, but we'll figure it out."

"You'll get to act like a spy." Gloria grinned. "My very own James Bond."

"You can help me pick out my double-oh number later."

"Deal." We shared a long series of goodbye kisses, and I left before my knees grew weaker. At home, I put on the disguise, checked my go bag, and added an old mobile which barely worked. With Clarence getting popped for making a video, I got a feeling APToo would crack down on phones. If they did, I meant to spare my good one. With my backpack full, I walked to where I parked the Caprice in the neighborhood. I'd left it on the street about a half-block from my front door. The decal in the windshield would identify the car as authorized to park in Federal Hill, but it would be easy enough to explain away if someone asked about it.

Once in the car, I texted Rich from the burner. *It's dark enough now. Heading to Brewers Hill. Will keep you posted.*

He fired off a quick reply. *Roger that.*

With ccps still directing traffic at intersections, the drive took much longer than it normally would have. I found a spot about a block away and curbed the Caprice there. The streets were dark in the residential area of Clinton Street. As I drew closer to the corner, lights from businesses like the Cardinal Tavern lifted some of the gloom. Citizens couldn't be happy. Basic services remained offline. If the hackers wanted to gin up the mob, I figured it wouldn't be too difficult.

I walked up the opposite side and stood outside the Cardinal Tavern. This required me to share the airspace with two men polluting it by smoking, but I ignored them as much as I could. The houses across Clinton looked mostly the same, an artifact of Baltimore rowhouse design. All were narrow, three stories, and could boast of no rooftop decks. The one T.J. identified was the only home with two doorbells. A camera kept an electric eye on the front. I wondered if another did the same for the back.

A short jaunt down Hudson brought me to an alley running behind the house I wanted. I stopped a couple buildings away. Outdoor lights from other homes were bright enough to show another camera mounted above the back door. Gaining access to most residential surveillance systems was trivially easy for any competent hacker. As I counted myself among this group, I pulled out my phone, took a few steps closer, and used an app to look for nearby open devices.

I got a hit on the device in question. A quick Google search of its make and model revealed the default credentials. APT00 would have used them to break in. They probably didn't expect anyone to come behind them, so making changes would have been low on the priority list. I entered the base values and got in. A view from the camera showed me I stood a few feet out of its range. Perfect. I recorded a minute of nothing and fed it back into the system on a loop. If anyone watched the output, they would see a very brief glitch in the video but nothing else amiss.

In case any neighbors took an interest in me, I opened the gate and walked through the chain-link fence. Like most rowhouses, this one had a negligible backyard which was more concrete than grass. I made it to the rear entrance and left my good phone in an empty plant pot. A peek inside showed the kitchen. As far as I could tell, the first floor remained dark. My snap gun bypassed the lock in a couple seconds, and I padded inside. All the lights were off on the main level. I put an ear to the basement door but heard nothing. It would make sense for offices to be on the second floor.

Another interior door led to the stairs. They were wooden and looked original. No cameras monitored anything here, but I took my time to stay quiet. I stopped and crouched as I reached the second floor. A bathroom sat off to the right. The rest of the level had been converted into an office, and the entrance yawned open on my left. Quiet voices and the click-clack of mechanical keyboards told me APT50 remained at work even after dusk.

I stood and walked into the room. Two people behind desks looked up in surprise. Another man rose to meet me. He looked more like a football player than a keyboard warrior—the guard Clarence mentioned. Before he could draw the pistol strapped to his belt, I booted him in the stomach. He backed off a step and launched a kick of his own, which I dodged. He rushed me with a flurry of punches. They came hard and fast but with no thought of defense. Once the initial volley slowed, I hit the guard with a quick jab in the solar plexus. He sucked wind and retreated.

Before he could recover, I gave him a hard right in the gut and then elbowed him in the side of the head. He dropped to the floor but remained conscious. I thought about hitting him again to turn his lights out but remembered I would need to work with him if I joined the group. I couldn't make an enemy of him. Instead, I grabbed the gun from his holster. "Stay down." He coughed and gave no indication he was in a rush to stand up again. "Hi, everyone. I'm Foxtrot. Your friend Cold Frost recommended me."

I glanced around the room. Six desks formed a loose semicircle. Each held two large monitors. Only two were currently occupied. A door on the side of the room opened, and a man stepped out holding a pistol. I fought the urge to raise mine, but I shifted so I could duck behind a desk if I needed to. "So you're Foxtrot," the newcomer said.

"Factor Zero, I presume."

He inclined his head. The group leader looked to be about my age. He was shorter than me, probably five-eleven, and looked slender enough to fear strong winds. I wondered if firing a gun would cause him to fall over. He didn't have the wild hair or Che Guevara tattoos I expected. The man standing before me was clean-cut and clean-shaven. "Nice work on the camera system. I guess you messed with the feeds." I didn't say anything. "I heard from Frost. He was an idiot." I shrugged. "He put in a good word for you, though." Factor Zero drew closer. His gun remained pointed at me. A chill crawled up my back, and I remembered a hidden assassin stepping out of the shadows at the harbor to shoot me twice. "Put the gun down."

I stuffed it into the back of my waistband. "Best you'll get."

"You're pretty good at fighting for a hacker."

"I was bullied for being a geek in middle school," I said. "My parents insisted I take martial arts." I shrugged. "I've kept at it."

"Good for you," he said. "I've heard of you, but I'm not sure I trust Frost after what he did."

"Guess I should've brought my résumé."

"How about a test? You break into a system, and we let you join the group."

"And if I don't?"

Factor smiled and waved the pistol.

CHAPTER 10

"I THINK you've seen *Swordfish* one too many times," I suggested.

"Maybe." Factor Zero kept the pistol trained on me as I sat at one of the open desks. "I know what you're talking about. Hugh Jackman cracks some fancy crypto while a maniac holds a gun to his head."

"Pretty much."

He stepped closer. If I needed to, I could push off the desk with one hand and make a play for his gun with the other. I hoped it wouldn't come down to such a maneuver, of course. "I'm going to ask you to break into something which should be easy for you. We want the city's HR records."

"I'm surprised you haven't gotten them already," I said.

Factor shrugged. "Didn't need them before. Hell, we might not now, but it can't hurt to have them. A lot of IT people bailed for bigger checks. I want to know who's left."

"Fine." I opened the city's public website.

"You can see we run Kali Linux," he said. "It's a custom build with a few modules added. You should have everything you need to get me what I want." He looked at the drab clock on the wall. "You have ten minutes."

I got to work. Navigating to the employee portal was easy. Proceeding without the right credentials, however, would be impossible. I used some of the computer's tools to check for common vulnerabilities. None I could use popped up on the scan. I tried a few common injection attack techniques, but the login screen simply reloaded. "Eight minutes," Factor said.

I broadened my search. Developers and administrators often leave notes in online repositories like Pastebin and Github. The former held a bunch of text but nothing I could use. The latter contained credentials for a privileged account used to access and assess the system. I entered the user name and password and got in. "Not bad," the group leader said. He lowered the gun, resting it in his lap. If I needed to grab for it, his relaxed posture would make it easier.

The internals weren't organized in the most sensible way, but I eventually found a server containing the HR department records. I felt squirrely handing it over to this hacking group. I also felt I didn't want to be shot again. Besides, my nine minutes of work weren't unique. If APToo recruited people with some decent skills, any of them could have done the same. "I think this should be what you want," I said as I scooted my chair back.

"And with fifty-five seconds left on the clock," Factor said. "Not very dramatic, but I like the results. Fine. You want in?"

"I do."

"Why?"

"Because institutions rot from the top, and the city is rancid." I believed the first part of my statement, and while I would never like Vincent Davenport, the second represented a huge reach. Still, if this sentiment got me in the door, I could call the mayor an asshole all day long and never tire of it.

"Welcome to APT Double Zero," he said. "You have a phone?"

"Of course," I said, "why?"

"Let me see it." I took the old model which barely worked out of my pocket. "Put it on the desk." I did. Factor Zero took the pistol by its business end like a hammer and smashed the mobile with the grip. The screen cracked, glass flew away, and he kept at it until the Android model was beyond dead. "Clarence's phone got him in trouble. We're lucky it didn't compromise us. I'll give you a simple model you can use. Nothing else."

I pretended to be upset, throwing up my hands and slapping the desktop near the remains of the mobile. "What the hell am I supposed to do when your op is over?"

"Buy the latest and greatest," he said. "You'll have plenty of money."

I didn't belabor the point. "Fine."

"You start tomorrow. We'll be in a new location. I'll probably change every two days . . . more often if I think we need to. Keep an eye on the cell I give you."

"I will." He retreated to his office, handed me a very basic burner model straight from a decade ago, and showed me the numbers already programmed into it. "There's an app on there we can use, too. Otherwise, it's pretty locked down. Don't try to root it. We'll see you tomorrow."

I stood. The guard had recovered in the interim. "No hard feelings," I said. He didn't say anything. I left via the back door, collecting my real phone before I walked away.

———

I drove warily from APToo's base. No one followed me, and I did a loop of the block to be sure I hadn't sprouted a tail. Once I knew I was in the clear, I texted Rich while I waited for an officer to wave me on at an intersection. *I'm in. Location is going to change tomorrow. No one's following me, but I'll need the safehouse info.* He responded with an address a couple minutes later. I thought it was near Patterson Park, and plugging it into my phone's GPS confirmed this.

The house sat on South Curley Street. Patterson Park was massive, and the BPD's place was a short walk from its easternmost end, mostly walking trails and baseball diamonds. I found a spot a few houses down and left the Caprice there. As I approached the house in question with my bag over my shoulder, Rich appeared in the doorway. He waved me in with some urgency, so I hustled inside.

Leon Sharpe sat on a drab couch in the living room. Whoever furnished these houses for the police department pinched their pennies. The carpet was apartment grade and needed to skip mere replacement for a trip to the incinerator. Worst of all, it probably covered hardwood floors which only needed a little buffing and maintenance to be perfectly usable again. A smallish flatscreen TV sat on a dedicated stand. It probably got donated when some BPD official upgraded the one in their bedroom. I nosed into the kitchen and saw worn countertops and mediocre appliances. At least whoever maintained the residence stocked a coffee maker. Before I returned to the living room, I left APToo's phone in the fridge in case the group spied on its operatives. "Are the accommodations to your liking, sire?" Captain Sharpe said.

"They'll do." I sank onto a comfortable recliner. It didn't look like much, but it was a great chair. Rich plopped down near Sharpe.

"Tell us what happened," my cousin said.

"I found their house, looped the camera feed, and broke in. The leader put a gun to my head and made me hack into something. It was a test."

"I guess you passed."

"Yeah. Don't blame me if you get a lot more junk mail in the coming months, though."

Rich rolled his eyes. "I'm not sure I want to know. You going to keep us posted as to the new location?"

"When I can, yes," I said.

"Some people in the department want to move and arrest the hackers now," Sharpe said.

"I think it would be a mistake. You'd never get anything out of them."

"I know. I'm trying to preach patience. Doubly so with the damn feds sniffing around. The current thinking is to get them while things aren't too bad."

"Nothing like presuming your adversaries are idiots," I said. "These guys could have things set to run at certain times . . . or if someone isn't there to stop it. I'm glad the city has been able to adapt to the current disruptions, but a strike now could make things a lot worse."

"You think they have fail-safes in place?" Rich asked.

"I don't know. I won't have any idea until I get a chance to poke around what they've done. I'd work off the assumption they do. Smart groups will."

"All right," Sharpe grumbled. "I'll hold off the wolves. As long as the commissioner listens to me, we'll be good." He pointed a meaty finger at me. "You should work quickly."

"You can't rush greatness, Leon."

"I'm gonna hurry it along, then. Whatever you want to call it. We don't use this safehouse much, so someone beating down the door here isn't the issue. If your new friends make things worse, my voice might not be loud enough."

"Let's reiterate what happens if you kick the door in," I said. "I know I'll get led away like everyone else. We need to keep up appearances and all. What then?"

"You'll get released as soon as possible," Sharpe said. "The commissioner and I are both involved in this. We're not going to leave you with a bunch of criminals."

"I hope not. I still have my phone, but I won't be carrying it while I'm working. They got paranoid after Clarence's little video. I'll keep you posted when I can."

"All right." Sharpe stood, and Rich did, too. I remained in the recliner. Another half-hour, and I might fall asleep in it. "Good luck. Remember . . . faster is better."

"Not what my wife tells me," I said.

Sharpe sighed. He and Rich left. I settled in to my new digs, hoping I wouldn't need to be away from Gloria more than a couple days.

———

The rest of the house was fairly standard. A living room, kitchen, half-bath, and dining room on the main floor. The second level featured two bedrooms and a bathroom which hadn't been updated in at least two decades. The hosts of several home design shows Gloria watched might have fainted if they saw it. The top level held the master bedroom, a large bathroom, and another space which someone converted to a walk-in closet. Maybe the BPD stashed informers with the largest wardrobes here.

A text came in on the hacker phone. It was from Factor Zero, whose contact displayed as Math Tutor. A pair of coordinates formed the entirety of his message. Since the device didn't come with a map program, I used my real phone to resolve them to an address. This one was a rowhouse on the other side of Patterson Park which held a law office until recently. The pattern held. I responded in the affirmative.

I left the APT mobile in the powder room and ran water from the sink while I sat in the dining room and called Gloria. "Did you pass your audition?" she asked.

"You're speaking to the newest member of a not-really-elite hacking organization," I said. She didn't need to know Factor held a gun to my head during my tryout. Gloria worried enough about me already.

"Should I congratulate you or tell you I'm sorry?"

"Maybe a little of both."

"Where are you now?" Gloria wanted to know.

"In a BPD safehouse. This one must've been on the books for a while. They couldn't afford to buy it in today's market."

"Is it nice?"

"The location is," I said. "I probably shouldn't tell you where just in case. Let's just say they didn't spend much on the interior. It'll get the job done for a few days. Hopefully, I won't need to be here any longer."

"If you are, I might need to plan a conjugal visit."

I smiled. "I'm a little concerned about security, honestly. The group gave me a flip phone. It's a dumb model. No Internet connection. I think they're spooked after the guy I replaced made a drunk Instagram post. It wouldn't surprise me if someone tried to follow me from their base."

"Did they try already?" Gloria said.

"Not tonight," I said. "The location changes every couple days. I'm not sure how they're moving the equipment, but it's a logistical hurdle. Probably can't spare anyone."

"Be careful. I know you expect me to say it, but I mean it. I need you to stay in one piece."

"I do, too. I'll talk to you when I can, but I don't know how often it'll be. Love you."

"Love you, too."

I ended the call and retrieved the other phone from the powder room. No messages or calls came in. I thought about connecting it to a computer and seeing what processes it ran, but if my attempt got logged, I would quickly be out of favor with my new co-workers. Considering the leader's love of a pistol and history of violence, it was a place I didn't want to find myself.

At least not yet.

CHAPTER 11

THE NEW LOCATION on the western side of Patterson Park would have been an easy drive under normal circumstances. Thanks to my new coworkers knocking the traffic light system offline, however, I elected to walk. It would take about twenty-five minutes. I woke up early enough to put my disguise on and arrive at a reasonable hour. A brisk pace in the chilly morning air even allowed me to pop into a coffee shop I'd never tried before for a nice cup of dark roast.

Java in hand, I made a loop of the block to ensure no one followed me. I saw no suspicious people or cars. For the rest of the jaunt, I changed sides of the street a couple times, but nobody mirrored me. The new location sat on the opposite side from where I stood. I waited a few minutes to see if I could catch anyone coming or going.

One other person walked in. I couldn't tell much about him thanks to his hoodie and heavy jacket. An overstuffed bookbag hung on his back as he rang the bell, waited a few seconds, and walked in. No one else came or went, so I jaywalked across the street and rang the bell which still carried a law office label. "Yes?" a harsh male voice said.

"Foxtrot reporting for duty."

He grunted. A quiet buzzer went off, and I entered the building. Owing to my experience with the prior site, I expected the action to take place on the second floor. It was nevertheless empty, and I didn't hear anything coming from the third. The main level was similarly vacant. I used my vast sleuthing powers to deduce the team would be working in the basement. A door off the kitchen remained slightly ajar. I opened it and took the rickety wooden steps into the cellar.

Like many in rowhouses, it wasn't full height. I couldn't stand at my normal six-two even between the beams. Gauging people's heights when they're seated can be challenging, but I guessed the other members of the team to be shorter than me. In addition to its effects on my posture, the area smelled musty. A few pillars went from the concrete floor into the ceiling at various and random spots. Rather than the organized look of the work area in the prior site, the basement forced a chaotic configuration. Factor Zero didn't enjoy his own office here, but he did segregate his workspace from everyone else's. "Welcome to the team," he said without getting up.

The security guard I'd dealt with the prior day glared at me from a small station near the back of the area. Besides the sentry and leader, four other people worked behind two-monitor setups. One remained empty. Factor Zero stood and walked to me. He didn't offer a handshake, fist bump, or any other greeting, and neither did I. "You might try getting here a little earlier tomorrow."

I glanced at my watch—a reliable G Shock model instead of the smart one I normally wore. I didn't want anything to tie my alias of Foxtrot to my actual life. Reducing the potential attack surface helped. "Sure," I said.

"All right. I'll give you a quick intro to the team. Then,

you can dive in to some shit Clarence was working on. I think you'll be an upgrade for us. Chaos is what we do."

I offered my best fake smile at his little slogan and hoped the colored contacts in my eyes conveyed sincerity. "Can't wait."

———

I met my four new teammates in rapid succession. First up was Iceman. I remembered Deng telling me about him. Factor Zero introduced him by his actual name also—Darrell. Darrell was a short, pudgy black guy who looked to be a few years out of college. He typed on an old-school mechanical keyboard which filled the compressed space with click-clack sounds. A thin woman with an angular face sat near him. She barely looked up when Factor introduced me. Shelly (hacker name Honeybee, and I'd heard of her) didn't seem interested in meeting the new guy.

The next two were a little more receptive. Javier wore the hoodie I'd seen from across the street a short while ago, and the jacket hung from the back of his uncomfortable looking chair. When Factor introduced him as Paradice, Javier took care to tell me the second syllable was spelled like the kind you throw in craps and Dungeons and Dragons. As a fan of the latter, I understood, and we commiserated over the pain involved with stepping on a four-sided die while barefoot or in socks. Rounding out the team was Marc Turbowski, who introduced himself as Turbo. He stood, shook my hand, and told me how nice it was to meet another hacker he'd heard of. Turbo kept his head shaved and wore a bomber jacket. I wondered if he'd ever been in the military, and if so, how he reconciled it with his current activities.

With names and handles out of the way, I took my seat.

The chair felt as dreadful as I imagined. A full day in here would require a massage afterwards. All the computers looked alike, and they reminded me of the gaming rigs I'd built in my high school and college days. I enjoyed the same dual-screen setup as everyone else. Jiggling the mouse brought me to the Kali Linux login screen. I knew the default credentials but figured they wouldn't work. Sure enough, they didn't. "Let's see if you can get in," Factor said from his desk.

Considering I'd already given this jackass the city's HR files, I didn't feel like another test was in order. However, I rolled with the punches. The previous user was Clarence AKA Cold Frost. One could have been the user name and the other the password. This group wouldn't make it so easy. They'd want things to be more complicated in the event anyone got popped—like Clarence did. So far, he'd given the police nothing of value besides getting me in to take his place.

I lifted the rubberized mouse pad. Nothing hid underneath it. Ditto the basic white keyboard. I felt along the bottoms of the monitors until my fingers brushed a small piece of paper. I plucked the sticky note from its hiding place and read it.

Admin

Operat1onB@ltimore

Downw1thD@venport

I presumed the first two to be the credentials I needed, and entering them got me in. The third string must have been the root account password for running privileged operations. APT$_{00}$ enforced least privilege. It made sense. If someone tried to hack them back, processes would only run with the permissions of a user account. The damage would be limited. I'd respect the operational security if I weren't trying to sabotage the whole thing from the inside.

"We don't really do surveillance," Factor Zero said as he walked around the area. "We're going to be changing locations, and I want a minimum of teardown and setup. We have a guard whom you've met, and each computer runs a keylogger. I want to be able to know what's happening.'

"Understood," I said even though it complicated what I wanted to do. I couldn't defuse a logic bomb if every key I pressed left a trail. I pondered ways I might get around this while the leader kept talking.

"We'll work until our job is done. We want Baltimore and its mayor to pay."

"For what?"

"It's a long list," he said. "Stick around, and I'm sure you'll hear us talking about it. In the meantime, you'll find some things Clarence was doing in a text file on the desktop. Those are your projects now."

I wondered exactly what mess I'd gotten myself into as I looked over the list.

———

I spent the day doing a lot of reconnaissance work. It was important—like soldiers, hackers needed to know the battlefield before they stepped onto it. Considering the group had already launched a few attacks, I still felt surprised to be gathering so much information at this point. It became clear they wanted to target more and more systems and either force the city to pay millions in ransom or suffer with absent or degraded services.

"Do I clock out at the end of the day?" I asked my fellow keyboard warriors.

Turbo offered a hearty laugh. "We don't have timesheets

or anything. If your work is done, and there's nothing else you want to get into, you can go."

"I feel like I finished a lot for my first day." During the course of my work hours, I made sure to get up and stretch as best I could in the tight space. In addition to keeping the blood moving, I wanted to see what my teammates worked on. Trying to do this without being obvious complicated matters. I saw a lot of code on screens but couldn't read any of it without broadcasting my true intentions. Shelly used some kind of anti-glare screens which made whatever she did impossible to read from a distance. Factor Zero set his area up so we could only see him in profile, and I didn't want to raise his alarm by wandering too close.

On the whole, the day didn't feel productive. I did a lot of busywork a computer science undergrad could have performed for minimum wage. On top of it all, I didn't learn much about APToo's next targets. If Rich and Sharpe expected me to assemble a dossier for them, they would be disappointed by the initial returns. I packed up my stuff, shrugged into my jacket and backpack, and bid adieu to my not-friends. Walking up the stairs felt great because I could actually stand up. I hoped someone equipped the safehouse with a massaging chair, and I expected to be let down.

The official start of winter was still a little ways off, but dusk settled over the city early nonetheless. The lack of streetlights didn't help in the residential areas, either. Even Patterson Park remained dark and thus mostly vacant, with only a few determined dog walkers braving the early evening chill and gloom.

A chocolate Lab turning its head to look behind me clued me in to the fact I'd sprung a tail.

I used the large side mirror of an obnoxiously huge pickup truck to confirm it. Who the hell would be following me? The police knew where I was. Rich and Sharpe wouldn't put anyone on me, but Commissioner Ngo might. He didn't like or trust me and may not have been willing to wait for a subordinate to give him a nightly debrief. The FBI remained a possibility, too. If Agent Zellhoefer kept his boss in the dark —and I suspected he did in the interests of lightening his own workload—Hess could have put someone on me.

Then, I pondered the possibility of Factor Zero wanting me followed.

It made the most sense. I carried a name in the community and came recommended to him. However, the source of said recommendation may not have been the best. Clarence acted like an idiot and got caught, and his actions put the entire team in jeopardy. I wondered if Factor suspected Clarence nominated me because the cops put him up to it. The man seemed to be more than a little paranoid.

I didn't want whoever followed me to realize where I was going. About a half-mile remained in my walk back to the safehouse. The prevailing darkness might help me lose someone, but my backpack made me easier to spot. I couldn't get rid of it. Maybe I could stash it in something else long enough to fool the shadow on my six. I ducked into a small Italian restaurant and ordered linguine bolognese to go. Then, I sat near the entrance and waited. My team-issued burner phone made an effective mirror to see my tail pace awkwardly across the street.

A few minutes later, my meal was ready. "Can I have a very large to-go bag?" I asked the hostess. "I'm happy to pay extra for it." She provided a white paper bag with sturdy handles. It would be big enough to hold my dinner and my bookbag. I pointed toward the rear of the building. "Is your restroom there?" She nodded, and I headed toward the corridor marked EXIT.

In the john, I turned my brown jacket inside out. It wasn't reversible, and it would look a little ridiculous, but it would also look black to anyone following me. Outside the men's room, I made a left toward the rear of the restaurant. Sure enough, a back door led into an alley. A cook enjoyed a smoke break behind the building. A hair net and white baseball cap held his mullet in place. "Twenty bucks for your hat," I said, holding out a Jackson. He smiled and accepted it.

The cap smelled like grease, and I wished I carried disinfectant wipes, but I sized it for my dome and put it on. At least it touched the wig and not my skin. Now, instead of a man in a brown coat with a backpack, I was a man in a black coat, white hat, and large takeout bag. It wouldn't win prizes for disguise, but I hoped it would do enough to fool the guy tasked with following me.

I exited the alley, got my bearings, and continued the walk back to the safehouse. The man who had been on my tail remained across the street from the restaurant. He left his post a couple minutes later. When he walked behind me for a block, I wondered if I'd done enough to trick him. To my relief, he turned at the next intersection.

I kept going and didn't see him again.

CHAPTER 12

MY ITALIAN CARRY-OUT grew cold after I dodged my pursuer and walked back to the safehouse in the chilly dusk. The kitchen featured a large microwave on the counter, so I heated dinner up and carried it to a nondescript table. I caught up on email as I ate a pretty good meal. It likely would have been better if I'd gotten to eat it while it was hot the first time. No crises waited in my inbox. T.J. told me she paid a couple bills, advised a prospective client with a cheating spouse to look elsewhere, and informed someone else I'd be back in a few days.

She also reminded me she held dibs on my car in the event of my demise.

The phone vibrated as a call came in. I put the other in the fridge again before answering. The number made me think it originated at City Hall, and the mayor's voice a second later confirmed this. "Mister Ferguson. I was hoping I might trouble you for an update."

"Getting desperate?" I asked.

"What do you mean?"

"You could have had the commissioner ask me. He probably likes me about as much as you do, but he'd make the call if you told him to. There's also Captain Sharpe and my cousin. Any of them could've talked to me and relayed a message."

"I'm taking care of this personally because I want to know. I don't want to hear what's going on second or third-hand."

"Fair enough," I said. "Right now, there's not much to report. I spent the day working with the hackers. They tasked me with pretty basic things . . . information gathering, basically. They definitely want to do more damage and rub your face in it."

"And you're going to help them," Davenport said.

"I'm going to do my best to appear to be one of them. I tried to get some intel on what they're planning, but I'm the new guy. Only one person is really outgoing. The rest don't talk to me much, and it's hard to look at their screens without being obvious."

"Are you being monitored?"

"The leader keeps an eye on everyone," I said, "and he has a keylogger installed on every computer. If I went rogue and tried to sabotage something, he would know. Maybe not in real-time, but the jig would be up for me."

"I admit I'm a little disappointed." Davenport sighed. "Maybe I just don't have the right expectations. I think I've become too enamored of undercover operations thanks to movies and TV shows."

"I wish I could solve it quickly. Even with me on the inside, I think this is still going to get worse before it gets better. You need to be prepared. Have you brought in a proper incident response company?"

"They're coming tomorrow. I asked for a recommendation from my former CTO. He mentioned a company out of Pennsylvania."

"I don't need the whole story," I said. "Let them work. The best thing they could do is contain the damage. If you're lucky, they'll be able to bring things back online." I paused. Davenport didn't say anything. "You should give Charlie a raise and promotion, too."

"I think he's earned one," the mayor said. "We'll see how things go with the IR firm tomorrow. I'm still keeping all my options open, so paying these bastards remains on the table. I know you disagree, but I have the city to think about."

"Which is one of the reasons I disagree. You pay now, and where does it stop? Every asshole with a ransomware tool will make Baltimore a target for a quick buck. You'll need to replace your IT staff in triplicate to keep up."

"I understand your position. Maybe you'll come to understand mine."

"Stranger things have happened," I said, and I ended the call. My dinner grew lukewarm while talking to Vincent Davenport. I hoped the IR contractors would convince him his back-pocket plan was a fool's errand. It didn't seem likely.

———

Despite plenty of room for a king, the main bedroom in the safehouse held only a queen. Two plain nightstands, a dresser, and a treadmill rounded out the room. Exercise equipment made sense. The BPD wouldn't want the people it stashed here to be seen running the streets. I didn't want to be, either, especially not after getting followed for part of my walk home. I texted Gloria goodnight and went to sleep a little earlier than normal.

My alarm woke me at the beastly hour of seven-thirty. I lingered in bed for a couple minutes before changing into some workout clothes and getting on the treadmill. It was a poor substitute for the mean streets of Baltimore, but it kept me away from prying eyes. I started out with a normal walk, made it brisk after loosening up for a few minutes, and then turned the speed up to a run. The machine allowed me to adjust the incline, but it didn't include any courses or programs which would do it automatically. I keyed in a couple uphills and downhills for variety.

While I ran, I pondered my current predicament. Steps I could take to bypass the keylogger would initially get recorded by it. Factor Zero could have disabled the on-screen keyboard option, and a good enough piece of malware would capture those, anyway. I knew of a few programs which could encrypt inputs and shield them from a logger, but the question of how to get to them remained. If I typed in a web address, the group leader would know about it. Even if he didn't monitor everyone in real time, he could see the results in a file later.

I would need something on a website he wouldn't give much notice to. My Foxtrot alias owned a blog, and it spent the last few years gathering a lot of electronic dust. If I could get the right file up there in advance, the site itself might be harmless enough not to draw attention. It was my best bet. I cut my run short and drank some water while my laptop booted. The gaps in my blog's history could draw attention if Factor went to the website. I signed up for a free trial of an artificial intelligence writing assistant and let the AI compose a few mediocre entries. After backdating them, my site looked like it had at least been nominally active over time. I found a good key scrambler and added it to the files section. This wouldn't be a perfect solution, but it was the best one I could come up with for now.

After a shower and a bowl of cereal—the best of the quick options in the pantry—I texted T.J. and gave her the aliases of every member of the team in addition to their first names. I felt surprised Factor volunteered this information. He didn't offer anything about himself, of course. Still, association with the other members could open some more avenues of pursuit, and the leader didn't strike me as the type to keep his head down and be quiet, anyway.

She told me she would get on it. I'd gone over research techniques with her a few times. She knew the more interesting places to look when avenues like Google and common online repositories failed. Before I left, Rich texted and wanted to know the location of the hacker hideout. I sent a reply. *I hope you're not planning on raiding it today. I need more time to get some intel and try to reverse what they've done. It's not going to be easy.*

He responded a moment later. *Not going after them today. Sharpe wants to give you time to work. The commissioner is a little itchier. We want to know if there's a pattern to the places they use.*

It made sense, and I sent him the address before I left for my walk there. Ngo wanting to ramp up the timeline didn't surprise me. He was a tool of Davenport—and a tool in general from my limited interactions with him—so if the mayor wanted something done, he would try to make it happen. I hoped Sharpe could hold him off long enough to allow me to get some meaningful work in.

———

After stopping for a badly-needed ginormous coffee, I arrived at the location a couple minutes late. No one glared at me this morning, and even my pseudo-boss didn't seem to care. Everyone else already sat at their desks. I took my seat and logged in. Factor Zero stood a moment later and moved to an area where we could all see him better. "Good morning, everyone. Now that we're all here, I want to talk about what we're doing today."

My fellow hackers stopped working to pay attention. I pondered trying to slip the key scrambler onto my machine, but this seemed like a poor time to stand out from the crowd. My inner individualist grumbled, but I listened to the group leader. "Our first attack was good as a proof of concept," Factor continued. "We knew the city had been hit before, and we suspected they were still vulnerable. They were. Combined with the brain drain in their IT department, this was the best time to hit them, and we succeeded. All of this said, we managed to disrupt some aspects of life but not really stop anything. The cops are probably hurting without some of their important files, but fuck them."

I fought a smirk. Some data remained missing, but the police regained access to more than Factor Zero thought. If I could, I'd throw more wrenches in the works. "It's time to start leveling up what we're doing. We're going after the nine-one-one system today." I frowned. The team would probably succeed. A prior attack years ago knocked the system offline and forced the city to use its failover. It didn't go well, and I doubted things had improved in the intervening time. This would be a major blow to normal operations.

"I know what some of you might be thinking," Factor said as he held up his hands. "People legitimately need to call for emergency services. It's not just the cops. I get it. I do."

"You're going to kill someone," Shelly said, providing the voice of reason. "Some old man is going to have a heart attack, and paramedics won't reach him in time."

"I get the concern," Factor said, "and it's valid. However, you all know we need to break some eggs to make an omelet. A few people might die, yes, but our goal must remain the same. Davenport is out of power. The police bend their knees to public accountability. A corrupt city loses its stain. The people who die will do so for many others to live or live better."

This seemed to placate Shelly, who nodded as Factor spoke. I hated the whole thing. It was one thing to go after the bureaucracy of a city, state, or country and do a little damage. My friends and I did this in Hong Kong. We spent a few years poking the big red bear of the Chinese government, but no one died because of something we did. "Couldn't we just open a carton of egg whites?" I asked.

"What?"

"No need to break any eggs. You can still make an omelet."

"I heard you don't like Baltimore," Factor said, and I felt everyone else's eyes on me.

I shook my head. "Not entirely accurate. I don't like Davenport, and I don't trust most institutions. I get wanting to make change. I just don't see the value in killing people to get it done."

"By the end of this, you will. Sacrifices need to be made. No progress in human history has come without it."

I remained quiet. Factor Zero was a madman, and everyone else seemed content to go along with him because he could make his points well. Continuing to argue could get me booted from the group, and then I'd be no good to the BPD or the city. I sucked up my distaste for the man, what he stood for, and what he hoped to do. I could only hope my part in all the chaos would be small.

CHAPTER 13

WITH WHAT PASSED for a motivational speech done, we all got to work. I knew the 911 system remained vulnerable. The city didn't manage it outright—as calls traversed the cellular and public switched telephone networks, data carriers held some responsibility, also. Finding out which one took me about two seconds. Going after Baltimore's networks would be one thing. Trying to knock over a multi-billion-dollar international corporation with good security would be quite another. Of course, the city's part of the operation represented the low-hanging fruit.

When the emergency response network dropped a few years ago, the failover plan went into place. Planning for a disaster formed an important part of conducting any sort of business online these days. While a redundant system could pick up the operations, switching to the alternative wouldn't be instantaneous, and capacity remained the biggest challenge. The current situation already taxed things more than normal.

Shelly was right. Someone was going to die. The worst part about it was I couldn't warn anybody and not out myself as a plant in the process. I needed to go along . . . or at least appear to. With everyone else looking at their own workstations and Factor Zero back at his spot, I opened a browser. The keylogger would capture my attempt to go to my blog online. I couldn't fool it, but maybe I could hide the signal in a bunch of noise. I also brought up a text editor. For every real character I entered in the address bar of Firefox, I typed a word in a new document. At the end of the process, I opened the site I wanted and was the proud owner of a document made up of gibberish.

My plan remained far from foolproof. I might have tricked the keylogger—and the chance existed I did not—but any software which monitored system or web activity would know where I went. It was a risk I needed to take. I downloaded the application, compiled it, and installed it locally. If all worked well, my keystrokes would be scrambled at the CPU level, so anything Factor Zero got from his logger would be gobbledegook.

Hopefully.

If I wanted to do my part to help the city, I needed to act like it worked, so I got down to business. Code came to me from teammates. I looked it over and saw what it could do. Once all the pieces were combined, the resultant malware would knock out the 911 system. Nothing I saw indicated the failover would also go offline. Either the hackers didn't know about it, didn't care, or chose not to cripple emergency response completely.

I took my turn writing functions into our package and sent it along for others to look at. Factor Zero reminded us the final eyes on the project would be his. We spent a couple hours writing the malware and testing it in a controlled virtual environment. It worked, and it did its job quickly and repeatedly over multiple simulations. "Thanks for all your work," Factor Zero said in the early afternoon. "I've reviewed everything, and it looks good. We'll wait until just before rush hour to turn this one loose."

Could I get away? My leaving would draw attention, and if APToo's attack later failed, everyone would connect the dots. No, I needed to stay. If I bailed now and reversed what happened, my time with the team would be finished, and the city would lose any insight into the operations against them. As much as I didn't want to be involved in this, I needed to stick it out. I felt a little sick. The clock on the wall showed less than an hour until our attack would launch.

My teammates worked on other aspects of the agenda, including a lot of information gathering, probing, and network mapping. It was hard to have too much information. Maybe I had some time to lessen the pain. Again, I operated as if my key scrambler worked. If it didn't, I would find out the hard way soon enough. I checked online code repositories for inserting a backdoor into our little program.

Given time, I could've written my own, but I didn't have the luxury. I browsed a few well-rated ones which provided the capability I required. I needed to do this blind. Testing it in our virtual lab would raise red flags. I picked a good one, found the code we collectively wrote, and added it in the right place. It came close to the end, so someone giving the product a cursory glance could miss it. I would be able to log back in and turn off the malware . . . presuming Factor Zero didn't take a careful look at everything before he deployed it. This whole situation required me to cross my fingers a lot, and I didn't care for it. The sooner my time on the inside ended, the better.

The clock struck four. "We've made rush hour a complicated affair," Factor said. "Traffic lights are still down. Much of the city will be dark in a couple hours. The police are overtaxed by waving their hands at intersections. It doesn't look like a big win, but I think it is. Now, it will be even bigger. I'm pushing our beautiful code out into the world." He made a big show of pushing a button on his keyboard. His screen— now shared on a large TV—showed a few lines flash by. It didn't look like much, but then again, most attacks didn't until you really crawled under the hood.

"Chaos," he said, and everyone smiled. My expression came from the fact he likely didn't review anything before deploying. I crossed my fingers under the desk.

———

"We'll have another new location tomorrow," Factor Zero announced. "You'll all be notified where later tonight."

"Seems sudden." Javier said. "We were only here two days."

"We're ramping up. Taking more things down, doing more damage. We have to presume the city is going to spend some resources looking for us. Maybe even the feds."

"The feds?" I asked, trying my best to inject some nerves into my voice.

Factor Zero waved a hand. "It's inevitable. They're going to get involved because the city can't keep up. I'm not worried about them. I'm sure we've all been running circles around the FBI for years. Nothing's changed."

We dispersed a short while later. Only Darrell remained behind with Factor. A couple of my compatriots chatted on the way out, and they headed off together. I wasn't invited, and it didn't bother me. I preferred to interact with them when I needed to. I wasn't a trained undercover operative, and I didn't want to slip up and reveal some aspect of my life which shouldn't be associated to Foxtrot.

I walked in the opposite direction back toward the safehouse. Despite periodic checks behind me, I didn't see anyone on my tail. As I did the prior night, I popped into the small Italian bistro for carryout. This evening, I didn't need a large bag and a side order of subterfuge. No one followed me from there, and I made it back to the safehouse. As I approached, I noticed a few cars outside including a familiar blue Camaro.

"Shit," I muttered as I unlocked the door and walked inside. Rich, Captain Sharpe, and Agent Hess sat at the dining room table. "When did you two start slumming with the feds?"

"We're all after the same thing," Hess said. I moved to the kitchen and microwaved my dinner for thirty seconds. It gave me time to remove the blond wig and colored contacts. After collecting some actual silverware, I sat as far from the trio as I could. Rich eyed my bolognese. I broke off one piece of garlic bread and pushed the other toward him. He accepted it as Sharpe frowned.

"I guess a welcoming committee comes with the territory of staying in a house owned by the BPD," I said. "I hope no one saw you come in."

"We were careful," Sharpe said.

I grunted around a mouthful of pasta.

"We can wait until you're finished," Hess offered.

"I like to savor my food. You might be waiting a while."

"Fine. We want to raid the location."

I shook my head. "Too soon."

"We're handling the nine-one-one system being down," Sharpe said. "The backup is a little more robust than before. Having more cops out and about for traffic might be helping us, too." I wondered if Factor Zero considered this in his deployment calculus. Probably not. He struck me as a zealot more than a strategist.

"You couldn't get a warning out?" Hess asked.

"Not without blowing my cover," I said. "Don't they teach stuff like this at Quantico?"

"Of course." He rolled his eyes. "This might be your first time in a situation like this. Your friends here seem willing to give you a fair bit of rope. I just don't want you to wrap it around your neck."

"I'm doing my best to blend in. Thanks to the guy who got popped, we all only get basic phones. I can't exactly send a text every time something happens." I took another bite of my dinner. "It also means I'm hard to reach. I won't get any warning if your men kick the door in. What happens in this case?"

"You'll get arrested with everyone else," Hess said. "It has to be done."

"I know," I said. "The cops have told me the same thing. What I want to know is how I'll be treated. Basically, I want your assurance some overzealous asshole isn't going to disappear me to a black site."

"Of course not." Hess leaned back as much as the uncomfortable wooden chair would allow. "We'll make sure you're kept away from everyone else, and we'll release you." He paused. "You know where they'll be tomorrow?"

"Not a clue," I said. "I've provided the locations I know so far. Probably not enough to look for patterns or predict anything yet. They seem to be using offices rented by small businesses which folded or moved."

"Could be hundreds of places," Sharpe said.

"Probably. The two I know of have both been in rowhouses." I shrugged. "Less security than going to an actual office building where you can run into guards or people from other companies."

"It's a start," Hess said. "You know how they move sites?"

"No idea."

"Seems like it would be hard for them. They couldn't just pay a moving company. They need the job done at odd hours, and whoever does it can't tell anyone about it."

The FBI man raised a good point. The operation would take at least a few men to pack all the equipment, carry it to and fro, and at least stage it in the new location. Doing so in a discreet manner and under cover of darkness required money. So far, the city hadn't paid APT$_{00}$ a single cent. Did they get cash or cryptocurrency from other ransomware projects? Clarence told us they were a loose group who came together recently. Probably not a lot in the coffers, then. Did a benefactor stake the project? More questions stewed in my mind, and I knew how I might go about answering a few of them.

———

Once the law enforcement brigade cleared out, I put on the hat I'd paid for the prior evening. I could walk to where we worked today, but I would both get there and be able to escape faster if things went sideways if I drove. Once nearby, I found a spot just past the next cross street and curbed the Caprice there. For about an hour, the only things happening were people moving around and doing whatever they normally did.

A white box truck pulled up, and I slumped lower in the driver's seat as its headlights washed over the area. The vehicle double-parked, and the two men who got out looked like they could have picked it up and carried it to the curb in a pinch. They peered around the area and moved with a loose confidence. These weren't gym bros moonlighting as movers for an extra buck. They were professional muscle on someone's payroll. The question of course being whose?

The Sinew Siblings disappeared inside the building. Despite the truck's flashers remaining on, drivers honked and cursed as they approached and passed it. A lane remained open for traffic to get by on the one-way street. A few minutes later, the duo loaded two servers into the back of their truck. A few more trips saw them bring out the monitors, desktop PCs, and networking equipment.

I couldn't read the plate on their vehicle from where I sat, but I got the feeling it wouldn't matter. If they were pros, either the truck or the tags would be stolen. Maybe both. Factor Zero appeared, shook hands with both, and climbed into the back. One musclehead secured the cargo while the other fired up the engine. A minute later, they were rolling and coming my direction. I tried my best to sit low and not be visible. As their truck passed my position, I saw no distinctive markings on the side or rear. Plain and white and probably with stolen plates. No chance of finding it or tracing it back to them.

I considered following them but decided against it. They could spot me, and then the jig would really be up. The downside risk didn't make the upside worth it. Unless they led me to some secret base of operations, I would learn our next working location in the morning. I could wait until then, and so could the BPD and FBI.

CHAPTER 14

MY TEMPORARY PHONE woke me up the next morning. I rubbed sleep from my eyes and stared at the screen until it came into focus. It was 6:45. "Dammit," I grumbled looking at the message from Factor Zero. Like before, it came as a set of coordinates. Because latitude and longitude numbers meant nothing to me, I entered them into the GPS on my real mobile. They resolved to a business still listed as an art studio near the Camden Yards stadium complex and Horseshoe Casino.

I showered and trudged downstairs. The fridge held a surprising amount of food. I wondered how often the BPD restocked the perishables when no one used the safehouse for its intended purpose. They couldn't have a revolving door of witnesses in and out of here. Someone would be bound to notice. I set coffee to brew while I scrambled some eggs which still had a few days left before expiring. There was no fresh bread, but whoever placed the groceries left a loaf in the freezer, so I made toast with it.

Considering our location would be a lot farther away today, I needed to drive the Caprice. Normally, I'd go through the city. With traffic signals still down, however, I took the longer route of going to the highway and getting off at I-395. As it became Howard Street, I passed the stadiums on my left, found the studio on a small side road, and parked in the alley behind it. A camera eyed me from the back porch, and another did the same as I approached the main entry. I wondered if they came with the place or if Factor Zero set them up at each location. He seemed paranoid enough to do the latter.

This time, we were on the main floor. Newer houses touted their open-concept floor plans. The challenges of taking down load-bearing walls in rowhouses made it rare, but whoever owned this place pulled it off. A few beams painted to blend in with the ceiling—I only knew to look for them thanks to Gloria's affinity for home-buying shows—held everything up and made it easy to move from the front to the back. Perfect for a studio and small gallery.

Two desks remained empty. For once, I wouldn't be the last to arrive. One desk sat off to the side in what once served as the kitchen. Factor Zero sat there engrossed in his work—and as normal, we couldn't see his screens. The rest of us were in what would have been the living room and dining room. I dropped onto a chair. Shelly walked in a minute later, frowned when her eyes scanned the room, and took the last spot. Our leader looked up. "Good, you're all here."

"Maybe we could get the casino to put some lines on the books for us," I said. "Will the city pay the ransom? Yes at minus-one-fifty. No at plus-one-thirty."

Factor Zero grinned. "I'd rather keep us a little more anonymous. We're getting enough press already. All right, our nine-one-one takedown has made the news. The mayor and the police commissioner are trying to downplay it, but I know it's working. We're putting the squeeze on them one system at a time. At some point, they'll have no choice but to pay, and we'll raise the rate as we go."

"Or they have the feds work against us," Shelly said.

"Nothing they do should surprise us. Let's not put too much stock in the FBI, Honeybee. They have some good cybercrime people, but they're few and far between. We're better. Besides, if we knock over enough resources, they'll have to triage the most important ones. It'll allow us to keep going."

He didn't mention anything about the backdoor I inserted in the code before it went live. Yesterday, I didn't think Factor gave everything a final review before pushing it out. He struck me as the type who would call attention to someone messing with his plan. As the weekend loomed, the 911 network would become more important. The police were overworked. Things could get worse quickly. So long as my backdoor remained, I could restore things and spare Baltimore a little chaos.

"We have more targets," Factor Zero continued. "Our work is good but not complete. Let's make these bastards pay."

"What if they hold out?" Turbowski asked.

"I didn't just mean money. Davenport and this city have a lot to answer for."

———

I performed reconnaissance work on public utilities for the rest of the morning. The city didn't control electron flow, but they owned a stake in the infrastructure. Things like water and sewage fell under Baltimore's stewardship even if contractors performed some of the work. So far, APToo managed to inconvenience citizens and probably raise the level of anger and unease. The 911 system remaining down would fan the flames. Taking away things like water would pour gasoline on the fire.

This seemed to be exactly what Factor Zero wanted I remembered Deng telling me he wanted to tear down the power, and he enjoyed a true believer working under him in Iceman. If things kept getting worse, a large segment of the population would want the mayor's head on a platter. The cops would get cast as villains for trying to maintain order and prevent widespread violence. There would be riots in the streets, and my city would make the news for all the wrong reasons again.

As the morning wore on, Shelly and Turbowski circulated interest in lunch. The latter loomed over my desk. "You're local, right? I've heard Baltimore has a good food scene." He patted his normal-sized belly. "I won't say I take jobs where I might be able to eat well, but it's a consideration, you know?"

I wished he'd learned to modulate his voice indoors. "Are you asking me for a recommendation?"

"Yeah. We want some pizza. Know any good places? I'm sure there are a lot around here. The stadiums and all. People will want to eat after a game. They—"

"There used to a place called the *Sotto Voce* Cafe," I said. Turbowski stared at me like he didn't get the hint. Of course. "They went under, though. We're close enough to Little Italy if you're driving or getting delivery."

"Shelly and I will pick it up," he said.

"I'd recommend Brick Oven Pizza in Fells Point or Rizzo's in Little Italy." My onetime friend Gabriella Rizzo owned the restaurant her father opened decades ago. In addition to leaving her an eatery, he also passed down his title as head of organized crime in the city. Gabriella and I had been on the outs for a while. Even if a large lunch order would help our recent truce, Turbowski's motor mouth would ruin it.

"Cool. Thanks, man." He clapped me on the shoulder. "You a pepperoni fan?"

"I'll take anything except fruit, fish, or olives," I said.

Thankfully, he moved on and chatted up everyone else in the process of putting an order together. When he and Shelly left a few minutes later, I said I wanted to get some fresh air. I found the cameras on the local network and checked the feeds. The one in the rear showed the porch and about half the yard but nothing beyond. Perfect. I headed out the front door and walked around to the back. In my car, I used my real phone to send a text to T.J. *We've moved again. Near the stadiums now. Any progress on the names I gave you?*

She answered a moment later. *Not much out there, boss.*

Keep looking. Make sure you're on the VPN and using a VM.

I am. I do listen when you talk, you know. Sometimes.

I put the phone away and returned to my desk. I never closed the camera feeds, and a few minutes later, this proved to be a good thing. Several men clad in body armor and carrying long guns advanced on both doors. Memories of Hong Kong played in my head, and my pulse quickened. "Guys, I think we're about to get raided."

"Shit," Factor Zero said. "I'll start a wipe." He hit a few keys. As the men outside moved closer to the house, I could see the *FBI* on their jackets. How the hell did Hess and the feds find us? The team fanned out. I couldn't hear them, but they used hand gestures, and their intentions were obvious.

The front and rear doors burst in at the same time. Two agents shouted the usual commands at us. Along with everyone else, I raised my hands. A beefy agent ordered me to stand only so he could wrestle me to the ground. I refrained from commenting on the inefficiency of the process as he forced my arms behind me and slapped the cuffs on. Raised voices sounded from all around me. It was hard to hear any specific person. I got hauled to my feet, and at least one pair of hands gave me a rough shove toward the front door.

I could only hope Hess would keep his word.

I got shoved into the back of a van with blacked-out windows. There were a few others on the street along with a phalanx of FBI vehicles. Red and blue flashing lights stretched for a couple hundred feet in both directions. A few minutes later, two male agents climbed in the front of the van. No one else joined me in the back. We left the neighborhood, and being in a federal vehicle got us past every intersection where a cop directed traffic with ease.

We made the ride in silence. I didn't want to play the Hess card yet. My fellow hackers needed to see me getting hauled away and treated like them. Neither fed asked me anything. I wouldn't have answered if they did. We got onto the Baltimore Beltway and rode to the FBI field office in Milford Mill. It was a long brick building taller at one end than the other and surrounded by the black metal fencing which always made important places easy to identify. After passing through the security gate, the van stopped near an entrance at the single-story end.

The two agents were about my age and size. They didn't try to push me along, but I also got the sense they wouldn't let me stand around and gape at the pictures of J. Edgar Hoover on the walls. We rode an elevator to the bottom floor and stepped off into a gloomy hallway. Only about two-thirds of the overhead lights were on. The duo led me into a large room. I sat on the far side of the table, and they cuffed one of my wrists to a sturdy bar mounted on it. They then left without a word and locked the solid wooden door behind them.

I didn't see anyone else on the way in, and I couldn't hear anything happening outside the room. To make everything look legit, I would continue the ruse for a while, but at some point, Hess needed to turn up and honor his end of the bargain. This wasn't my first time in an interrogation room, but all of them had been much smaller than this one. Behind me was a good hundred square feet of unused space. Pipes hung from the ceiling and brought a musty aroma with them, but nothing else was in the area.

My watch remained on my wrist. About twenty minutes passed with nothing happening. I began a study of the ceiling. Rather than tiles, it was concrete, and the plumbing and HVAC ran above my head. I didn't relish the idea of being in the basement. It crept toward black site territory. A nice interrogation space on the main floor would have been fine. Another half-hour elapsed before someone came in. He was about my height but burlier and dressed all in black. A nightstick hung from his belt. He didn't wear a badge or any ID I could see. "So you're one of the hackers messing with the city," he said in a voice with a slight drawl.

I remained silent. The newcomer stared down at me. He had brown eyes and sandy blond hair. A mustache and goatee encircled his sneering mouth. "Not gonna talk?" After a pause confirmed this for him, he continued. "I didn't think you would. Assholes like you love to crow about your rights." He produced a key from his pocket. "I'm gonna adjust your cuffs." He undid the one around the bar. "On your feet." I stood.

He moved me backwards, looked up, and stopped. "Arms up." I complied. He put the cuffs around a pipe and locked my other wrist. Thanks to the brackets coming from the ceiling, I could move forward and backward but couldn't get away. My pulse picked up. This didn't seem like standard operating procedure. Regardless of what happened to my sort-of teammates in other rooms, I needed to keep control of this situation. "Hess knows I'm on the inside," I said. "We've talked about it."

The agent scrutinized me. "You could get his name from Google."

"Maybe, but you could call him and verify what I'm telling you. I'm working with the Baltimore police."

"You a cop?"

"Private investigator, but I was the best person to send undercover."

He shook his head. "Sounds like bullshit. Cops wouldn't send a civilian in, and there's no way Hess would sign off on it."

"I'm telling you the truth," I said.

He took the nightstick from his belt and grinned like a predator. "I guess we'll find out."

CHAPTER 15

"I THINK this has gone far enough," I said.

"You don't get to tell me what's going on," the guy said. He tapped the nightstick into his open palm. "You and your friends have already knocked a bunch of services offline. Disrupted life for a lot of people. Nine-one-one is taking it on the chin. Pretty soon, I'm sure our geeks will tell us what else you had planned. You think you get to skate?"

"I told you . . . I'm working with the police. They sent me in. The commissioner and the mayor signed off on it. Hess knows everything about it."

"Easy to drop a name and a couple of titles." He stalked closer. My pulse thudded in my ears. I was several levels underground with no idea if anyone knew my current whereabouts. The FBI field office would never count as a black site, but with this jackass cuffing me in a vulnerable position and clearly threatening me, the distinction seemed trivial.

"It's also easy to call your boss and check," I said. "It'll save us both a lot of trouble."

"Hess doesn't pull my strings." He walked a circle around me, tapping the nightstick the entire time. "My job is to get actionable intel to stop an ongoing operation. You got anything you want to say?"

"Other than what I've told you already? No."

"Have it your way." He whacked me in the back of the right knee. My leg buckled, and my hands being cuffed over the pipe prevented me from collapsing. They didn't prevent my shoulder and ribs from feeling like someone wrenched them, however. I fought through the pain and made it back to a standing position. "I kinda like it when people hold out," he said.

"You're real tough when you hold all the advantages."

He moved to my front again. "I told you why I'm here. Make it easy on yourself and tell me something."

"Fine," I said, "you're an asshole. A petty bully hiding behind a badge." He scowled and stepped forward, swinging the nightstick into my exposed midsection. I'd managed to clench my abs before the blow thundered home, but he put considerable force into it. It still hurt. A lot. I struggled for breath as he smiled.

"You're not special, you know," he said. "I've seen a lot of criminals. Young. Think they're smart. It doesn't matter. They all give up their friends if we apply enough pressure."

"You need to call Hess," I wheezed.

He gave me another whack in the ribs, and it hurt even worse than the first. "You don't get to tell me how to do my job. I'm not inclined to listen to criminals." He put the short end of the tonfa under my chin and bent my head back. "I want to know who you're working with and what your next move is. You're not interested in talking? Fine. But I think you can see how this is going to go for you."

As he paced away, I focused on the basics of respiration. Inhale. Exhale. It grew easier. Telling this prick to talk to Hess wouldn't work. For all I knew, Hess signed off on what currently transpired. It wouldn't be the first time he'd let me down. I watched as my captor inched closer again. The hell with him. I was done playing nice. "I'm working with the Baltimore police," I said, "and my next move is going to be ending your miserable career."

He sneered and shook his head. When his arm went back, I gave him a quick snap kick in the groin. It stopped his swing and bent him over. Being held mostly in place by cuffs meant I couldn't follow up like I wanted to. Still, I could slide my restraints forward and backward along the pipe. The space between brackets gave me a few feet to maneuver. I took advantage. Before my tormentor could recover from my first kick, I hit him with a second one—much harder—under the chin. His head snapped back, and he fell over. The night-stick clattered when it hit the floor.

I came to the end of my range. He and his weapon lay just out of reach. "Got some fight in you." He got to all fours, picked up the tonfa, and stood. "Just makes it more satisfying for me in the end."

"Do your worst," I said. He stalked forward. I wouldn't surprise him again. When he readied another strike, I tried to boot him in the gut. He blocked it, however, and my limited ability to move prevented me from doing much else. My adversary gave me a solid jab in the ribs and then followed it up with a hard whack across the face. My cheek and jaw blazed with pain, and I blinked a few times to clear the cobwebs.

"I don't much care what you have to say at this point," he said. "I think I'm going to enjoy this for a while."

Before either of us could do anything else, a key turned in the lock.

———

The door swung in. Rich, Leon Sharpe, and Agent Hess walked toward us. "What the hell is going on here?" the FBI man demanded. "We don't treat prisoners like this. Especially not ones who are cooperating."

"He was telling the truth?" my captor said.

"Did he tell you he was working with us?"

"Several times," I said. "All I have to show for it are some facial bruises and maybe a couple cracked ribs."

"Put your nightstick down, Brubaker," Hess said. The guy complied. "Stand over there." He thrust a finger toward the corner opposite the door, and his compatriot moved to the appointed area. "C.T., I'm sorry this happened to you." Hess reached into a pocket and produced a small set of keys.

"I'm used to you falling short of expectations," I said.

He grunted but didn't have anything to say in his own defense. Hess stood uncomfortably close as he undid my right wrist and then my left. I took a moment to rub both.

"No hard feelings," Brubaker had the audacity to say.

I spent another few seconds making sure circulation returned to my hands.

Then, I sprinted forward, picked up the nightstick, and clobbered Brubaker upside the head with it before he could muster a defense. He dropped like a rock. I raised the tonfa again and let him have it in the gut. The fallen man grunted and folded in half. Rage flowed through me as I raised my arm again, but someone grabbed my wrist and lifted me away. A beefy black hand held my forearm. Sharpe carried me with as much effort as he might exert hoisting a sack of groceries and set me down about twenty feet away. Hess and Rich moved to stand between me and my former tormenter.

"What the hell?" Hess said.

"He deserves more. Let go of me, Leon."

"I think it's best for you if I don't," he said. I had a basically zero percent chance of escaping the powerful captain, so I stopped struggling. Brubaker coughed a couple times and managed to raise himself to a kneeling position.

"Now, there are no hard feelings, you miserable prick."

"I was doing a job," he sputtered.

"Fuck you and your job," I said. I tossed the tonfa down. Sharpe released his hold on me, and I took a few steps forward. "When this is all over, name your place and time. No badges, no weapons, no friends. You and me. We can settle this like men."

"You got it."

"This is ridiculous," Hess said. "We're in the middle of a major investigation. This is an unwelcome distraction."

"Tell it to your man there."

"He's not 'my man.' Brubaker is a Bureau contractor."

I snorted. "Right. Just means you get a little more soap to wash your hands with at the end of the day when he goes off the rails. I hope you're not too attached to your *contractor*, Hess, because I'm going to kick the shit out of him when this is done."

"The hell you are," Brubaker said, but everyone ignored him.

"I presume I'm free to go?" I said. Hess frowned. "If you think you and your man can keep me here, you're welcome to try."

"I could arrest you," Hess said.

"I promise I'll resist."

He shook his head. "Fine. You're lucky Captain Sharpe was able to restrain you so quickly."

I stepped forward and got in the special agent's face. "No, Hess. *You're* lucky. You and Brubaker both."

"We should at least talk about the case," Hess said. "Let's go upstairs."

I jerked my thumb toward the contractor, who had regained his feet. "I'm not coming if he does."

Hess stared at his hired hand. "Take the rest of the day off, Mike."

Brubaker grumbled, glared at me, and stomped out of the room. As we walked toward the door, Rich whispered, "I wouldn't have let Hess arrest you."

"Your help would've been great fifteen minutes ago," I said as we left the area.

———

We rode the elevator in silence to the second floor and walked to a small conference room. I eased myself onto the hard plastic chair. With the adrenaline of the moment wearing off, the pain of my mistreatment came back. "You all right?" Rich asked, frowning in concern.

"I'll live. I don't know if anything is broken. My face will probably swell up and bruise in a couple spots, but I won't need to see the orthodontist."

"I'm sorry again for what happened," Hess said.

"Go to hell," I said. "Let's get our briefing over with so I can leave this shithole."

"Fine." Hess adjusted his tie. "We arrested four people including you. There were a couple other work spaces, though. Was anyone not there?"

"Two people just left for lunch."

"Who are they?"

"Honeybee and Turbo."

"What are their actual names?"

"Probably not Honeybee and Turbo," I said, "but I didn't sign their birth certificates."

"This will go a lot better if you cooperate," Hess said.

"Your man downstairs said the same thing."

"We're not getting anywhere this way," Sharpe broke in. "Hess, why don't you tell us where the Bureau stands on the people arrested so far?"

"Sure. The other three are being processed. The leader has a lawyer. Some fancy asshole I've heard of." I wondered how Factor Zero came into such esteemed representation, but Hess didn't need to know my suspicions. "We're probably going to release him pending charges. The other two will be staying a while."

"Why are you letting him go?" I asked.

"We have to build a case," Hess said. "A federal prosecutor will work on it. We could push for remand, but his lawyer will fight it. There's strategic value in it, too. He might mess up. Might lead us to some more people . . . like the pair who made a lunch run right before we showed up."

I shook my head. "He's not going to help you with anything. He's a true believer. Chaos all the way, burn down the institutions . . . you name it. You know, if he torches this building for what happened today, I'll be sure to bring a bag of marshmallows."

Hess rolled his eyes but didn't take the bait. "We have all the IT assets, of course. Early word is there's a lot of encryption, and he claims not to have any of the keys. I'm not sure how much actual data we'll be able to recover."

"I'm not surprised." When Hess maintained his gaze at me, I added, "I don't have the decryption keys, either."

"Would you give them to me if you did?"

"I would remind you of the applicability of the Fourth Amendment," I said.

"I think we can use the events of today," Sharpe said.

Rich nodded his concurrence. "I agree. What happened sucks, but the leader might take it as a good sign."

They had a point. My shabby treatment at the hands of the FBI could win me points with Factor Zero. "All right. I'll reach out to him later today once I have all my stuff back."

"I'll be sure you do," Hess said. He made a call, and a few minutes later, a junior agent handed him a bag containing my wallet and burner phone. "I don't think we'll be releasing him for an hour or so. You might as well get a head start."

"Right." Rich and Sharpe left with me. The captain rode away in his chauffeured SUV. My cousin gave me a lift back near the APToo location in his Camaro. We stopped about a block away so no one saw us together. All the FBI cars and vans were gone. "I know you're pissed at Hess," Rich said. "I would be, too. He's going to do the right thing."

"I don't really care what he does," I said. "He sat on a pile of evidence I gave him connected to Samantha's death. You can go to bat for him all you want, but he's a bureaucrat and a clown. I'll be fine without him. Thanks for the ride." I climbed out of Rich's car, got back into the Caprice, and drove to the BPD safehouse. Whoever stocked the freezer left several bags of vegetables, and I put them to use covering my ribs and my face. The cold felt good for a while, and I put everything back before opening Noize to contact Factor Zero via a secure message. *Just got cut loose by the feds. They got rough with me, but I'm out. Ready to get back to work.*

He didn't answer for at least a half-hour. Maybe the FBI took their time processing him out. *Good. I'm out, too. We need to pick up where we left off. I need to get a few things ready. What happened with the FBI?*

I didn't tell those bastards a thing even when I got beaten on with a nightstick.

Right on. I'll send a new location tomorrow. Our work will continue. The feds are on the list, but we'll finish what we started first. Thanks for holding out. I put the phone away. At least I would have the remainder of the day off. The way I felt at the moment, I needed it.

———

I rested and iced my face and ribs as much as my tolerance for cold would allow. The main bathroom had a bottle of Tylenol in the medicine cabinet, so I took two. After a couple hours, the swelling on my cheek and around my mouth subsided, but both bruising and pain remained. Once this whole mess was in the rearview mirror, Brubaker and I would settle our differences once and for all.

Later in the afternoon, I stashed my APToo mobile in the fridge and called Gloria on my real phone. My goal was to catch her after her workday, but she ran her own business now. Hours were flexible. Once she heard what happened, she wanted to see the evidence, so we added video to our chat. "Oh, my god," she said when my feed went online.

"Normally, I like hearing you say those words."

"Different context. Are you sure you're all right?"

"I'll manage," I said. "I don't think he cracked a rib. My face hurts, but the swelling is down, so it seems like nothing is broken. I'll just look like I caught the bad end of a boxing match for a few days. So far, I know our leader is out. He lawyered up. We're starting up again tomorrow." I rubbed my cheek. "If anything, this helps my cred with the hackers. They think holding out on the feds proves I'm devoted to the cause." I shrugged. "In a way, they're right."

"What's going to happen to the guy who did this?" my wife asked.

"Probably not much. He's a contractor, which gives the Bureau some level of deniability. I told him we'll settle this once the case is over."

Gloria frowned. "Don't go rushing off to fight someone."

"He has it coming," I said. "He's a bully, and he needs to know not everyone is going to knuckle under just because he works for the FBI."

"Still . . ." Gloria closed her eyes and took a deep breath. ". . . do you need to be the one to teach him that lesson?" She answered her own question a beat later. "Of course you do."

"Of course I do."

"I'm not going to talk you out of this, am I?"

"Nope," I said.

She nodded. "All right. Nevertheless, I want to see you. It's hard for me to know you're in pain somewhere and forced to be by yourself."

"I'm trying to be careful. Someone tried to follow me home the other night. I lost him and don't know who sent him."

"So be careful," Gloria said. "We won't meet at my house. I'll get a room somewhere. You figure out a way to rendezvous without anyone following you."

"I brought a cloak with me. Too bad I left my dagger at home."

She grinned. "You said you had the rest of the day off. Come spend some time with your wife. You can go back to whatever you're doing tomorrow."

"All right," I said. "Text me the details. I'll find my way there . . . dagger or not." We hung up, and I packed an overnight bag. Before I left, I grabbed the burner phone from the fridge. Gloria was on to something. A night of sort-of normality with my wife would be a nice recharge for the rest of my time with the hackers.

CHAPTER 16

ONCE I LEFT the confines of the city, I took a needlessly complicated route most of the way to the destination. I got off and back on the highway twice, took the wrong exit once I got close, and drove around the block a couple times as I neared the parking garage where I would leave my Caprice. I didn't risk the S4 and its built-in GPS. Once I was confident no one followed, I left the car on the fourth floor and called a cab company whose information I looked up before leaving. Services like Uber and Lyft left a trail. Anyone could call a taxi, pay in cash, and not provide a name.

A light blue Toyota Camry pulled up to the curb a few minutes later. The driver, a Japanese woman, didn't try to make conversation after the initial hello and confirming where I wanted to go. I wore a baseball cap and sunglasses and tried to keep my nose pointed down as much as possible. It all gave her poor odds to see the bruising on my face, which would be a distinguishing feature should anyone follow us or ask her about me.

You're not paranoid if they're really after you.

We reached the end of my time in the car. I paid the fare and a generous tip in cash. Nondescript restaurants stared back at me from each side of the street. Once the cab disappeared, I walked a block to the Hyatt Regency Hotel. Gloria told me she booked a room under the name of her foundation, and the middle-aged desk clerk confirmed this when he handed me a keycard and wished me a pleasant stay.

I felt a bit silly busting out all my amateur spy tradecraft, but I used a little more. Gloria's room was on the sixth floor. I rode the elevator to the fourth, took the stairs to the fifth, got in another lift to go to number seven, and then hoofed it down a flight. All I needed were a sharp tuxedo and a Walther PPK to complete my transformation into an MI6 field agent. I slid the keycard into the lock and opened the door.

Gloria sat on the bed. She stood to greet me, and the smile on her face turned to a grimace when she saw my bruises. "You should see the other guy," I said in my best Sean Connery voice—which would convince no one I was a Scottish actor.

Her hand caressed my cheek. "I'm here to see you . . . even if you look a little rough and can only do a bad Bond impression."

"My spycraft is pretty good, though."

She grinned. "I'll take your word for it." We shared a few lingering kisses. "I've missed you."

"Me, too."

"We have dinner reservations," Gloria said. She kissed me again, and my resolve to leave the room wavered.

"When?"

"Twenty minutes." She patted my chest. "Easy, tiger. We have all night."

As we were in Hunt Valley, Gloria booked us a table at one of the country clubs in the area. This one featured a dark wood motif highlighted by some lighter pieces. The dining room gave off a country lodge vibe. The only things missing were animal heads mounted on the wall. I didn't mind their omission. The menu was American with some rustic options to go along with the theme. The staff dressed like they worked in a nice restaurant rather than in flannel, at least.

Gloria and I split an appetizer of scallops risotto. Our server dropped it off, refreshed our waters, and took our entree orders. My wife continued a seafood evening by opting for salmon, and I embraced the lodge milieu and chose hunter chicken with wild rice. I asked if a man with a musket shot the fowl this morning and got a strange look for my answer. Some places could only lean into a theme so hard.

"I can't believe what happened to you," Gloria said as the waiter left. The dining room wasn't overly crowded on a weeknight, and she kept her voice quiet.

"I'd like to think he was a rogue asshole . . . someone Hess couldn't control." I spooned about half the appetizer onto each of our plates. It smelled fresh and buttery.

"Are you really going to seek him out when this is over?"

I nodded. "He needs to learn he can't treat people like crap. The lesson starts with me."

"You have an interesting code."

"I don't like bullies," I said. I cut a scallop in half and tried it. Perfect. It had a nice sear on the outside but remained tender. The risotto—a dish I had seen end the journeys of many cooking show contestants—served as a great complement. Gloria sliced her scallops into smaller bites, a habit she started to improve her fitness for tennis tournaments a couple years ago. I'd always been the faster eater, but I routinely lapped her now.

The trend continued over dinner. The hunter chicken here featured a couple varieties of mushrooms and some small diced potatoes. The dish of my youth had been more simple. I preferred this one. The sauce and rice meant it ate more or less like a hearty stew.

"Do you know what you'll be doing tomorrow?" Gloria asked as she cut her fish into pieces requiring an electron microscope to find.

"More of the same, I think. I know the leader is pissed, but he wants to stay on point for now. I don't know how much of what we did will survive the raid. Could be a long day."

"Good thing we're here together tonight, then." She grabbed my hand and squeezed while flashing her best high-wattage smile. It buoyed my spirits and made me look forward to when this mess would be behind me.

A short while later, Gloria got half her entree packaged to go. She paid with her business credit card, and we drove back to the hotel room. No sooner did she close the mini-fridge door on her leftovers than she pulled me in for a kiss.

It was a great night, and I needed it.

———

I woke up early in the hotel room. It felt nice to have Gloria beside me again. The temptation to put my head back on the pillow and enjoy the morning a little longer nearly overwhelmed me. For now, all remained quiet from Factor Zero, but I expected to hear from him with a new location. Gloria stretched, and the sheet shifted to reveal her nude upper body. I almost leaped back under the covers but refrained. "You leaving already?" she asked in a sleepy whisper.

"As much as I don't want to, I need to."

"I hope your case doesn't go much longer."

"Me, too," I said. "Your business probably can't afford many more nights like we just had."

She grinned. "We'll manage."

I got dressed and put my disguise back in place. Gloria strummed an air guitar when she knew I was looking at her. "How can you be sure I'm not a drummer?"

"You'd rather be closer to the front of the stage."

"You know me all too well," I said.

I packed my bag, kissed my beautiful wife goodbye, and fought the persistent urge to rejoin her in bed before I left the room. I called the same cab company as the prior night and rode to a random business about a hundred yards from the garage where I left my car. As I approached it, I wondered how the FBI found us yesterday. I didn't give them the information. Rich or Sharpe—or someone above the captain— might've shared it. It would be like Davenport or Ngo to try and foster a collaborative process or whatever other absurd buzzword they chose.

Once the coast was clear, I checked the Caprice. In the right rear wheel well, my hand passed over something hard and plastic. The flashlight on my phone illuminated a small black box with a tiny green LED blinking intermittently. "A tracker," I said to no one. "Son of a bitch." I gave it a good pull, and it popped off. The back of it remained sticky. I walked down the row, found an obnoxiously large pickup, and stuck it in the same spot. Let the feds chase their tails.

As I drove back toward I-83, Rich called on my personal phone. "The nine-one-one system is still down," he said. "The backup is starting to strain. It wasn't really designed to be in place for days."

"Maybe it should've been."

"Didn't you say you had a way to bring the primary one back?"

"I do," I said. "Or I did. After your FBI friends raided

everything, we'll need to hope I can still get in. Did you know they put a tracker on my car?"

"I'm not surprised. What did you do with it?"

"Stuck it on some massive pickup."

"You know the feds might chase whoever owns it," Rich said.

"Maybe they should. Someone needs to enforce gas mileage requirements."

He sighed. "Let me know if you're able to get things up and running."

"I will," I said. "I'm on my way back into the city now.' I ended the call. Twenty minutes later, I curbed the Caprice near my house, checked for people spying on me, and went inside. APT30 used the cloud for most of their infrastructure, so the FBI taking computers would have a minimal impact. This required the online resources to be configured in such a way the feds couldn't find them, of course. I didn't want to presume competence.

The group set things up correctly. I reached our deployment server, logged in, and checked the script. It still ran, and my backdoor remained. I executed it, authenticating with a system default credential, shut the program down, and cleared it from the repository. Once I disconnected, I called Rich. "Should be back up now."

"Thanks. I'll let everyone know."

After we hung up, Factor Zero sent a message with coordinates to the burner phone. *Let's assemble ASAP. We have a lot to go over.*

I figured we did.

———

I drove to the new location. This one sat a little north of Penn Station and about a block east of the Charles Theater. If we weren't able to compromise another system, maybe Factor Zero would take us to see a play. I snagged a spot in a public parking lot and made the short jaunt to what had been a psychiatrist's practice according to the sign still mounted above the front door. A few members of the team probably needed a shrink. I wondered if anyone would make a comment about our latest venue.

We were on the main level again with all the desks and equipment setup in the large open-concept living area. Most of the computers and monitors were missing. Older laptops and smaller screens sat in their places. Networking gear was easy enough to replace, and a new router and switch sat near Factor Zero's desk. He only had one screen now, and the back of it faced the room. I wondered where the budget came from for everything. The FBI wouldn't return any seized equipment so soon, and I couldn't imagine a small group keeping a stash of replacement hardware in reserve.

I needed to poke harder at the money angle. T.J. could do a lot of good work while I remained indisposed.

"Damn, man," Turbo said as he peered at my face. It made everyone else look at me, too. "What the hell happened to you?"

"A fed got rough with me." I jutted out my chin. "Didn't tell him shit, though."

"You been arrested for hacking before?"

"Not in this country," I said, which was mostly true. "Those FBI guys were amateurs." Despite the eagerness with which he used his nightstick, Brubaker couldn't measure up to the guards in the Chinese prison where I spent nineteen days.

"Appreciate you holding out," Factor Zero said. "I didn't

think anyone would find us this soon. We had safeguards in place of course, but I want to keep the cops and feds spinning their wheels as long as possible."

"Yeah," Iceman concurred. "Good job. Sorry it happened to you."

I shrugged like I got beaten by overzealous FBI contractors every week. "I'm no snitch." I looked around at the assembled crowd, which was a little smaller than normal. "Where's Javier?"

"Paradice is still in custody," Iceman said. "Have to hope he's stonewalling them like you did."

I wondered if he got stuck without the fancy lawyer to get him out. Maybe there was a hierarchy for who got to use the services. "Yesterday sucked," Factor Zero said. "You all know it even if you managed to avoid getting rounded up."

"What's the plan now?" Iceman wanted to know. "I want to stick it to these bastards."

"We will, but everything in time. For now, I'm kinda pissed." His eyes narrowed. "Our nine-one-one hack is offline. The system is back up."

Iceman threw up his hands. "What the hell? We need to get it back."

"It's a setback," our leader said, "but it'll be temporary. Foxtrot, you checked it out this morning." Everyone's eyes moved to me again. "What happened?"

"Hell if I know," I said. "I wanted to be sure it was still working after the FBI seized all our stuff yesterday. Looked like it was still up and running when I checked."

"You're sure?"

"I am." My teammates continued to stare at me. I knew this would be the result of what I did. As the last person to authenticate to the server, I'd bear the brunt of the questions. I could have erased the logs . . . which would have created another entry describing what I did. I hoped the signs of my mistreatment by the feds would carry the day here.

"You were the last one to log in," Honeybee said.

"If someone is the last person to see a murder victim alive," I said, "it doesn't make them the killer."

She glared at me. "Sounds like a cop's analogy."

She had a point, and I didn't think about it when I said it. "We've all watched shows like *NCIS*, right? Or movies where the police are trying to figure out who killed someone. It comes up a lot."

"It's fine," Factor Zero said after a few seconds. "We'll take you at your word. You certainly took your lumps for us."

Honeybee leaned closer. "Would you do it again?"

"Get the shit kicked out of me with a nightstick, you mean?" I asked. "All things being equal, I'd prefer not to, but if someone else hauls us away, I'm still not going to be a snitch."

Her head bobbed slowly. My answers seemed to sate everyone except Iceman who kept looking at me. I ignored him as Factor Zero got on with new business. "Like I said, I'm pissed this is offline, but our mission continues. We're sticking to the plan. Davenport and his city are going to pay." He glanced around the room. "Let's get back to work."

CHAPTER 17

IT TURNED out to be a slow morning. We retained access to our cloud resources. No one in law enforcement made the association. Like most groups, we were good at not making attribution easy even when it came to assets. The city ramped up its defenses in the intervening time, however. "First, the nine-one-one system comes back up," Iceman grumbled, "and now this. What the hell is going on?"

"We assumed they'd respond at some point," Turbo said. "Making things harder shouldn't be a surprise."

"We planned for this," Factor Zero added. "The city is down on its IT staff, but they could have brought in outside consultants. It doesn't matter. They all use variations of the same playbook."

Iceman stared at me for a few seconds before returning his attention to his own screen. He struck me as the most devoted to Factor Zero and his plans. Whatever cred my bruises earned me stopped mattering to Darrell in short order. Ever since he learned I logged in last before the 911 system came back online, he'd been zeroed in on me. I felt his eyes boring into my head again. "I know I'm handsome," I said, "even if a bit less than normal now. However, whatever answer you're looking for isn't written on my face."

"I got my eye on you."

"I can tell. How's your work coming along?"

"Screw you," he said. "I don't take orders from some newbie."

"Gentlemen," Factor Zero broke in, "let's focus on the task at hand. The city has upped their game. We'll do the same."

We spent some time testing the new defenses. Charlie must have passed my recommendation of an incident response company up the chain. The first thing they would want to do after an initial assessment is contain the damage. This took a few forms. Fewer city websites remained accessible to the public. Credentials we'd found to gain unauthorized access no longer worked. I didn't know which operation Davenport called, but they did a pretty good job of locking the basics down. We'd be able to get around their new defenses, but it would take more time.

A short while later, a news alert said Baltimore restored its traffic signal system. The article made no mention of street lights, CCTV, or incident response contractors. Score another one for the good guys. Everyone in the room remained calm and focused on their tasks, so they either didn't see the information or didn't care about it anymore.

I got hungry a couple hours later. Turbo left for lunch, and I ducked out a couple minutes later. A message waited for me on my real phone. The mayor wanted another update, this time in person. The drive to City Hall would be easier without having to wait for someone to wave me along at most intersections. It still wasn't a short jaunt, and with suspicious eyes on me, I didn't want to be gone too long. I drove a few blocks away, made sure I wasn't followed, and called Davenport's office.

After a few minutes, I got connected to the conference room. "I have Captain Sharpe, Commissioner Ngo, your cousin, and Special Agent Hess here," the mayor said. "We're honestly pretty happy right now. The IR company has turned things around for us."

"I've noticed," I said.

"We were hoping you'd be joining us at City Hall."

"Too much chance of being seen. Does the turnaround mean you no longer want to pay the ransom?"

"At the moment, I don't see a reason to. I'm sure your friends are going to keep trying to work us over. It will depend on how badly they can hurt us. I won't endanger the people of this city, especially not in the interests of looking tough or grandstanding."

"We still advise against it," Hess chimed in.

"I need to know something," I said. "The leader of the group seems to be aware of what's happened to the city in terms of IT workers leaving. I don't remember hearing a lot about it."

"We tried not to advertise it," Davenport said.

"I understand. I'd still like to know what happened. There are a few things about this guy which don't quite add up for me."

"Not much to say. I'd probably have to ask HR for a lot of the finer points. Basically, a bunch of our IT staffers left for better-paying jobs. I know a few of them went to work for the same company."

"Which one?" I asked.

"I never heard the name. I think it's based in Pennsylvania. Easy drive up Eighty-three."

"Didn't you say your former CTO recommended an IR firm from there?"

"You're right," Davenport said. "I didn't make the connection. I doubt they're the same place. None of the people we've met so far worked for the city before."

"What about your leader concerns you?" Sharpe wanted to know.

"The group is pretty new," I said. "Hasn't made a name for itself yet. Stands to reason there's not a lot of money in the coffers. He has an elaborate moving operation in place every day or two. A couple of guys who look like professional muscle. Then, after we got popped by the feds, a fancy lawyer gets two of the guys out. Maybe Factor Zero is independently wealthy. I don't know. I've asked my secretary to dig around on him."

"Keep us in the loop," Davenport said.

"I will." I glanced at my watch. "I should go. Probably need to turn up with some lunch or people will get suspicious. I feel like I'm already getting a few scrutinizing stares. I guess it takes more than criminal abuse from the FBI to satisfy some people." A sigh came through the connection. Probably Hess.

I ended the call, found the closest carry-out place, and drove back with a greasy cheesesteak and fries. I wondered what kind of reception awaited me.

———

It didn't take long to get an answer.

"Where the hell did you go?" Darrell asked from about two inches in front of my nose.

I held up my white paper bag which featured two large spots turned translucent by grease. "Lunch."

"Long lunch."

"Are you the timekeeper?" I said. "I didn't know we were getting paid by the hour."

He managed to get even more in my space. "First, we get arrested. Next, our nine-one-one hack is gone. Now, you take a long lunch."

"Back up, or you're going to regret it." The security guard I had to deal with when I first joined the group never returned after the FBI raid. Maybe he didn't qualify for fancy lawyer status.

Darrell kept staring at me, but he took a couple steps to the rear. "I still wanna know."

"I went to lunch," I said. "I'm not in this part of town a lot, so I drove around to find a place. If you want to streamline the process, publish a list of approved joints. Otherwise, piss off."

He pointed forked fingers from his eyes toward me. "I'm watching you, man."

"How nice for you." I walked to my desk and set my lunch down. "While you're at it, why don't you figure out why the FBI would have abused me if I'm the one who tipped them off."

"Let's try and be productive," Factor Zero said. "Darrell, I don't think Foxtrot needs to prove himself to us at this point. He's done good work, and he caught the brunt of it when the feds rolled up. Take it easy."

"Yeah," Darrell said, and his glare gave me some insight into how he got the Iceman moniker.

I opened my bag. The time driving back plus arguing with my teammate left me with lukewarm food. Fries in particular tended to get dreadful as they lost heat, and these were no exception. The place didn't have a microwave--any useful appliance left with the previous tenant--so I made the best of it. Before I finished eating, however, Factor Zero stood and paced the area behind his desk.

"I'm not happy," he said. "We're down a member, and we weren't a big team to begin with."

"We going to recruit anyone else?" Turbo asked.

"I don't think I want to. We've had a lot of disruptions in the last twenty-four hours. Bringing in someone new makes everything a little more complicated. We can finish the work with the team we have. Maybe we'll get Javier back soon."

"You think he's ratting us out?" Darrell said.

"I doubt it. Even if he gave the feds some answers, he didn't know about this location. We're safe here . . . even so, I think I want to find a new spot for tomorrow. Recent circumstances mean we'll need to be more transient than we first thought."

"What's the plan, then?" Honeybee said.

Factor showed a humorless smile. "We're going to bring the city to its knees. Nothing changed. It might be a little harder than it was at first, but we'll still get it done. This is a strong team. I have a good feeling about what we can accomplish. Our targets remain the same. We want to sow chaos. It'll be worth it when Davenport goes down. Maybe then, when Baltimore is at rock bottom, they can start to rebuild."

I didn't like the plan at all. As much animosity as I might have held for Vincent Davenport, he'd done a pretty good job during his time at City Hall. I wondered if Factor and the group bore a grudge against the city or its current mayor. Regardless, massive disorder would lead to needless injuries and death. I hoped I could put up a convincing front and act like I went along with everything. If Darrell watched me as closely as he threatened to, my attempts to tank the group from within would be much more difficult.

With the battleground changing, we needed new intel.

The IR firm Baltimore hired made our jobs harder but not impossible. This would be good enough against less determined adversaries. In many cases, people who avoided being the low-hanging fruit were safer because hackers wanted easy marks. Thanks to our leader, however, APToo made it our mission to knock over as much of Baltimore's infrastructure and operations as possible.

To do this, we needed to map their networks again.

New defenses prevented us from sending the required traffic from the outside. "We could spoof an internal host," Turbo suggested.

"But the firewalls and routers know it's not coming from the inside," I said. "Compromising them will take a lot longer."

"You got a plan, then?"

"What if we use a box we already owned?"

"Maybe," he said. "You try it. I'm going to poke a bunch of their web apps and see if I can find a way in."

Early in the hack, the team took over a computer used by someone in public works. The credential remained on file in a large document, and it let me in again. I only had a user account at the moment, but this employee enjoyed administrative privileges on his department's servers. His email showed a message from the city's IT department advising everyone of new administrative logins. The username changed, so I made a note of it. The password came in a separate email.

The contents were encrypted.

The city used ID badges as smart cards, so without the physical token, I couldn't decipher the message contents.

Users loved to take shortcuts, however. If they weren't system administrators by trade, having the extra duties counted as a burden. People and burdens rarely interacted well. I searched the employee's hard drive for credentials stored in files and found one such text document updated earlier today. From his PC, I remotely connected to a Windows server and input the user ID and password.

I was in. "I got it," I said as I added the updated local admin information to our file. For a moment, the thrill of breaking into something made me feel like I was back in Hong Kong again. Working with friends against the Chinese government. Trying to help dissidents and foreigners. Instead, I sat in a former shrink's office helping a lower-rent version of my old team take down my city. A deep breath flushed the zeal from my system. I needed to do my job well enough for Factor Zero to keep me around, but my obligation ended there. The rest of the time, I would try to undermine APT∞'s efforts.

At the moment, I was the only one with a way to finger-print the network. I downloaded a couple of tools—the city hadn't yet locked down browser use on its servers—and set them to work. Everyone stopped by periodically to check my screen as we gained a better picture of the updated network. A few minutes later, I saved the output file. We now had operating system info, physical and IP addresses, installed patches, and critical services running for every host on the network. I uploaded it to one of our cloud-based file shares.

"Good work," Factor Zero said. "It'll pay off in a few minutes."

"What do you mean?" I asked.

"I redid our nine-one-one takedown. Made a few improvements this time." His fingers flew over his keyboard. "I think we should do work like this in Java for now. The city loves using old versions of it according to your scan. Anyway, I'll have this ready to go shortly."

"What about their backup system?"

"We know a little bit about it now," the leader said, "again thanks to you. The telecom maintains most of it, but the city has some responsibility now. Something they changed since last time, but your work caught it." I tried to keep my expression neutral as he kept talking. "We'd need to do a lot more to get it offline, but I think we can degrade the performance. Should be enough to scare them again."

I wanted to tell Rich and Sharpe what to expect, but excusing myself for a few minutes now would draw way too much suspicion. Using my laptop to send a text wouldn't work, either. I'd never reinstalled my key scrambler this morning. With the team focused on Factor's work, I visited my old blog, snagged the files, and set it up. Before I could do much with it, however, he made a show of hitting a key. "It's live."

The rest of the team looked happy, so I gave them my best fake smile.

———

Factor Zero dismissed us for the day a couple hours later. "I'm going to stick around and monitor the chaos," he said with a sincere grin pasted to his face.

"I wanna see it, too," Darrell said. "People got a lot to answer for." He made a point to look at me. "You sticking around?"

"No," I said. "I figure I'll drive around for a couple hours before I find a place to get dinner."

My comment earned me a smirk. It was progress. In case anyone followed me, I drove a terrible and circuitous route to my office. People who never visited Baltimore before could have found a more direct way, and my brain hurt by the time I pulled into the lot and parked the Caprice next to T.J.'s Mustang. She snickered when I walked in, and I remembered I still wore my disguise. She strummed an air guitar as I poured myself a cup of coffee. It smelled a couple hours old, but I didn't care. "Thanks for not banishing me to the drums," I said as I took a seat.

"There's no way you'd hide at the back of the stage," my secretary said. This meant I lived and worked with women who knew me well. Somehow, I doubted this could be positive. Nevertheless, I was about to agree with her assessment when she added, "How else will you show your flowing blond locks to the crowd?"

"You're fired."

She smiled and didn't miss a beat. "I found a couple things on your leader. Maybe I can tell you before I pack up my desk."

"Maybe you could."

"He's done a good job of staying under the radar. The dark web never forgets, though. Seems he used to go by the handle of Factor one . . . the oh in 'one' being a zero, of course."

"Still don't know the name," I said.

"I doubt you would," T.J. said. "His most active times came while you were running a business. Besides, he's spent most of his life on the west coast."

"He got tired of perfect weather one day and decided to come after Baltimore?"

"Like I told you, there's not a ton to find. This guy is dangerous, I think. There are rumors that Factor one killed someone he used to work with."

My coffee mug stopped halfway to my mouth. I remembered him pointing a pistol at me when we'd first met. He definitely wasn't unfamiliar with handling a gun. "Nothing definitive?"

T.J. shook her head. Her natural blonde ponytail wagged better than my fake hair ever could. "He left shortly after, of course. The handle went dark. Factor Zero emerged a few months later, this time operating out of Pennsylvania." I frowned. "What?"

"It's probably nothing."

"Spill it."

"The city hired an incident response firm recently," I said. "They've helped. Davenport said his former CTO recommended the company, and they're based in Pennsylvania. I also heard several IT folks who left went to work for a place up there."

"It's a big state," T.J. said.

I nodded. "It is, but now we have a coincidence."

"And we don't like coincidences."

"I don't hate them. I just believe they're rare in our line of work."

"Let me guess," T.J. said. "You want me to keep digging into Factor Zero."

"Yes," I said.

"And find out about this IR company."

"Yes."

"And see if there's some kind of a link there."

"Yes."

"Are you getting me a Christmas bonus?"

I almost answered in the affirmative on autopilot but paused. "Nice try." T.J. grinned. "Maybe we go down this rabbit hole, and there's nothing there. Fine. Pennsylvania is a big state. Thirteen million people live there."

"What are the odds two specific ones know each other?" my secretary asked.

"Extremely small," I admitted, "but not zero. We can't trust a coincidence."

"I'm on it. Be careful around your new boss. If he figures out what you're really up to, he'll probably want to kill you."

I remembered Darrell's baleful glare from earlier in the afternoon. "He'll need to get in line."

CHAPTER 18

I DROVE BACK to the safehouse from my office. When I walked inside, Rich and Sharpe waited in the living room. At least they left me the comfy chair, which I dropped onto. "It's a good thing I'm married and not bringing a bunch of women around. You two would be cramping my style."

"Did you know nine-one-one was going to get screwed up again?" the captain said. He leaned forward and blotted out much of the natural light pouring through the windows.

"Not until it happened. I couldn't exactly run out and send a text. I'm starting to draw some suspicion."

"You need to break this off?" Rich asked.

I shook my head. "No. It was a couple things. My long lunch to cover our chat was the bridge too far for someone."

"Not the leader?"

"His chief zealot," I said. "If the two of them talk enough, I could have a problem." When I left, of course they were huddled together. Even if I'd lingered, they probably would've waited for me to leave before getting to the meat of their conversation. Factor Zero was dangerous according to T.J.'s research. He'd pulled a gun on me once already. I didn't want to give him any incentive to do it again. "Did something change with the nine-one-one configuration?"

"Yeah," Sharpe said. "We wired an old call center in for some extra capacity on the backup system."

"We found it. Thanks to the IR contractor and some of their remediations, we needed to re-map the whole network. Your little improvement came up in the scan. I don't think anyone knew what it was." Except for Factor Zero, who made sure to take it offline with his new and improved script. Which he wrote and compiled pretty quickly.

"Being in December helps . . . or it would if this were a normal month. People are on edge after the lights and signals went down. I don't know how long our capacity will hold up. A surge in crime is going to screw us."

"Can you get more capacity?" I asked.

Sharpe shrugged his massive shoulders. "Probably. The commissioner said he'd look into it if we need it."

"It'll be too late by then."

"Same thing I told him. Verizon would have to make some changes, but I think it would work. Not immediately."

"How much longer do you think the group will be working?" Rich said.

"I wish I knew. I'd like to be done with this as soon as I can."

"Any idea?"

"The FBI raid set us back two whole days," I said. "My guess is maybe three more." I paused and considered sharing what T.J. told me. I didn't want them to get concerned and try to pull me out, but they should know the full picture of the opposition. "T.J. hasn't had much luck finding out stuff on the crew. Nothing beyond the basics. Today, she dug up a little dirt on the leader."

"Factor Zero or whatever the asshole calls himself?" Sharpe said.

"The same. He used to live on the west coast and went by Factor one. We don't have all the details yet, but he's suspected of killing someone and fleeing east." I held up a finger as Rich started to talk. "No, I don't want you to pull me out. I think we're better off leaving me on the inside so I can try to learn what they're planning. Factor's dangerous, Darrell is a true believer, and the other two will just shrug and go along. I don't think we want to be flying blind."

"Keep getting us some intel, then."

"I'm trying."

"No backdoor in the code this time?" Rich said.

"No," I said. "Factor did it all himself. I never even saw it."

"Do what you can, I guess."

"You don't think I am?" I spread my hands. "I already feel helpless sitting around while these assholes wreck the city. It's hard to not jump in and try to stop it, but I don't want to give myself up too early. They have bigger things planned. Remind the mayor and the commissioner. This crew wants to sow chaos and make the city look as bad as possible."

"We know you're doing what you can," Sharpe said. "Going undercover is hard. A bunch of cops never go on their second assignment. You're doing fine."

"I wish I could do more," I said.

———

After Rich and Sharpe left, I walked a few blocks to get dinner. I'd eaten a lot of Italian recently, and I didn't want another greasy sub. Google showed me a small but well-rated Mexican place nearby. Armed with a variety of tacos and a container of refried beans, I headed back to the safehouse. To minimize my time being visible on the streets, I ducked in and out of alleys when I could. I popped into the one which ran behind my temporary home. A car I hadn't seen on my way out sat near the entrance.

A few seconds later, footsteps rushed toward me from the right. I ducked on instinct, and a wild haymaker whizzed over my head. The punch left whoever launched it unbalanced, but he recovered quickly and pivoted around. I set my food down near the fence and stood in a defensive posture. A light in the alley illuminated the face of my attacker.

The guard APT00 used.

He rushed me again, and I blocked his two punches. When he tried to knee me in the groin, I turned and raised my leg to blunt the attack and shoved him hard in the chest. "Guess the feds cut you loose, too," I said. "What the hell are you doing?"

The only answer I got came in the form of more punches. The guy knew how to use his hips to get power, but his strikes lacked sophistication. He was big and strong, and most men with those attributes got by without a lot of refined knowledge. Size meant they wouldn't get picked on, and power ended fights against unskilled opponents quickly. When a right cross came at me, I shifted to the side, hit the outside of his arm, and walloped him with a left to the face. He spun, lost his balance, and fell on his ass.

While he struggled to get his bearings, I rushed forward and drove my knee into his chin. My opponent's head bounced off the concrete, and he groaned. I kept a vigilant watch, but the alley rang his bell. After a couple minutes, he slowly pulled himself back to a seated position. "Why are you following me?" I said when his eyes struggled to focus on me.

"Darrell told me to."

It figured. I knew Iceman didn't trust me, but I never suspected he'd send someone to follow me. "Did Factor sign off on this?"

"Yeah," he said. "He and Darrell talked about it."

For the second day in a row, I would need to wonder what kind of reception greeted me when I met my teammates. "You been following me for long?"

He shook his head, winced, and almost fell over again. "No. Lost you on the way back. I happened to pick you up again leaving Little Italy. I didn't know which house you went into here, so I stayed in the area."

"I have no clue what Darrell expected," I said, "but I'm on the up-and-up. If he has a problem with me, he can settle it himself. Same goes for your boss."

"You fight pretty well for a hacker."

I shrugged. "Like I said at the beginning, I got bullied, and my parents insisted I take martial arts. Turns out I liked it."

"This is twice you got the better of me." He held out a hand. I stared at it for a few seconds before extending mine and helping the guy to his feet. He spent a few seconds bent over at the waist and breathing hard. I took a step back in case he vomited. Eventually, he straightened up.

"Let's not have a third time, then," I said. "It won't be the charm." He nodded. "What are you going to tell Darrell?"

"You're legit," he said. "Not a threat to the group."

"Good. Because I'm not. I don't really care what Darrell thinks. If all goes well, we only need to work together for a few more days, and then we never need to see one another again." I wondered how this man came to work security for APToo. No time like the present to find out. "Factor hire you when this all started?"

"I guess. He went through the company I work for. We do basic security work."

"You from around here?"

The guard shook his head. "Pennsylvania," he said.

————

Another Pennsylvania connection. When I got to the safehouse, I texted T.J. *Tomorrow, focus hard on the PA angle. The guy who works security for the group got hired from there. I think something's going on.* She confirmed she would. I reheated my tacos and beans, ate them, and then fired up my laptop. Maybe I could get a head start on the commonwealth angle.

Plenty of security companies would hire out a guard. Most proclaimed their employees were licensed and bonded. A normal business would insist on this for liability concerns. A group of hackers couldn't care less. Eliminating the firms on the up-and-up represented a logical leap I wasn't prepared to make. It just meant I'd be swimming in a wider pool. I spent a few minutes crafting a good search and then scraped all the companies' relevant data into a CSV file.

Several businesses—mostly LLCs—owned a few of the security firms. Unscrambling them could take a while. Some people were quite adept at chaining shell companies together. T.J. and I would walk through the webs if need be. I conducted some further research until I started yawning. None of the corporations I'd looked into raised initial red flags. I compiled my notes into a document and sent it to T.J. along with the spreadsheet.

The next morning, I woke up early and got on the tread-mill again. It still paled to a run on the streets, but a glance through the window showed a light rain falling outside. I called it a draw today. After a short warm-up, I did three and a half miles on the motorized belt. My thoughts strayed to the guard. Too many people coming from Pennsylvania to call it a coincidence. But what did they have in common besides a nearby geographic origin? Maybe I should've pushed harder in my research last night. I'd come to rely a lot on T.J. these last few months—she certainly proved indispensable when I worked cases like this one—but I also needed to do the lion's share sometimes. My name was the one on the door, after all —as she pointed out several days prior.

Once I showered and dressed, I checked the APToo phone. Another new location today, but I could walk to this one. The coordinates resolved to an interior rowhouse on South Linwood Avenue. It sat a block to the west and a couple south of my current location. My GPS still identified the photo studio which must have recently vacated the premises. I guzzled a cup of coffee, grabbed a couple granola bars from the pantry, and headed out.

As before, a camera spied on passersby on the street side. This time, there was no partner unit mounted at the rear of the house. I walked inside to find everyone onsite except Darrell. Excellent. "Iceman should be here in a few minutes," Factor Zero said. The guard barely looked at me. I wondered if he'd talked to the boss yet—and what his message would've been. If he still smarted from the initial beatdown I gave him, his update could have been very different than the one we talked about yesterday.

I set my bag down and went out to walk a few houses to my left. With my hood over my head, Darrell may not recognize me. If he approached the house from the front, I would see him. Sure enough, he moved toward our location from the opposite end. He turned to enter the alley at its northern mouth. I ran to intercept him and staked out a position near the rear fence before he got there. When he walked past me into the yard, I followed him.

Darrell turned out not to be the most observant fellow out there. When he neared the door, I put my hand in his back and shoved him forward. His face bounced off the brick, and he grunted. I let him turn around so I could put my forearm across his throat. His eyes widened. "Anybody ever tell you it's not nice to have someone tailed?"

"What the hell, man?" he croaked.

"Don't try to deny it. The guard told me it was your idea, and you got Factor to go along with it." I leaned a little harder into him. He tried to shove me away, but my body pinned his arms. He lacked the leverage.

"Fine. I don't trust you."

"You'd better learn to," I said. "I'm legit. I'm on the up and up. Maybe you're trying to throw suspicion off yourself." He frowned and coughed. I eased up a little. "I wonder what Factor will think of my theory."

"Screw you," he said. "I'm straight. Factor knows he doesn't gotta worry about me."

"Great. The problem is I don't know if I believe you. I'll look past what you did this time for the good of the team." I stepped back a half step and hit him with a jab in the solar plexus. Darrell gasped anew. "Have me followed again, and it's not going to end well for you. We clear?"

"Yeah," he managed to say.

I stormed inside. When Factor looked up as I entered the room, I said, "Anyone else want to question my loyalties? Darrell is out back reconsidering his earlier suspicions."

"Easy," Factor said. "Iceman had some concerns. I didn't necessarily agree, but I figured it couldn't hurt to put a tail on you." He didn't add "again," so I pondered who followed me a few nights ago. "I don't think anyone needs to wonder about you."

"I got it a lot worse than any of you from the feds." I stared at each of my coworkers in turn—including Darrell, who stood near the door. "They wouldn't abuse one of their own, and they wouldn't rough up an informant. Anybody has a problem with me? Come talk to me about it. I know I haven't been a part of the team as long as the rest of you, but I think I've proven myself."

Factor Zero smiled, and I didn't care for the expression. "You're certainly about to."

CHAPTER 19

I LIKED his words even less. "We're taking the cops offline. Well . . . you are."

I'd landed solidly in the soup on this one. My real phone remained at the safehouse a few blocks away. I could try using the burner Factor gave me to text Rich, but I'd be using the device in full view of everyone. Proving myself meant doing it in public, so sneaking away to fire off a quick message would draw suspicion. I also couldn't rule out the possibility Factor logged everything the phones did. "Pretty big job," I said after a momentary pause.

"You should be good for it, I'm sure."

"Yeah," Darrell said, putting both hands on my desk and leaning down. "A guy who's on the up-and-up like you shouldn't have any issues doing this."

"I disagree," I said, "and it's for the same reason as the nine-one-one takedown. Sure, we're going to make things hard on the police, but it's going to have second-order effects on other people, too."

"All cops are bastards," Darrell said.

"Even if you think so, they'll have open investigations which are going to benefit a lot of people. If their network goes down, more than just the cops stand to lose something."

"You're right," Factor Zero said. He put a hand up to calm Darrell, who seethed a foot away from my face. "Everything we do is going to affect the people of the city. If we took public water offline, it would be a big deal. It would certainly get attention, which is what we want. The power structure in Baltimore is rotten. Davenport, the police . . . all of it. They've kept a few high-ranking officers despite their atrocious records. You ever hear of a Captain Leon Sharpe?"

I hoped my poker face still worked when I answered, "Name's not familiar."

"Maybe it should be. He's the worst of them all. Old-school to the core. He's the type to punch or shoot first and maybe ask questions later if the mood suits him." Factor shook his head. "Men like him should've been put out to pasture years ago. Maybe when the city has to pay us millions of dollars, they'll actually put a cost on keeping dinosaurs like Sharpe in circulation."

"Add it to our demands," Darrell said.

"I don't think we'll need to," Factor Zero said. "The city employs enough accountants and risk managers. Brain drain hasn't hit there yet. Someone will make the connection. For all his faults, Davenport understands money and losing propositions. Darrell, give him some space." Iceman made sure to keep glaring at me even as he backed away. "Thanks to you, we've fingerprinted a lot of the network. It should be pretty straightforward to identify the segments we want to knock over. I'll check your code before we deploy anything."

"Of course," I said. Bile rose in my throat. I didn't see a way out of complying with this demand. I knew a great deal about the BPD's network already thanks to Rich leaving his computer unguarded during my first case. In the aftermath of what APToo did, I wondered how well it would still serve me. The IR contractor already made things more complicated for us. "This is way beyond holding a few systems for ransom, though."

"I know," our leader said. "It all serves the purpose. We're causing chaos to bring change." He paused, and his eyes flicked to the guard. "If you're not up for doing this, Foxtrot..."

For his part, the sentry made sure to show me he carried a gun on his hip. The easy smile on his face conveyed how he would harbor no objections if asked to use it on yours truly. The only saving grace I saw was the time this operation would take. Maybe some way out—or at least a way to notify Rich or Sharpe—would reveal itself. I needed an epiphany.

"I'm good," I said, and I glumly got to work.

———

The more I poked and prodded the BPD network, the more I realized not much had changed.

Getting in proved a little different but far from an insurmountable issue. Once I gained access, however, the layout was instantly familiar. I'd been all over this digital space for the last four years, and the police either didn't know or didn't care enough to keep me out. For the first time in my professional life, I wished I'd never snagged Rich's computer info back then. Trying not to use the knowledge I'd amassed over dozens of cases proved difficult. I took a breath and slowed down.

"You're in," Factor Zero said from over my right shoulder. "Why are you stopping?"

"Getting my bearings. Think about how massive the

police department is . . . not just in terms of officers and case-load but bureaucracy. It's going to be huge."

"Yeah. And you're going to take it down."

"Unless you got some objection," Darrell added from the other side. I hated doing anything while someone looked over my shoulder, and now, the whole team basically stood behind me and watched. I tried to suppress the shudder crawling up my spine.

"No objection," I said. "Hey, Darrell . . . while I'm in here, you want me to print out the pages on how to get someone in a chokehold?"

"Screw you."

I shrugged. "What the hell do you two mean?" Factor Zero asked.

"Iceman and I had a little chat outside this morning," I explained. "I told him I didn't like being treated like a suspect and followed. I think we came to an understanding, but he couldn't talk very well for most of it, so maybe I'm wrong."

"Maybe if you talked less and typed more, we'd be good," Darrell said.

I took his advice and got back to the task at hand. Delaying would only buy me so much time, and I couldn't go to the well too often without getting everyone to join Darrell in being suspicious of me. I envisioned the police network as a road, and its many cross streets represented specific branches of the department or necessary functions. Homicide. Human resources. Current case files. Traffic enforcement.

Considering I did most of the work of fingerprinting the city's digital layout, I hoped no one on the team studied things too closely. I focused on the first router I came to. The user name of *admin* worked with the third captured password I tried. Even a good incident response company couldn't do much if the client made the keys to the kingdom so easy to find. The same password also worked for managing printers. I changed the credentials and rewrote the routing table so it would basically send traffic nowhere. "There."

"Nice work," our leader said, "but you only did one segment. I think you just knocked Sex Crimes offline. We want it all."

The guard came into my field of vision, and he took delight in flashing the gun on his hip again. I'd been banging away at the keyboard for a while. "All right. I could use some coffee, though. And lunch soon."

Factor Zero crossed his arms. "We'll order in. Keep working. We're all watching what you do."

"Cool," I said even though the situation was very much the opposite. I hoped the other routers I encountered would require different credentials to administer. One by one, these hopes were dashed. The IT department opted for convenience over security, and they would pay the price for it. As I hit each device, I changed the password to the same thing each time and made sure the routing table dumped traffic in a digital black hole.

"I almost wish I still had my 'Send all feedback to /dev/null' T-shirt," Turbo said.

"They can recover from this, you know," Honeybee pointed out.

"I know," I said. "So long as they know how to login to their routers again, which they don't. Without being able to authenticate, they'll have to hard reboot the entire infrastructure and configure it again. Even if they go virtual, it's going to take time, money, and manpower, and I don't think they have enough of any."

"This is good," Factor Zero said. "Keep going."

To my dismay, I did. We ordered lunch. I didn't get a

break other than a couple times to pee, and I didn't risk taking the burner phone with me. The BPD would already be having problems, and things would only get worse for them throughout the day. Factor Zero had bigger plans for something after they were dead in the water. Once the network was completely offline, he clapped a few times, and the rest of the hackers joined him. I held my applause.

"Thanks to Foxtrot, we've basically made the police useless," our leader said. "Their desktops will still turn on . . . for all the good it'll do them."

Darrell smiled like a kid who realized he enjoyed unfettered access to the cookie jar. "Now what?"

"Now, we move on to phase two."

I didn't know what it would entail, but I felt confident I wouldn't like it.

CHAPTER 20

FACTOR ZERO STRUTTED around the room. It wasn't a big space, and it made him look ridiculous, but he didn't seem to care. "We've done a lot since the FBI came for us." His smirk took us all in. "I wonder if they'd raid us again if they knew how well we'd respond to it. The emergency response system is limited, and the police are basically dead in the water. It's time to put the screws to Davenport. Check this out."

We all gathered around his large monitor. A new message appeared, and he was careful not to show anything else. "Considering what we've done in the last twenty-four hours," he said, "I think it's time we updated our ransom demand. I've just added some more victims, too, so the message will spread farther into the city's workforce. Davenport will need to do something."

I read the new screed.

Robber baron Davenport,

You've had long enough. We're tired of waiting for you to act. Your beloved police are basically helpless. Citizens will struggle and die, and it'll all be on your head.

It's what you deserve. We have to break a few eggs to make this omelet. They're sacrifices for the greater good. You'll be deposed and go back to being just another rich thief and crook.

The ransom for undoing all the damage is now $40 million. We're not going to negotiate a lower figure. Your personal wealth won't cover this unless you also believe in sacrificing for the greater good. Pay us in Bitcoin by the end of tomorrow, or things will get worse for the city and you.

"Love it," Darrell said. "The best part is things are going to get worse no matter what."

"How do you mean?" I asked.

"I've been in touch with some contacts on the dark web," Factor said. "These are the kinds of people who have their hands in a lot of pots. Connections into pretty much every corner of society. Situations like these call for public rallies, and those are things we can direct and exploit. So we will. Whether Davenport comes up with the money or not, we're going to have chaos."

"Sounds violent."

"It will be. The country will watch how Davenport directs his jack-booted thugs in the police to attack the good citizens of Baltimore. If what we've done doesn't get him thrown out of city hall, a good old-fashioned riot will do the trick."

"You should be happy." Darrell glared at me for about the hundredth time in the last two days. "I thought you hated the city."

"I'm not a fan of innocent people dying," I said.

"It's the only thing which leads to real change," Factor Zero said. "Cops across the country do terrible things every day. We only seem to wake up and take notice when they're on video murdering an innocent person. The world will be watching. Yeah, a few people will die. The fucking cops won't be able to help themselves. Once everything settles, whatever the cost, we'll see real change. Baltimore will become a better city, and it'll do it by casting a thief like Davenport aside."

Factor's latest missive certainly zeroed in on Davenport. It wasn't about the city so much as making its mayor look bad and getting everyone to blame him for the string of terrible events. I wondered what he'd ever done to piss Factor Zero off so much. I didn't like Davenport and never would, but everything the group talked about went way beyond the pale. I needed to go along for now, at least. I remained badly outnumbered, and the guard wouldn't be the only person with a gun and the willingness to shoot me.

"All right," I said even though my words made me feel a little nauseated. "Let's break a few eggs."

———

Toward the end of the day, our leader made another announcement. "Pack a bag. Maybe two. We're going to stop squatting in places like this. I've made us some hotel reservations. It's all on the down-low. We'll have access to everything we need, and the goddamn cops and feds won't look for us there. I'll send you all messages with the details shortly. Make sure you're there tonight."

I left a few minutes later and walked a little out of the way to discourage anyone from following me. Once I made it inside, I called Rich. "You could've warned us our network was coming down," he grumbled.

"I couldn't, actually. We're going to a hotel later. All part of the next phase of this op. You and Sharpe should get over here ASAP."

"The captain's busy. Hell, I am, too, but I'll be there in a few." He ended the call, and I hurried upstairs to get a bag ready for a couple days. I texted T.J. and told her we'd need to figure out the next steps later. I got the feeling every member of the team would get searched on the way in—maybe me a little more vigorously than most—and my personal phone and computer wouldn't be allowed. We would need a solid Plan B.

The rumble of a V8 announced Rich's arrival, and I let him in a moment later. "I don't have long," I said once he situated himself on the sofa.

"I probably don't, either. We're all basically running around like our hair is on fire. We're dead in the water. What happened?"

"I got ordered to take the police network down. Everyone watched. I didn't have a chance to get away or send a message. They also made it clear I'd get shot if I didn't comply."

Rich blew out a deep breath. "All right. You think your cover is blown?"

"I don't know." I shrugged. "My little run-in with Brubaker bought me some cachet at first, but it's gone now. No one seems to suspect I'm working with you, but they're giving me the hairy eyeball a lot more. I think some of it stems from the nine-one-one hack ending after I checked on it. You and I aren't the only ones who struggle with coincidences."

"Got any tips for getting our network back up?" Rich asked.

"On the scale it operated before, no," I said. "At least nothing quick, cheap, or easy. I know you roll your eyes when I mention getting onto the network, but I've spent a lot of time there over the last few years. I know how you organize it. Routers are down, so you can't get anything from one group to another. Switches are still up, though. The group was so impressed with what I did, they didn't ask me to go any deeper."

"You know I need a translator when you speak geek."

"Switches deliver local traffic. Same network segment only. In your buildings, it means one team or one floor. They'll still be able to talk to one another. My advice? Set up a desktop to connect to every switch and use it as a file server. Your IT folks will know how. If you really want to get geeky, they can probably restore some cross-team functionality with virtual LANs."

"I'll nod and pretend this all made sense," Rich said.

"It doesn't matter if you understand it. I honestly don't expect you to. There are deeper fixes, but this one is the easiest and quickest. Just remember what I told you so you can relay the message."

"I will."

"Let me know when the medal ceremony is," I said. "I think I should get one this time."

"I'll see myself out," Rich said.

After he did, I finished packing. I liked this op less and less the longer I remained involved, but I was committed at this point. Even if it got uglier, I needed to stick it out to try and help the city dig out.

———

Sure enough, Factor and the security guard—whose name I still didn't know—searched everyone's bags outside our block of rooms on the third floor. "I told you no personal devices, Shelly," he said, handing his brawny compatriot a phone confiscated from a sullen Honeybee. She, at least, avoided the pat-downs the rest of us got. While the sentry gave me the once-over, I wondered how the group scored reservations at the Residence Inn without drawing a lot of unwanted attention. This was a national chain, not some little local place which rented rooms by the hour. "You're clean," he said. Factor Zero handed me a keycard, and I walked into my room.

Once inside, I knew why our leader chose this place. A small kitchen—complete with oven, microwave, full-sized fridge, and dishwasher—meant we wouldn't need to go anywhere. This made managing the group much easier. Services like Instacart would deliver groceries and other supplies, and combining those with what the hotel provided meant we had everything we needed.

And so did Factor Zero. His team now lived and worked under one roof, and the ban on personal devices meant he controlled communications. I set my overnight bag atop the queen bed farther from the door and my backpack on the desk. Though empty of all but a few facility-provided extras, it offered enough space to work. I wondered if anyone else would be staying in here with me. After about fifteen minutes of no activity, I figured I had it to myself—which would be far better for everything I needed to do.

The outside of the hotel looked free of balconies, but my room featured a small one. This side faced the neighboring Hampton Inn. Most rooms on the lower four levels offered a small walkout space. Starting on the fifth story, guests clearly couldn't be trusted to avoid taking headers onto Grant Street below. Someone knocked on my door. I walked back into the room and looked through the peephole. Factor and my favorite guard waited. I opened up. The guard shoved a laptop bag at me. "Your computer," Factor said.

"Cool. We getting some supplies?"

"Like what?"

"Fridge is empty," I said.

"Got a delivery coming later. A lot of staples."

"I'm going to head to the gift shop and get a few things." Neither of them moved, and both kept looking at me like I'd sprouted an additional head. "Is there a problem?"

"No," Factor Zero said. "Don't be long."

"Sure." I took the stairs down to the main level and found the hotel shop between the front desk and the elevators. A middle-aged couple browsed the shelves, so I puttered around until they left. I grabbed a couple bottles of soda and a few small bags of nuts. The clerk was a young woman with a round cheerful face and a head full of pink-streaked blonde hair.

"Anything else for you today?" she asked as she scanned all my items. The total came to a rather usurious $22.40 with tax.

"Yes, actually." I set a fifty on the counter. She eyed the Grant suspiciously. I kept talking before she could rattle off some corporate policy about large bills. "Can I use your phone? I need to send a couple texts." She frowned. "It's nothing weird. Mine's . . . lost, and I can't get a replacement soon enough. You can watch everything I do, and you can keep the change."

She glanced to the money, to me, and back again a few times before finally saying, "All right." After taking the bill and putting my items in a hotel-branded plastic bag, she slid a recent iPhone onto the counter. "You said I could watch what you do. Make sure I can."

"No problem," I said. I opened the messages app, entered T.J.'s number from memory, and jotted off a quick text. *It's C.T. Borrowing a phone. I need you to look into the IT worker angle. Need to know more about the ones who left and where they went. Also need you to bring a phone for me to the Resi-dence Inn downtown.*

She replied a moment later. *Will do, boss. Be there in about twenty. Where should I look for you?*

Side facing the Hampton. Third-floor balcony. Can you make the throw?

My answer came in the form of a strong emoji. I deleted the text thread from the clerk's phone and handed it back to her. "Thanks."

"If you don't mind me saying, sir, you must have a strange job."

I smiled. "You have no idea."

———

I hoped T.J. didn't overestimate her arm strength. She was tall, and her time away from the streets allowed her to fill out her frame better. Still, throwing a device like a phone over thirty feet in the air with some degree of accuracy would be a challenge. If I didn't think my actions would be scrutinized, we might've been able to make the handoff in the lobby. Factor Zero chose this location for a reason, and I suspected an ability to view important camera feeds to be part of it.

A few minutes before the appointed time, I wandered onto the small balcony again. It was devoid of furniture or decoration. Only a five-foot translucent plastic barrier topped with a metal bar prevented me from toppling to the pavement below. Lawyers signing off on the liability surprised me. I looked for my secretary, but she hadn't arrived yet. Grant Street was mostly a glorified alley in this stretch, so no one passed by below.

Foot traffic between the two hotels increased while I waited. Plenty of stores and eateries were a short walk away, and cutting down Grant made sense especially from the Hampton Inn side. Finally, a familiar blonde young woman made an appearance. She scanned the facade of the building. I didn't want to draw too much attention by waving, but when she didn't spot me right away, I took the risk. T.J. walked farther along until she stood below the balcony with her back to the neighboring hotel. "You good?" she said.

"More or less."

"I presume you're not the only one staying here."

"Nope," I said.

She nodded, and I knew she would understand. Despite this being her first real job, T.J. displayed a lot of smarts and some good intuition. "I have what you want."

"I was hoping."

T.J. held the phone in her hand. I again hoped she could make the toss. If she missed—or I dropped the blasted thing— we would require a fortunate set of circumstances to get a second attempt. She put her left foot forward, drew her arm back, and stopped, quickly tucking the mobile away. I wondered why until I heard Factor Zero's voice from the balcony next to mine. "What the hell is going on out here?"

CHAPTER 21

T.J. REMAINED silent as Factor Zero stared between her and me. "Foxtrot, what are you doing?"

"It's been a lonely few days," I said, hoping T.J. would run with me on this even though it promised to be awkward. "I saw this fine-looking girl walking by and started chatting her up."

"You need a woman, I can get you one," he said. "I know people who can make it happen . . . pretty much whatever you want."

"I'm not paying for it." I pointed to the street below. "Not when hotties like her just walk by."

Three stories down, T.J. shrugged. "I don't like it when men holler at me, you know, but most of them don't look like him. So I stopped."

Factor Zero snickered. "He's not even very good-looking. Nothing personal."

"Better him than you," T.J. said.

"He works for me." Factor pointed to himself. "I'm his boss."

"Maybe he should be the one in charge. I like him better."

"Seems like she has good taste," I said. "Nothing personal."

"Whatever," he muttered and went back inside.

"So what's a nice girl like you doing outside a hotel like this?"

"Some jerk asked me to stop by," T.J. said. "Didn't even have the courtesy to come down and meet me."

"I'm sure it's a complex situation. He sounds very handsome, though."

"Meh." She fished the phone out of her jeans pocket again. I gave her a thumbs-up. T.J. stepped forward, drew her arm back, and let it fly. She showed a throwing motion a lot of young ballplayers could emulate. The phone rotated end-over-end as it soared through the air. I wasn't sure it was going to make it high enough, and the wall prevented me from providing a lot of help. I leaned over as far as I could. When the cell neared my hand, I reached down and squeezed it. Hard plastic settled between my thumb and first two fingers.

I brought my hand up slowly as T.J. moved closer to the balcony below. If I dropped the mobile, she would be in position to catch it and try again. I held on, cradling it in two hands when I brought it over the plastic barrier. It was already on and showed an Android home screen. "Thanks," I said. "Nice toss."

"I played softball in high school . . . before I dropped out." She paused to flex her biceps, walked back up Grant Street, and I returned to the room. I admired the bathroom as I ran water in the tub.

Between my own eyes and an app on the phone, I checked the suite for bugs and cameras. To my surprise, I found none even after a second search. T.J. called. I turned the TV on to add some more background noise before picking up. "I never want to flirt with you again," she said. "Ew."

"I'm glad you could roll with the punches. The feeling is mutual, by the way."

"I'll look into the city workers like you asked."

"Sooner the better," I said. "I have a hunch something dirty has been going on. It makes me wonder if Davenport hired a real incident response company or some shady outfit who's tied into everything else."

"All right . . . I'll get on it."

"Check on Rich, too, when you have a moment. The police network is pretty much down. I talked him through a way of getting some functionality back. When I won't draw too much suspicion, I'll try and do more."

"Sure," my secretary said. "Anything else he'll need to know?"

"Yeah," I said. "The cops should have people keeping an eye on the dark web. If not, maybe they can ask the feds for some help. Our leader is posting something about a rally in Baltimore. It's supposed to look legit, but it's really a front for violence. His end goal seems to be chaos, and I don't think he cares how many people have to die to make it happen."

"Jesus Christ. I'll make sure Rich knows. You have any other details?"

"Not yet."

"You really landed in the soup on this one," T.J. said. "Your boss or whatever he is seems suspicious, too. You all right?"

"For now, I think I am. They're paying more attention to me than some of the others, but it's nothing I can't handle."

"Be careful."

"You don't need to worry about me," I said. "Make sure the word gets out." I ended the call.

———

I couldn't leave the water running forever. If Factor Zero bunked down in the next room, he would get suspicious. I left the TV on and turned it up a couple clicks before calling City Hall and asking for the mayor's conference room. A staffer I didn't know picked up. Once we established the situation, I asked if Charlie were still on the clock. She told me he was and connected us. "How are things on the inside?" he asked.

"Interesting, and I mean it in the ancient Chinese curse sort of way." I kept my voice low. "I can't talk too loudly, so I hope you can hear me."

"I can, but it's not great. Is there a TV on?"

"Yeah, and it needs to stay on. Long story, but this is the only way I can speak. I presume you've heard about the police network?"

"It's been the topic of conversation all day."

"I figured," I said. "Don't hate me, but I'm the one who did it. I had to if I wanted to stay on the good side of the grass."

"Sounds like they're on to you," Charlie said.

"I think the leader and his believer-in-chief are naturally suspicious. For now, I think I'm all right." I hoped I could continue to make this claim. While I kept a pocket knife in my jeans, it counted as my only weapon. A pistol wouldn't have gotten past the search.

"Did you call me because you want to try and bring the BPD back online?"

"Yes," I said, "but it needs to be a staggered approach. If it just reverts to full-go all at once, I might end up in a wood chipper tomorrow. And I'm not sure these guys would have the courtesy to stuff me in head-first."

"Ugh." Charlie fell silent for a few seconds. "There's a visual I didn't need soon after dinner."

"Sorry. I can tell you how I did it. For now, I'm only on a phone. It can get online, but I'm trying to minimize those sorts of escapades at the moment."

"I got you. Walk me through it."

"It was all layer three. I found a credential someone should've deleted. From there, I logged into the routers, changed the passwords, and dumped the tables."

"Might be out of my league here," Charlie said. "We'll need a network engineer."

"I hope you still have one," I said.

"We do."

"Good. I told my cousin . . . he works in Homicide . . . local traffic will still work over switches. Not sure what he was able to do with it, though."

"You know the password you put on all the routers?"

"Sure. I'll email it to you. Caesar cipher."

"Okay." He sighed. "I don't know if we can get anyone back in here tonight. Might not be able to do anything until the morning."

Ordinarily, I would use my phone to connect to a computer in my office, access the resources I needed securely, and no one would be the wiser. With our leader in the next room, I didn't want to make the attempt. If he brought a device to capture and decrypt wireless traffic, I wouldn't be talking my way out of anything. "I'm sure they'll be happy to have things restored," I said. "Just tell the engineer not to do it all at once. Maybe one router an hour or something. I can't have too many eyes on me."

"I'll make sure he knows," Charlie said. "Good luck. Sounds like you're sticking your neck out on this one."

"A lot more than I expected to, yeah." We ended the call.

I sent Charlie an email with the password he would need. The Caesar cipher was a simple one which moved all characters three places in the alphabet. It probably worked very well when few people in the world could read. It almost counted as a joke now, but even if someone intercepted my email, they wouldn't know the significance of the content let alone the idea of shifting each letter and number three spots.

Charlie sent back a short confirmation message. I'd done what I could for tonight. Tomorrow, the police would get their capability back, Factor Zero would be pissed, and I expected things to go off the rails from there.

Maybe I needed a gun after all.

CHAPTER 22

THE NEW VENUE meant we didn't need to gather in abandoned buildings anymore. We all stayed in our rooms and worked on tasks Factor Zero sent via text. I missed the large central space where we would all hammer away on our keyboards, but I didn't miss having our leader pace the room and keep an eye on everyone. Of course, he could do so electronically. The laptop's webcam could be activated without turning on the light to alert the user, and I knew a keylogger would capture all my input.

I took the same steps as before to defeat it. Multiple windows with every third or fourth keystroke going to the browser. I downloaded the key scrambler, installed it, and hoped for the best. When no one barged in with a pistol after fifteen minutes, I figured I was good. A message came in on my burner phone. *Everyone downstairs, breakout room 2, no computers. Come now.* I ensured my disguise was in place and took the stairs to the first floor. I found the appointed room near the back of the hotel and took a seat at the large round table. We filled half the eight chairs. Factor and his pet guard remained standing after shutting the door.

"This has been a complicated op from the start," our

leader said. "We changed personnel, got raided by the feds, and we're still down a man." I wondered what happened to Paradice. He wouldn't be clued in to things like our current location, but as an original member of APT00, he might have known details of the endgame. If the FBI released him, he'd done a good job of making himself scarce. "This morning, the police network is coming back online."

"What the fuck?" Darrell banged his fist on the table. He lowered his voice when Factor Zero moved his hand up and down. "I thought they were cooked."

"They were," I said, "but it was their routers. Someone could've figured it out. We can't presume everything we do is going to work indefinitely, especially with the city hiring an IR firm."

"How do you know what they've done?" Darrell asked.

I shrugged. "It's on the news. The body count is an evergreen topic in Baltimore, but this time of year, the only other things they talk about are the weather, the Ravens, and Christmas. Doesn't take much to make the paper or get on TV in December."

"You're local," Factor Zero said, "so I guess you would know." I didn't care for the edge in his tone, but he didn't threaten me, so I let it go for now. "We can knock the police offline again later. More than just a layer three takedown, too. Our plans continue. When the time comes, they won't be able to do anything to stop us. We're going to focus on some specific targets today. I'll text you assignments, and I'll be popping into your rooms to check on things." He looked at me when he asked, "Anyone object?"

"No," I said in unison with the rest of the team.

"Good. We'll get a food delivery soon. Make sure you eat and stay hydrated. This should be a busy day. We have a lot to prepare for."

Honeybee and Turbo left the room. When I stood, Darrell moved in front of me. "I still got my eye on you." He jabbed his finger at me, and it took all my self-restraint not to grab it and snap it. "Maybe you let the cops come back online."

"It wasn't a crippling attack." I swatted his finger aside, and he glared anew.

"How'd they get the passwords for the routers?"

"How the hell would we get them? They figured it out. Always a risk. You want to knock them offline, you write the goddamn code."

"Guys," Factor Zero said, "this isn't productive. We're nearing the end of this op. Let's keep it together until then, okay?"

"Sure," I said. Iceman grunted and stormed out of the room. I planned to give him a wide berth when I exited. Factor and the guard remained behind, and the latter nudged the door. It remained slightly ajar. I headed toward the stairs and stopped. Why did they stay behind? Was the leader telling his goon to put a couple rounds in the back of my head? I flattened against the wall and padded closer.

"You sure about this?" the sentry whispered.

"We talked about it," Factor Zero said in a similar hushed tone. I peered through the small opening. "The op needs to survive me getting arrested or whatever at the rally." He took something from around his neck. It was a slender silver chain with something hanging from the end. The more I looked at it, it bore a strong resemblance to a small USB flash drive. "Keep it safe."

"You know I will."

I backed away and headed toward the stairs again. What did Factor really give the sentry? If it was in fact a flash drive, what did it hold? I didn't want to wait for some violent rally to get answers.

———

The Instacart delivery brought several assorted fridge and pantry staples. It was a smart tactic. Factor Zero could keep the team working in our rooms. No need to go anywhere and get anything. No risk of exposure, drunken social media posts, or plants in the organization letting the cops know what went on. I still wanted a pistol and help doing some research, and I couldn't order those from a delivery service.

I put the TV on, called T.J., and made arrangements. "It's early for lunch," she pointed out.

"Bring breakfast, then. I don't care."

"All right. You want the forty-five?"

My Sig Sauer .45 ACP was my favorite gun. In a chaotic environment like a rally turned violent, however, I reasoned it would be wise to trade stopping power for magazine capacity. "Bring me the nine," I said. "I don't know if Factor got a look at you last night, so do something like pulling your hair under a hat."

"I got it, boss," she said. "What's your room number?"

"Three-forty-four."

"All right. Be there soon."

"Bring your laptop," I added before she ended the call. In the meantime, I worked on what my esteemed leader sent via text. *Find a better way to take down the police and fire department networks. I want to cripple these bastards. No good response at the rally and whatever comes of it. Use Java because they do. We have all the classes we need in our repo.*

An idea flickered in the back of my brain, so I replied. *You don't want me to make a custom class?*

Factor Zero responded a moment later. *No. Use what we have. It should do whatever you need. Plus, I won't need to check those parts of your code. Don't let me down again.*

Now, the idea blazed. I didn't bother texting back. This prick would get what was coming to him soon enough. I needed to make things look convincing, at least, so I poked around the fire department's network while I waited for my secretary. It took a few minutes to map and fingerprint everything. Whoever set it up used a similar structure to the BPD's: organized mostly by division and location with a few segments used for specialized functions. There weren't as many branches because a local fire house didn't get subdivided into nearly as many different groups and functions like a police precinct did. The BFD's network would be even easier to disrupt.

A few minutes later, someone knocked on the door. I looked through the peephole. T.J. stood in the hallway. She held a pizza box with a paper bag inside a plastic one atop it. Her delivery person attire consisted of jeans, a loose-fitting hoodie, and a cap which held her long blonde hair. I opened up, and Factor Zero did the same next door. He looked over at us and frowned. "What the hell? We just got a delivery."

"I wanted something else," I said. "Problem?"

He grimaced and scrutinized the delivery girl. Between the rather formless sweatshirt and Orioles cap, T.J. didn't look like the attractive young woman from outside the balcony last night. "Where'd you get pizza at this hour?"

"I'm local, remember? I know the owner. Want a slice? Jalapeño and anchovy."

He wrinkled his nose. "No. Just make sure your work is done."

"Aye-aye, Captain." He returned to his room. I confirmed the hallway was clear before ushering T.J. in. "Thanks for coming." I kept my voice low and turned up the TV volume another couple clicks.

"Jalapeño and anchovy?" she said as she set everything on the unused bed. I inserted one of the 9mm clips, racked in a round, and set its safety before stowing it in my waistband and pocketing the extra mag.

"Pretty low odds he'd want those toppings," I said. "We needed him gone. Where'd you get the box, anyway?"

"You're lucky I hadn't taken out yesterday's recycling yet."

"At least you're still eating well on the company dime."

She smiled and patted her flat stomach. Ah, to be very young and have a metabolism to match. "What are we working on?"

"I need to do some stuff for the team," I said. T.J. frowned. "Don't worry. I'll split my time. I want you to focus on the IT workers who left the city. Where did they go . . . and was it for some place in Pennsylvania?"

"I'm on it." She took her laptop and an older, smaller model of mine out of the pizza box, used her cell phone as a hotspot, and got down to business by turning the bed into a makeshift workspace. I finished fingerprinting the fire department's network and uploaded my results. I also checked our code repository to see what Java classes we had access to for writing code. The standard options were there along with several custom ones. A team-specific one called *Compromises* held a lot of good attack scripts. I could work with it.

First, however, I wanted to gather some information with T.J., so I connected to her mobile hotspot. The city's IT department brain drain was real. They'd lost a lot of long-tenured workers and only replaced a handful. Tons of institutional knowledge walked out the door and didn't return. I paused with my fingers hovering over the keys. After our first attack on the city, Factor Zero summarized everything with a speech. I couldn't recall the whole thing, but one bit stuck out to me now. *Combined with the brain drain in their IT depart-ment . . .* The only people I'd heard use the term worked for Baltimore. It wasn't something people went around saying all the time. Thus, it made an odd phrase for a young hacker like Factor Zero to use.

A few minutes later, T.J. said, "I have something." She remained sitting on the bed but turned her laptop around so I could see the screen. "I used the LinkedIn scraping tool you showed me. Haven't found all the folks who have left yet, but I'm at about sixty percent. So far, they've all gone to one of two companies."

"Good work." I looked at her results. Both places were in Pennsylvania, and I'd never heard of either firm. This alone didn't mean anything, but two unknown places poaching a bunch of IT workers from the state to the south struck me as unlikely. A few employees posted status updates, and they consisted of the usual new-job platitudes. "Let's run these companies down."

We each took one and compared our results. A different LLC owned each, but the same company was listed as the parent for both. It didn't take long to unravel the owner.

Dale Willett.

"Holy shit," I said. "This guy used to work for Davenport. Gloria and I went to a speech where Davenport specifically thanked him for some process improvement."

"It seems the admiration isn't mutual," T.J. said.

"Definitely not based on recent events. This doesn't mean Willett sicced APT double zero on Baltimore, but it all has to be connected."

"What do we do with this info?"

"Untangle the webs," I said. "Let's also hope the mayor

hasn't done something stupid." It didn't take long to discover he had, though unintentionally. One of the shell companies also owned an incident response company. One second on Google showed me it was the same one the city hired—the firm recommended by someone at Davenport's current company. "They're screwed." I pointed to my screen, and T.J. read over my shoulder.

"I thought you mentioned things got better."

"They did. It all seemed pretty basic to me. An attempt not to be the low-hanging fruit. I haven't heard of any forensic work this place has done. They made a few things harder to do, but if the company is in league with Willett, Factor Zero might already know how to bypass any new defenses."

"This is going to keep getting worse," T.J. said.

I nodded. "Yeah. I need to let Davenport know. Normally, I'd enjoy telling him he bungled something. Not this time."

———

The mayor could wait. We needed to know more first. I split my time between work for the group and research with T.J. Between the two of us, we put together a pretty good dossier on Dale Willett. Davenport told the story accurately when he made his speech before all hell broke loose. Willett was a product line manager overseeing hamburger and hot dog buns for D&S. Whatever improvements he made to the company's processes didn't register to me. I've baked two loaves of bread in my life, and one came out a disaster. Whatever Willett did, it helped the company a lot.

We couldn't find a lot of data on the falling out the two men had. What we uncovered indicated Willett wanted credit for the process and not just in terms of having it named after him. Davenport declined, and he continued to use the improvements even after Willett left the company. A few months later, Willett filed a business permit in Pennsylvania for his own bread company. It never got off the ground, however, because his brother died in police custody a short while later.

Today, such a case would make the news and stay in the national consciousness thanks to social media. Nineteen years ago, it faded quickly. State police investigated and found no wrongdoing. The Willett family sued everyone they could attach to lawsuits at different levels of government, but the US Justice Department declined to prosecute on a criminal basis. The plaintiffs reached a civil settlement with the county and state for an unknown amount. "Now we know why he hates Davenport and the police," T.J. said.

"But not the Baltimore police. This all happened in PA."

She shrugged. "All right, let me see something." After a few seconds, her eyes lit up. "Scranton PD got hit by a massive denial of service attack a few weeks ago. Some of their systems still aren't back. They've had to farm out some work to the state police and surrounding districts."

"Must not have been a big news story down here," I said. "I don't remember hearing about it."

"It's not getting a lot of coverage to the north, either. They've kept a pretty tight lid on things. A few smaller outlets are running with it."

Larger papers needed access to the police department for stories and quotes. Their corporate overlords may have erred on the side of not reporting something which would embarrass the local cops. "Leave it to the indies," I said. I compiled what we'd found so far into a document and sent it to everyone I could think of . . . including the mayor. Someone needed to stop him before he paid the ransom.

"Looks like Willett came into some money recently," T.J. said. She turned her laptop around again so I could see the screen. "He's sold off a few companies or his shares in them. Raised quite a few million dollars."

"Certainly enough to bankroll a bunch of hackers," I said. While T.J. dug into Willett's millions, I poked at the companies he created which got entangled in the Baltimore mess. The city's former IT staffers all worked for a couple consulting firms which boasted no clients. Getting paid to sit around and do nothing must have been nice. I looked into all the employee rosters and found an interesting entry.

Francis Ziegler. "Check this out." I showed T.J. my display. "Does a certain asshole look familiar?"

She smirked and nodded. "He's your boss. Totally looks like a Francis, too."

"I pegged him as more of a Frankie," I said.

"You going to use it on him?"

I shook my head. "No point in showing my hand this early. There's still a lot of work to be done. I have an idea to make the group's upcoming attack a lot less potent."

"How are you going to do it?" she asked.

"Factor wants us to use Java. It calls on classes for a lot of functions. We have one called *Compromises* out in our code repository. There's a Cyrillic character called *es* which looks identical to our C."

T.J. frowned for a second, then her eyes widened, and she bobbed her head. "You're going to duplicate the existing one, and the name will look identical."

"Yep," I confirmed. "I'll copy what's there for the new one, but I'm also going to add a time limit. Factor will think he's taking the police and fire networks down—and who knows what else—and he will be . . . but only for a while."

"He's not going to notice?"

"I doubt it. He said he's not checking our calls to the repo. I presume this means he'll still be going over other pieces of code. It might be my only chance to slip one by him. Speaking of slipping, you probably need to go. The longer you're here, the better the odds someone discovers you."

"They'll hear your door open," T.J. said. She jerked her head toward the other end of the suite. "I'll go out the balcony."

"Unless you recently got bitten by a radioactive spider," I said, "I don't think the thirty-foot drop will agree with you."

She grinned. "No superpowers. I checked out the balconies when I came by last night. It's an easy drop to the one below. The railings are thick enough." I must have given her a skeptical look because she said, "I used to get in and out of hotels for a living, remember? It's not like I never needed to make a quick getaway in my past life." Before I could object, T.J. produced a backpack from the grocery bag she arrived with and stuffed her laptop inside. "Trust me, boss. I'll be fine."

I opened the balcony door and checked to see if anyone else enjoyed the midmorning air. No one did. T.J. climbed onto the barrier, hung by her hands, and dropped to the one below. My heart skipped a beat as she landed on the railing, rocked back and forth, and got her footing. She did the same thing again, dropping down to the first floor and then making the easy hop onto Grant Street. She waved as she headed off. I walked inside and got back to work.

CHAPTER 23

SHORTLY AFTER T.J. made her heroic departure, I finished my code. Once I'd finished fingerprinting the fire department's network, programming the actual attack wasn't complicated. What chewed up time was duplicating the *Compromises* Java class with my own little additions. I couldn't do a lot of testing to make sure I'd gotten everything right. If the timelines moved like I expected them to, my work would get tested live soon enough.

Factor Zero—I snickered as I thought of him as Frankie—sent a message to congratulate me on my work. If he checked what I'd written, he'd see calls to what he thought was a well-known Java class. The Cyrillic *es* character would look the same as a capital C on a screen. As the leader texted a reminder about the rally being tomorrow, my phone rang. I recognized the number and turned on the TV. "Mister Ferguson," Vincent Davenport said after I picked up, "I understand you've made some progress."

"Did you read my email?"

"I'm a busy man."

"Want to trade places?" I asked. "You could add 'not getting discovered and killed' to your itinerary."

"All right . . . I'm sure you've got a lot going on, too."

"I do, but I was able to track down a lot of what these assholes are doing. Have you heard from Dale Willett recently?"

"No, and I don't expect to. Why?" I didn't say anything and imagined the hamster wheels turning inside the mayor's mind. After a couple seconds, he added, "Wait, are you saying Dale is behind all this?"

"Looks like it," I said. "I put it in the email you didn't read."

Davenport sighed. "Maybe you could summarize it for me now. I'm about to walk downstairs to a press conference. Despite what our friends in law enforcement have told me, I'm amenable to paying the hackers and getting rid of the problems."

"Don't. For a lot of reasons, but the big one being Dale Willett will go a long way for a grudge. He set up a couple companies to poach a bunch of your IT workers and—as far as I can tell—pay them handsomely for doing nothing. The hacking group gets money from him, too. Whatever you did to piss him off twenty years ago must've really stuck." Davenport didn't take the bait this time. "It goes beyond you, too. His brother died under questionable circumstances in police custody."

"I didn't even know he had a brother."

"Any other former business partners or employees who might hate you?" I said. "For the good of the city, I think we need to know."

"A man like me will inevitably make some enemies, Mister Ferguson. I think Dale is an outlier in terms of how much he disliked me, his apparent resources, and how far he would go to get his revenge."

"Maybe whoever's left in the IT department can re-recruit some of their old coworkers. You could use the help."

"I'll mention it."

"It gets worse. The IR company you hired is also tied to Willett. It's all indirect, but I don't think you can trust the work they're doing."

"My CTO recommended them." Davenport sighed. "He's been with the company a long time."

"Did he overlap with Willett?" I asked.

"Yes, but I didn't have any reason not to trust him." He paused. "With all this bad news, I'm not sure what I'm going to say at this press briefing."

"Tell them you're not going to pay. I think I've managed to keep a lid on the worst of things. Make sure everyone's ready for the rally tomorrow, and I think we'll be good."

"The risk assessment looks a lot different for you than for me," he said. "I'm happy to be defiant now, but if things get worse quickly, I've liquidated assets and am prepared to pay."

"I hope you don't have to."

"Do your best to make sure I don't, then." He ended the call. I looked at my watch. Barely twenty-four hours remained until the rally APToo planned would kick off. A bunch of attendees would already be in town. Factor got the word out under the radar and repeatedly, including in communities where it would spread. Again, I found myself wishing I could have done more, but getting exposed wouldn't help the city.

———

Early in the afternoon, my phone buzzed with a text from T.J. *Someone's waiting for you in the gift shop.* I'd done my share of work for the day. If Factor or anyone else questioned me, I would tell them where I was headed. I opened the door to my room and stepped into the hallway. No one challenged me. I let it close quietly and took the stairs to the main floor. Inside the shop, Leon Sharpe stood against the drink case in casual clothes. Somehow, the lack of a police uniform made him look even more massive. "Leon." I opened a nearby glass door and pretended to browse the options.

"I got your message. Good work. You all right here?"

"For now," I said. "How'd you know where to find me?"

"Your secretary talked to Rich." Sharpe shrugged his massive shoulders. "He told me."

"What are you doing here?"

"Getting the lay of the land." The cashier, a middle-aged woman with a long nose and short hair, pretended to be interested in her book while she watched the captain and me. Sharpe kept his voice low, which I imagined came at significant effort for him. "Why shouldn't I arrest all your friends now?"

"First of all," I whispered, "they're not my friends, and a couple of them will tell you so without being prompted. Second, it wouldn't matter."

"What do you mean?"

"You realize attacks can be released on a schedule, right? Like anything else. They're just automated tasks designed to run at a certain time or with an if-then condition. You wouldn't stop whatever's already in the pipeline."

"Might stop the rally," Sharpe said.

I scoffed. "Come on. Factor Zero has spread the word far and wide. Malcontents, people who hate the cops, and shit disturbers from anywhere nearby are going to come out for it. Some of them are probably here already. You wouldn't be stopping anything."

Sharpe frowned and nosed around the bagged snacks. "I don't like doing nothing."

"Me, neither. Look, the group is going to take down your network again . . . the fire department's, too, this time. I've managed to put something in the code. Think of it as an expiration. After a certain time, whatever got done initially gets reverted."

"And everything comes back."

"It should," I said. "No guarantees when it comes to city IT assets. I would suggest you call the help desk, but I'm not sure you have one anymore."

"I'm not sure, either." He sighed as he kept perusing the shelves. We'd run out of square footage soon. "We'll be ready for the rally."

"I hope so. I don't think it's going to be people marching peacefully with a few picket signs. The plan is to cause chaos. Remember, Willett hates Davenport and police in equal measure."

"The commissioner read your email, too. We'll have an appropriate response."

"I don't want to tell you how to do your job—"

"So don't," Sharpe broke in.

"You know me, Leon. I'm going to anyway. You probably have a consultant or PR person talking to you about optics. Think of how it'll look if the cops come and punch everyone at a rally ostensibly against police violence."

The captain waved a hand. "People want law and order. Optics are for the news. You going to be at the rally?"

"I need to be," I said. "I'll do what I can to keep things under control. Probably no better time to out myself as working for the enemy." Recent memories of my arrest and awful treatment at the hands of the FBI prompted my next question. "I understand I'll probably get arrested along with everyone else, but you'll make sure I'm not given an enhanced interrogation, right?"

"Sure," Sharpe said. He grinned. "Just think of the optics there."

—————

I came back from the gift shop with a couple bottles of Gatorade and a bag of peanuts in case anyone saw me. Factor Zero's pet guard patrolled the hallway. He gave me the hairy eyeball even when I showed him my haul from downstairs. I returned to my room and checked on what I'd done. My take-downs of the BPD and BFD were in the pipeline. I wondered when they'd go live. Sharpe knew what to expect, so he could get the word out.

A couple hours later, I got a message on my team cell phone. *Downstairs breakout room, 5 minutes.* I spent a few minutes hiding my phone, laptop, and gun. There weren't a ton of great options in the room. I set the mobile under the Gideon Bible. Someone who opened the nightstand drawer and didn't take a careful look wouldn't notice. The laptop, while small, proved more challenging. I ended up stuffing it and the pistol under the mattress. By the time I made it to the ground floor, I was the last person to arrive for our meeting.

Factor situated his laptop so we could all see the screen. "I just pushed our attacks against the police and fire departments." He smiled like a predator eyeing a wounded animal. "In less than a day, we'll wreck this city. The Keystone Cops won't be able to coordinate anything. The fire department will be disorganized. We wanted chaos, and we're going to get it. Thanks to Foxtrot for his work on these."

"Happy to help," I said with as much sincerity as I could muster.

"I hope these work better than the last one," Darrell said with a sneer.

"Of course they will. I wrote them." This fact didn't seem to improve his mood.

"Turbo checked everything," Factor Zero said.

"Yeah, good work," he added. "You write clean code."

I shrugged. "Years of practice."

Factor queued up a document on his laptop. "This went to the mayor and every news outlet a few minutes ago. Davenport isn't going to be able to wriggle off our hook." I leaned in to read the text better.

Robber baron Davenport,

You've gotten a couple lucky breaks. No more. Your run of good fortune is over.

Right now, your police and fire departments are aimless and clueless. Their networks are down, and they're not coming back up until we say so.

Tomorrow, thousands of people will attend a rally to end police violence and the tyranny of autocratic mayors. We would invite you, but you wouldn't be a popular guest. Maybe you should just watch on the news. There will be a lot of coverage. You love cameras, don't you?

If you want to make things easier for yourself and your city, the price has gone up again. Pay us $55 million in cryptocurrency by 9 AM or things will only get worse.

"Steep price," Honeybee said once we'd all finished reading.

"It's one I'm not sure he can pay," Factor Zero said. "Davenport has money, but a lot of it is tied up in his company and investments. He probably can't liquidate enough to raise such a total. We know the feds will tell him not to pay. The FBI doesn't believe in it."

"What did you mean by, 'things will only get worse'?" I asked.

"I don't expect Davenport to pay. The reality is it doesn't matter. If he does, we're set for life. Whether or not he coughs up the Bitcoin, I have some additional plans for tomorrow. Way beyond what's happening now."

I tried to summon a smile at the news. "More chaos, then."

Factor Zero nodded. "A lot more. This city is going to burn, and Davenport will get blamed for holding a gas can."

CHAPTER 24

AFTER OUR CONFAB on the first floor, we all went back to our rooms. I finished my work of identifying a few obscure hosts on various segments of the city's network. I pegged them as security appliances. No one on the team expressed any concern in our Discord channel. Factor Zero told us all to eat well and rest up for the rally tomorrow. I feigned excitement before signing off.

No one discovered my other phone or laptop—or the 9MM—while I was downstairs. I checked online to see what people said about the rally. Local sites, forums, and subreddits were full of opinions. Some folks were uninterested, but those who wanted to attend struck me as the type who would cause problems. Many posts trashed Davenport. Ordinarily, I would've appreciated the jabs at his expense. In light of what may happen tomorrow, however, I saw them in a more sinister light. Some of the most upvoted replies promised destruction, violence, outright murder, and the targeting of police officers.

The dark web proved even worse. Although about half the folks using it at any given time were law enforcement of some type, a greater feeling of anonymity compelled people to say even more inflammatory things. Specific high-ranking members of the BPD—including Leon Sharpe—and city officials came under fire. Photos of them with targets over their faces were popular. City landmarks got the same treatment.

Factor Zero's plans had taken off in the most sinister way possible.

I flipped on the TV and called Rich, warning him to be ready for tomorrow. "We're monitoring a lot of the same things you are," he told me.

"People are calling out specific members of the department," I said. "Captain Sharpe. The commissioner. They're in graphics with big targets on their backs."

"You think it's never happened before? Ngo is pretty new here, but he's been in leadership elsewhere. Sharpe has been around the BPD for twenty years. I doubt either of them would be concerned about it."

"Someone should be."

"Look . . . we're going to have all hands on deck tomorrow. Sharpe told me he talked to you. I think arresting your crew wouldn't make a difference at this point. We need to focus on the bigger picture. If they'll all be there tomorrow, we'll be able to pick them up then."

"They will be," I said, "but your network is down. Worse than before from what I understand."

"You're not wrong," Rich said. "We learned a few things. The techs are helping teams share more in the precinct without needing to hit a file server. We're way below our normal capacity, but I also heard this isn't going to be permanent."

"As far as I know, no one's discovered what I did. Whatever is down should revert in under a day, but I can't guarantee anything."

"I know. We'll survive. This has been a pretty trying week. I think we've come through it stronger."

"Great," I said. "I'll be sure to look for the new batch of motivational posters the next time I visit you."

"I appreciate your concern," Rich said. "You going to be there tomorrow?"

"It'll give too much away if I'm not. Don't worry. I'll be trying to blend in with my teammates, but I'll be playing for the right side. I don't know how much help I can be in the grand scheme of things, but I'll do what I can."

My cousin chuckled. "Isn't going undercover fun?"

"Not really the word I'd use."

"I hear you," he said. "Now, you see why I don't do it."

"You also look like a cop," I pointed out. "Even in disguise, I can just blend in as the handsome fellow who needs a haircut."

"I could take you to see my barber."

"No, thanks. I actually like my hair." We ended the call. I kept looking online and feeling more anxious about tomorrow. People would be coming for the express intent of agitation. They would sow chaos. Incite violence. Take shots at cops. Despite Rich assuring me the BPD would be ready, I harbored serious doubts. As Mike Tyson taught us all, "Everyone has a plan until they get punched in the mouth." What if the BPD's comms went offline? What if the situation proved far worse than expected?

I had one pistol and two clips, and it felt like far too little.

———

I spent a while texting most people I knew. The message changed a little depending on the audience, but the crux remained the same—a rally in the city tomorrow seemed certain to turn violent. Get out of town or at least have a plan to leave when the shit hit the fan. Responses were mixed, which I expected. Anyone outside the confines of the city didn't think they'd be affected. Those who lived within the limits of Baltimore were split on a feeling of dread and thinking the whole situation would be much ado about nothing.

If she remained at her own house—and she confirmed she would—Gloria would be far removed from whatever happened. I called my parents last. My father picked up. When I mentioned getting out of town, he scoffed. "Son, you said the same thing a couple months ago when Vinny was out of jail. We can't head to the hills every time something goes badly."

"This isn't the same, Dad. This is going to be a mob scene disguised as a rally. If the police can't keep a lid on things, the violence will spread. You're in one of the old money neighborhoods. They'll string people like you up first despite your liberal bona fides."

"Thanks for the visual," he said. "How do you know so much about this, anyway?"

"I'm . . . working with the police. They requested it thanks to my knowledge of how hacker groups operate. See, I told you what happened in Hong Kong would pay off."

"Your mother's not going to want to go. She thought it was a little silly we left town over Vinny."

"Of course," I said. I affected my mother's voice and added, "Vincent was always such a nice young man."

"He was also a more direct threat," my father said. "Roland Park isn't exactly next to City Hall. Even if this mob scene burns most of downtown, it would take them time to get out here. If we need to evacuate, we will, but we're not going to pack our bags and go somewhere based on unlikely risks."

I couldn't find fault with his assessment, so I said, "All right."

"Working directly with the cops . . . this is new, right?"

"It is. Probably a limited engagement, too. Once we wrap this up, I'll go back to reminding them I'm right more often than they are, and Rich can resume his occasional seething about it."

"Good luck, son."

"Thanks," I said. "Keep an eye on the news. If things get bad, just go."

"Where are you going to be?" my father wanted to know.

"I'm a man of the people, Dad."

"Be careful. Don't try to be a hero."

"I don't need to try," I said. "I come by it naturally." We said our goodbyes and broke the connection. I took some time away from the computer to eat dinner in my room. The supplies we got delivered made for an adequate if unexciting meal. When I checked for new posts about the rally, I remained discouraged. The weather would be on the cold side but good. No rain or snow. I wondered if there were more I could've done along the way to cripple APToo before things got to this point. Letting the cops or feds in sooner might have made a difference. I closed the laptop and banished thoughts of hindsight. They wouldn't do any good now. Besides, Sharpe or Commissioner Ngo didn't need my permission to storm a house. They could've done it regardless.

I left the TV on and called Gloria. She would be worried about me at the rally, but I wanted her to know what would be happening. "Do you need to go?" she asked.

"I'm pretty sure I'll get compelled at gunpoint if I try and refuse."

"Sounds like it'll be chaos. You won't be able to control anything."

"I know," I said. "The whole thing is going to be a mess. I'll do what I can for the good guys."

"Please be careful," Gloria said.

"I will."

"You're an older man, so you wouldn't know what it's like to be widowed before turning thirty."

I smiled. "I'll be sure and wait until the summer before getting killed on the job, then."

"You're so considerate. It's one of the reasons I married you."

"I promise you'll be able to dote on me after this is all over."

"I'm going to hold you to it."

"You young people are so idealistic," I said.

———

My phone's vibrations woke me up early the next morning. I didn't have a chance to run water or turn the TV on, so I answered and kept my voice low. "My boss is back at work," Charlie said

The fog hadn't lifted yet, so I mustered an, "All right?" in response.

"He left a couple weeks ago. Told me the mayor reached out to a bunch of folks, and they're going to help get things sorted out. I don't know what you did, but thanks."

"Sounds like I might have pissed on your chances for a promotion."

"The city comes first," Charlie said. "The rest will sort

itself out. What do you know about the emergency response networks being down?"

"Don't worry about them. They'll come back up. Focus on shoring up the defenses. Did your boss mention the IR firm?"

"Told us we need to check everything they did. Might take a while."

"Stay safe today," I said. "I think it's going to get ugly."

"You, too. You'll be closer to it than I will."

"Yeah." I blew out a deep breath. "Don't remind me." I ended the call, took a quick shower, and assembled a breakfast out of the delivered supplies. Bacon, eggs, and toast. When you're about to stare down an out-of-control rally, always stick with the classics. Maybe I could make my own motivational posters. After I finished eating, Factor Zero sent a message to the group. I felt a breakout room summons coming and wasn't disappointed. *Meet downstairs, 10 minutes. Final prep for the rally.*

I threw on a hoodie and jeans, made sure my disguise was in place, and took the stairs to the first floor. This time, Darrell arrived last, and I made a show of looking at my watch as he strolled in. He gave me a one-finger salute before dropping onto an open chair. Factor Zero typed the whole time. He didn't offer any indication he even knew we'd joined him. After a few minutes, Honeybee said, "We're ready when you are."

"I'm not," served as his brusque reply. We waited a few minutes. No one said a word. Shelly's knee bounced under the table. So did Turbowski's. Only Darrell showed no hints of anxiety. "All right." Our leader turned his screen around. I recognized T@kedown, a popular command and control suite, and my stomach clenched. "As you know, I've been getting the word out about today. Even recruited a few like-minded folks who happen to have plenty of computing power at their disposal. The city is down, basically. A massive DDOS." A distributed denial of service knocked resources offline by overwhelming them.

Darrell clapped his hands. "There's no way they can even coordinate a response."

Until Charlie and whoever joined him undid whatever the IR firm put in place, they couldn't even get started on digging out of this. Such attacks usually need to get cut off at the provider level. I hoped those discussions already happened. While Iceman was correct, a lot more areas would be affected besides emergency services. If the damage covered the city's entire networks, every function of the government would be hindered. Road crews. Public education. Traffic signals.

Hospitals.

"I've added this to the ransom," Factor Zero said, "and doubled the price."

"There's no way Davenport can pay it," I said.

"Right." He grinned, probably thinking I made my statement in happiness. "He couldn't do the lower amount. This is way beyond him. The citizens of Baltimore will see their mayor for the fraud he is. If he doesn't play ball once the rally is over, we'll keep the pressure up. The DDOS stays in place until I turn it off. If they try to mitigate it, we'll be prepared."

I tried to summon some form of enthusiasm to match Factor's and Darrell's. Honeybee and Turbo remained neutral. They weren't true believers. Maybe I could use them to help me. I needed to do something. "Go back upstairs," our leader said. "We'll be headed to the rally soon. All our work is about to pay off."

CHAPTER 25

BACK IN THE ROOM, I sent private messages to Shelly and Turbowski. *I don't think you're zealots like Factor and Iceman. Hacking is one thing, but inciting a mob is something else. This is way more than I signed up for. You, too, I suspect. Want to talk about it and see if we can do something?* After a couple minutes, both responded in the affirmative.

Shelly suggested meeting in her room as it sat farthest away from Factor and the guard. In case they were more devoted to the cause than I suspected, I tucked the 9MM into the back of my jeans. I opened my door as quietly as it would allow, confirmed the coast was clear, closed it as softly as I could, and made my way down the hall and around the corner. The interior looked exactly like mine. Shelly and Turbowski each sat on one of the beds. I took the desk chair. One of them possessed the good sense to turn the TV on. "Thanks for talking with me."

"I don't know what to do," Turbowski said. "I'm kind of in the same boat you are. This is what I do to try and keep powerful groups in check. Davenport seems like a bastard." He shook his head. "This rally . . . or whatever it turns into . . . is going to kill people. I'm just not sure how to stop it all at this point. I know I didn't join up to watch people die."

"Me, neither," Shelly added. "Marc's right. How do we keep a lid on things?"

"I'm not sure," I admitted. "You guys were here before me. Anything come to mind?"

"I wish," Turbowski said. "Why are you doing this, anyway? You're local. Don't tell me you want to see blood in the streets."

"I don't." I paused, wondering how to address the elephant in the room. "You two are committed to try and keep casualties down?" They both bobbed their heads. "All right. I'm going out on a limb and trusting you here." I took the blond wig off. Both Shelly and Turbowski frowned as if seeing me for the first time. "I'm a hacker, but you might say I'm at least a little bit reformed. I work as a private investigator these days. I'm consulting with the police. Once Clarence got arrested, we leaned on him for a recommendation, and here I am."

"The FBI raid?" Shelly asked.

"I didn't get any advance notice . . . and their shabby treatment of me was legit. I have a score to settle with a certain contractor when this is over."

"Why didn't you let the cops haul us all away before then?"

"I thought I could still gather some useful intel," I said. "A captain in the BPD agreed. I don't think anyone expected Factor's little rally to blow up like it did. His real name is Francis, by the way. He looks like a Frankie to me."

Shelly snorted. "His buddy the muscle is Ronny. Jesus. Frankie and Ronny. Like a couple kids who think they're tough in fifth grade."

At least I knew the guard's name now. "We don't have a

ton of time before we're going to have to join the march. I doubt we can do much about the DDOS."

"Whole city is basically flying blind," Turbowski said.

"I may have an answer there. Factor told us to use Java and the classes already in the repo. I made a duplicate of *Compromises*, but with the Cyrillic letter *es* standing in for the C. He wouldn't notice the difference in code."

"Brilliant," Shelly said.

"Thanks. Part of it involved trying to undo everything we were planning. I built a timer into everything. After twenty-four hours, things should return more or less to normal." The DDOS could complicate this, but I hoped someone resolved it by then. "We can't count on everything to come back properly, but at least the city won't be degraded. They got a lot of their workers back today, too. Turns out there's a connection between our boy Frankie, a guy who hates the mayor, and a couple of shell companies."

"We'll see what we can do," Turbowski said. "The past few days have taught us a lot about how the city's networks are built."

"Besides poorly, you mean," I said.

He smiled. "Yeah."

I stood. Getting back before anyone realized I'd been gone would be the best play. "I'm trusting you two not to out me."

"You're good," Shelly said. "Maybe you can even put in a good word for us if we get rounded up."

"I'll do what I can," I said. I left the room, walked down to the second floor, and then came up the staircase closest to my room. The subterfuge didn't matter as no one took note of me. I awarded myself another point for spycraft anyway.

———

Three messages arrived in short order. The first came from Factor Zero. *Downstairs, 15 minutes. We're headed to the rally. It's a day to celebrate chaos.* "It's a day for you to get led away in shackles, you prick," I muttered to my empty hotel room. It possessed the good sense not to respond.

Shelly sent the next just to Marc and me. *Tried to check the C2 suite and couldn't get in.* I didn't think she'd be able to access the command and control software, but I appreciated the effort. Turbo chimed in and said something very similar. I had a feeling I knew the way to turn off the attack if the city couldn't get it blocked by their Internet providers. He'd be at the rally, too.

With nothing else to do, I made sure I was ready for a mob scene—if one can truly prepare for such an event. I put my bags in the car in case the police raided our rooms later. Hopefully, they would. Once back upstairs, I tucked my pistol into the back of my jeans again. The sweatshirt would hide it. I put the spare clip in my left front pocket. Finally, I took off my wig and popped the colored contacts out. I would wear the hood up. If it came down, I didn't need someone grabbing a bunch of fake hair. A pair of cheap sunglasses from the gift shop would hide my eyes from anyone who might notice the color difference.

I waited outside at the appointed time. "Good to see you all ready to go," Factor Zero said once we'd all assembled. Ronny remained conspicuous by his absence. I wondered if our leader stashed him away somewhere. It would make sense. I guessed the flash drive he wore around his neck held a way to disable the DDOS attack slamming the city. If Ronny never showed up, he couldn't get arrested and let the cops confiscate his interesting jewelry. "We're going to walk there. It's not far. I expect we'll see more supporters the closer we get. I'm expecting a good turnout.

The police will be overwhelmed. The mayor will have no choice but to make major changes before he resigns in disgrace."

"Damn right," Darrell added. No one else said anything. "Let's go." He led the way, and the rest of us followed. We walked east on Redwood Street and picked up Calvert going north. Foot traffic seemed normal when we began. As we approached Fayette Street and Battle Monument Park, however, the crowd density ramped up. The concrete landmark honored those who died during the Battle of North Point in the War of 1812. I imagined they would've looked on the assembled throng with significant disdain.

Hundreds swarmed around the black iron fence which encircled the monument, and thousands more roamed the streets headed toward City Hall. The seat of the city's government sat a block away, and from where we stood, it looked surrounded by an angry mob. Whoever helped Factor Zero rile up the people and get the word out did a hell of a job. Police in riot gear manned the immediate area around City Hall. Others in uniform patrolled the streets. So far, nothing violent happened, but I figured it wouldn't be long until the chaos our leader wanted ensued.

Trying to find Ronny would be impossible in this crowd. He was taller than me, but so were fifteen percent of the assembled thousands. If he were here, I hoped his marching orders would earn the attention of law enforcement. The cops wouldn't know the significance of what dangled from his neck, but I could explain it to them once the smoke cleared. As I thought of smoke, a black cloud billowed out from a small building on the far side of City Hall. A fire truck arrived with flashing lights and sirens. Only a few people bothered to move out of the way.

Shelly put a hand on my back and leaned closer. Hearing

her over the din of the crowd still proved challenging. "What the hell are we going to do?"

"Try not to get caught up in the hysteria," I told her. "Cops are out in force, and they're going to be on edge after the last week. If I were you, I'd turn around and go back to the hotel."

"What are you going to do?"

"Whatever I can. I only hope it's enough."

"I saw Ronny earlier," she said. "Factor sent him ahead. He's wearing a white baseball cap. Might make him easier to spot."

I saw no one fitting the description in the immediate area. "Thanks. I'll keep an eye out for him." Shelly offered a small smile before turning away.

The fire engine stopped as close as it could get to the blaze. The crew unrolled the hose. It reached the flames. Uniformed officers moved to ring the firefighters as the mob closed in on them. It was only a matter of time before this powder keg burst.

A scrum near our location provided another spark. A dozen men clashed with five officers who struggled to keep the situation under control. A few more in full riot gear joined them and beat back the attackers. This provided little discouragement to the five additional troublemakers who rushed into the fray. More pockets of fighting erupted throughout the area. I put my back against a building to avoid getting swept up in the mob. I looked around for Shelly but didn't see her. Hopefully, she did the sensible thing and got the hell out of here. Part of me wished I could have followed her.

Another fire broke out closer to where I stood. I didn't see what started it, but it wasted no time spreading. Flames burst the windows of the Hoodfellas Bistro. A few cops rushed inside to help people evacuate. "Fuck the police!" someone shouted near me. It was Darrell. He moved closer to the building and took something out of his pocket. A grenade. He pulled the pin, threw it at the restaurant, and then ducked to blend in with the crowd. I took a few steps back and shouted for everyone nearby to leave.

It didn't do any good. I stood a good hundred feet away, and hearing me over everyone else was probably impossible. The explosion rocked the building, blasting the door from its hinges and blowing holes in the stone facade. A cloud of dust and smoke spread as loose rocks fell and people screamed and fled the area. A couple cops emerged from the wreckage, leading patrons and restaurant workers to safety. As the smoke cleared, a few nearer what remained of the front door lay on the sidewalk.

One of the uniforms struggled to raise himself to a crouch. He coughed as he made it back to unsteady feet. As if sensing the man's injuries, Darrell emerged from the mob. The blast cleared a lot of people from the area. He would have an open path to cause more damage and carnage. A few other miscreants joined Iceman in moving toward the fallen cop. This could end very badly. I followed. As I drew closer, I saw the officer's face.

It was Rich.

CHAPTER 26

MY COUSIN STUMBLED about like he'd gotten his bell rung. He probably did. Based on where he lay a moment ago, he was close enough to the grenade to get caught in the blast. Darrell and a few others quickened their pace. Two other uniforms stirred, but Rich was the only one who'd managed to stand. He looked around like his eyes had trouble focusing.

Everything happened in slow motion. Darrell led a small group in moving toward the woozy Rich. My chest clenched as a nightmare scenario played out in my head—Darrell would wrestle Rich's gun away, execute him with it, and then turn it on the other fallen officers. No one seemed interested in stopping it. I sprinted toward Rich. Someone moved to block my path and ate an elbow to the face for his efforts. My dash allowed me to overtake Iceman and his fellow jackals. I reached the sidewalk before they did, drew my pistol, and turned to face them.

Darrell stopped, and the other guys rushing with him all did the same. They eyed me and my 9MM. "Traitor," Darrell said. I pulled my hood back, letting him see me without the disguise. "I knew you were a phony."

"Good for you. Now, back off. I'm not letting you kill wounded officers."

Another man stepped forward. He was middle-aged and overweight, and his ruddy face formed a scowl as he stared at me. "We don't like the cops. Don't like you for sticking your nose in."

"If you assholes liked me, I'd need to re-evaluate my life," I said.

"Get out of the way. You're one guy." Rich leaned against the damaged wall in my peripheral vision. "You can't drop us all."

I turned the gun on him and held it in a two-handed grip about a foot from his head. His eyes widened. "Maybe not, but I can guarantee *you* a closed-casket funeral."

"He's bluffing," Darrell yelled. "This man is a coward." He reached behind himself.

"Don't do it," I said, covering him with the nine. He ignored me. His right hand emerged holding something. I fired once, hitting him in the upper right torso near his shoulder. Darrell spun and fell to the asphalt. A few of the men who came with him—including the one who hollered at me—dispersed. Four others remained. "I have plenty of bullets left."

"So do I," Rich said. He stood behind me and held his own pistol toward the group. "Get out of here. Go home." They grumbled but lost interest and moved away from City Hall. More officers rushed toward us. Rich encouraged them to check on their injured brethren and Darrell. I stood over my fallen former teammate. He lay on the street, his left hand covering the bloody wound to his upper body. His right hand still held a knife.

"He's with us," Rich said to a couple cops who didn't

know me. "Tend to the wounded . . . including the idiot with
the blade."

"You all right?" I asked as Rich leaned on the damaged
edifice again.

"I'll make it."

"You might have a concussion."

He shook his head. "I don't think so. I've had one before."
He took in the mob scene. Our mini-fracas did little to
change things. "This is ridiculous."

"It is." I spotted Factor Zero across the street. He
narrowed his eyes when he saw me talking to the police.
"There." I pointed toward him, and blue uniforms closed in
on his position. "He's the leader. Make sure you get him. Feel
free to bounce him off a few buildings first." Factor Zero had
the audacity to look betrayed as three officers surrounded
him. Because he was a wimp, he didn't even put up a fight.
One slapped the cuffs on him, and two led him away.

"The chaos continues!" he shouted as they hurried him
along.

Unfortunately, he turned out to be correct. I'd managed
to save my cousin and a couple other cops, but the force was
still overwhelmed. They'd been burning the candle at both
ends since the lights and traffic signals first went out. If I
didn't hate Factor Zero, Willett, and everyone else involved, I
might've given them props for a well-executed plan. Rich
tried to use his radio. At least they still worked. The noise and
density of people in a small area must have made coordi-
nating a response impossible.

Engine noise grew in intensity. A state police helicopter
flew overhead. Suddenly, the prospects of keeping a lid on
things looked better. A few gunshots rang out from the other
side of City Hall. Rich headed toward them. I moved in the

same direction looking for any of my former crew in the crowd. Especially Ronny. I didn't see anyone. Another helicopter passed above us. Hummers rolled onto the scene, and National Guard troops hopped down. The reinforcements arrived.

As soon as they did, a few hundred people decided they needed to be anywhere else. Thousands more remained, but they would lose their nerve soon enough. A few would try to provoke anyone in Baltimore blue or military camouflage to try to get on TV and milk the situation for a lawsuit. With extra manpower, the BPD focused on arresting the worst offenders. A bunch of people got cuffed and led away. For the first time in a few days, I managed to feel optimistic about how this would end.

———

"We need to find a guy named Ronny," I said to Rich. His partner in Homicide, Sergeant Paul King, joined us, along with a few officers I'd never met. "He's the muscle in the crew."

"Why is he important?" King wanted to know.

"I think the leader gave him something we'll need. He's a big guy . . . taller and broader than me. Dark hair. I don't know how he's dressed, but I heard he's wearing a white cap." With the crowd thinning out, our chances of spotting someone in distinctive headwear must have improved. A quick scan of the throng showed me how wrong I was. Even with a portion of the assembled masses coming to their senses, the good guys were severely outnumbered.

A gunshot rang out near City Hall. Another followed. People ran in all directions to get away from the shooting. Several Maryland National Guard troops converged on a spot near the front of the building. The law enforcement presence would be greater there, but so would the chance for chaos. Causing damage. I ran toward the fracas, and several members of the BPD accompanied me.

My eyes focused on everyone's heads. It was possible Ronny took the white hat off or lost it in madness of recent events. It remained his most distinctive characteristic, so I would use it until I struck out. We reached Guilford Avenue, which ran along the western side of City Hall. A few guardsmen held a man to the ground. One of them stood with a boot on a pistol. Despite Guilford running one way southbound, most people leaving the scene headed north at varying rates of speed.

A tall figure in a white hat veered off from the crowd and turned down Lexington. "This way," I shouted, hoping the BPD officers could hear me. I took off at a sprint. Thanks to the number of people still on the street and sidewalks, I needed to vary my pace and weave left and right often. Still, I made it to Lexington much faster than I would've if I'd simply walked. The white-capped man moved toward Holliday.

Fewer folks gathered and milled about here, so my sprinting paid better dividends. Ronny didn't seem to be in a hurry. He turned his head to look at something to the left, and the profile view confirmed I pursued the right man. He paused and completed the pivot just in time for me to tackle him to the asphalt. Ronny shoved me off, rolled away, and got back to his feet. He drew a knife from his belt. I still carried my pistol, but the close quarters didn't give me a chance to draw it. I needed to play defense.

The BPD contingent lingered behind, breaking up fights and trying to encourage people to leave the area. Ronny swept the blade back and forth in front of himself. A slender chain hung from his neck, though most of it disappeared under his sweater. He reversed his grip and slashed out at me. I spun to my right and hit him in the jaw with a short jab. He scowled. My punch served to annoy him more than anything.

The blade came toward me again. I've never liked fighting people with knives. It only took one lucky swing to end things—perhaps forever. After I dodged his latest strike, Ronny tried to keep me at bay with short thrusts of his weapon. If I moved left, he stabbed in the same direction. It was an effective tactic, but it carried some limitations, and I could exploit them. I feinted right, and he fell for it. When he lunged toward where he expected me to be, I grabbed his hand with my right arm and hammered my left fist onto his wrist. He howled and dropped the knife. I swept it toward the gutter with my foot.

"You're overmatched now," I said. "Give it up."

"I knew you were a traitor."

I snorted. "Please. Don't try to give your cause some nobility. You're a band of jackals, and you've gotten what's coming to you."

Rather than engage in some repartee, Ronny launched a haymaker. I dodged it and hit him with a quick left. While he wagged his head, I followed up with a right cross. He stumbled back a step. I kicked him in the stomach. When he bent forward, I walloped him with a right. To his credit, he remained on his feet even if his legs wobbled. I grabbed a handful of hair at his nape and slammed his face into a metal newspaper box. He rebounded off it, his head hit the asphalt, and he lay still.

I drew my pistol and stood over Ronny. He remained conscious, but his eyes couldn't focus on me. His hat came off in the fall to the street. I waved over a couple uniformed officers and showed them my ID when they eyed me and my gun. "He's one of the hackers," I said. While two cops checked Ronny for injuries, I spoke to the third, a solidly-built woman. "The chain around his neck is connected to a flash drive. It might be important. I think Captain Sharpe will need it."

"You know Captain Sharpe?"

"Sure. We smoke cigars together at the Havana Club every Friday."

She scoffed. "No, you don't."

"You're right," I admitted. "But I do know him, and I've been working with him since this whole mess began." I grimaced and added, "He'd probably say I've been working *for* him."

"All right." Officer Donaldson gave me a curt nod of her head. "We'll take it from here."

I harbored no doubts they would. With the fracas dying down, I checked my phone. Gloria sent a series of concerned messages. I dashed off a quick reply. *I'm fine. Still have some work to do to wrap this up. See you at your house as soon as I can. Love you, too.*

As people started to leave the rally—or whatever the hell this mess turned into—I felt hopeful for the first time in days. Best of all, I'd get to see my wife soon, and we wouldn't need to pull off a cloak-and-dagger routine to make it happen.

CHAPTER 27

IT TOOK another hour or so, but the crowd kept losing interest in whatever they were supposed to be protesting and dispersed. Only a few stragglers remained, but no one offered them the attention they sought. This didn't seem to deter them. If anything, the police presence compelled them to shout louder. Once things were mostly back to normal, I found Rich near City Hall. "Going to suck up to the mayor again?"

"No better time than after a protest turns violent," he said.

"Maybe you'll even get another commendation on the back of my hard work," I said.

Rich rolled his eyes. "We can't all have a lacrosse trophy case."

Leon Sharpe approached. In his body armor and helmet, he managed to look even more enormous and menacing. If I were raising a ruckus, and he strode up to arrest me, I'd plop down in the street right away. "You two are coming with me to Central Booking. We have a few people to question. Wait here for a few minutes."

"You got it, Captain," Rich said. When Sharpe walked

away, my cousin locked at me again. "Thanks for your help with this. I know it wasn't always easy."

"Definitely not," I said. "Worth it in the end. Overall, I think the city's going to come through this pretty well."

"Let's hope so." A couple minutes later, Sharpe's black SUV stopped at the curb. Rich and I climbed into the rear for the short drive to Central Booking. I still didn't care for unrelenting gray in the interior, but I walked back with my cousin and the captain. We stopped in a hallway outside a collection of interview rooms. Through the small panes of frosted glass in the doors, I saw several of my former teammates sitting alone at tables.

"We're starting with the leader," Sharpe said. "No point in offering a deal to someone else first."

"He hasn't lawyered up?" I asked.

"Tried." Sharpe shrugged. "Ever since we started working with the cops in PA, his attorney has been incommunicado."

"What a shame."

"I'm not sure how much we'll get out of him, but he hasn't asked for any other counsel. Let's see what he says." The captain led the way. As usual, two chairs sat on the other side of the table. Rich and Sharpe remained standing, so I did, too. Factor Zero looked at everyone. His eyes settled on me and narrowed.

"I should've gone with my gut. You're a traitor."

"Spare us all the wounded bird bullshit," I said. "I didn't give up state secrets. You and your band of assholes don't deserve loyalty . . . Francis." He scowled. "Yeah, I know about your cushy, phony consulting gig with Willett."

"Aren't you smart?" he said with a sneer.

"To put it mildly, yes."

"Let's get down to business," Sharpe said. He stood

across from Francis and dropped onto a chair. He didn't sit on it as much as dominate it, and with the only light in the room behind him, Sharpe actually cast a shadow on the prisoner. I knew him well enough to understand he used this to his advantage. "You and your friends caused a lot of damage to this city."

"Good," Francis said. "You deserve it all. Would've been a lot worse if you didn't have a plant on the inside." He glared at me. "You a fucking cop?"

I snorted. "Please. I have way too much self-respect." Rich and Sharpe both cleared their throats. "Private investigator who's also done a lot of the work you have."

"So you really are Foxtrot."

"I guess I've burned the handle now, but yes."

"You shot Iceman."

"He'll live," I said. "If he wanted to avoid a bullet, he shouldn't have been so bloodthirsty."

"Right." Francis jeered again. "Just do as you're told, citizen, and nothing will happen. Spoken just like someone in power."

Sharpe slapped the metal tabletop. It sounded like a bomb going off, and Francis flinched. "Enough. We want to clean up the last of what you did."

"I'm sure you do," he said.

"Turn off this attack, and maybe we'll go easy on you."

"Go to hell."

"Willett's not helping you," Sharpe said. "Once we learned he was involved, we've been working with a few police departments in Pennsylvania. They'll find him. Or the feds will since we've crossed borders." Francis grimaced at the mention of the FBI. "Make it a little easier on yourself. Maybe you won't die in prison."

"For hacking your shitty systems?"

"We're doing a deep dive on all the effects of your little tricks. Traffic signals down. Street lights out. Nine-one-one diminished. All we need to do is prove those hampered the city's ability to save one person. It's not murder one. I'm no lawyer, but I think you're looking at manslaughter in addition to whatever else you get charged with." He paused. "How old are you, Francis?"

"Twenty-six."

"All right. If you want to spend the second half of your fifties breathing fresh air, I think it's in your best interest to help us."

Francis spread his hands as best he could with one cuffed to the table. "I'll take my chances."

"The state's attorney is going to throw the book at you," Rich added.

"I'll take my chances," Francis said again. "Not helping you pigs."

"Your benefactor isn't bailing you out, Frankie," I said. He rolled his eyes at the nickname. "He's in the wind. He's thinking about himself. You should do the same."

"Some of us can be loyal to a cause."

"Get over yourself."

"I'm done," Francis said. "I want a public defender. You pricks aren't getting one more syllable out of me."

Sharpe stood. He blotted the light even more. "Have it your way. You won't fare very well in prison. My guess is guys'll be passing you around within a month."

Francis held true to his word and didn't say anything else, though Sharpe's barb made him grimace. We left the room. "We don't need him to cooperate," I said. "Leon, did anyone tell you about what the guard wore around his neck?"

He bobbed his large head. "I heard about it. A flash drive?"

"Do you have it?"

"I know where it is. Why?"

I opened the door to Francis' room again. "By the way, you and Ronny have shitty taste in necklaces."

Color drained from his face. It took him a few minutes, but he sputtered, "Lawyer. I told you I want a damn lawyer."

"Eleven syllables." He frowned. "You said not one more. I counted eleven." While Francis stewed, I closed the door again. "We need the flash drive."

"Let's get it," Sharpe said.

———

Commissioner Ngo joined us as Sharpe retrieved the flash drive on a chain. It was a small silver model. From a distance, it might have looked like a brooch. Up close, the connecter gave it away. "You think this is what we need?" Sharpe said.

I nodded. "Francis entrusted it to Ronny. Both of them getting popped probably wasn't the plan. Besides, this would just get put in a bag as part of someone's possessions."

"It's an envelope in most cases," Ngo said.

"Thanks for putting one burning question to rest," I said.

The commissioner didn't take the bait. "Should we talk to this guy and make sure?"

"I'm on the clock with hazard pay for today, so it's your money."

He grunted, and we walked back down the series of hallways to Ronny's interrogation room. Ngo stepped up to the table. Sharpe remained closer to the door with me. It was odd to see him not take charge of a situation. I'd never experienced him being outranked in an investigation before. He crossed his arms and let out a long, slow breath. Maybe he hadn't experienced it often, either. "This mean anything to you?" Ngo held the drive and chain toward Ronny.

"Sure. It was my grandma's favorite. She got it in nineteen-sixty."

"Call the press, Leon," I said. "This prick's grandmother was a time traveler." Ronny shot me a confused look. "USB wouldn't come around for another thirty-six years."

"My grandma was a smart lady."

"Too bad you didn't inherit any of it."

"Is there something on here which will turn off your attacks?" Ngo asked.

"Dunno, man. I'm just the muscle. I ain't so smart."

"We don't need him," I said. "Let's go directly to the source."

We left the room, and Sharpe walked ahead to make a call. By the time we reached the front of the building, he put his phone away. "Our forensic team is still processing the hotel. They haven't collected the equipment yet."

"Good," I said. "Tell them to leave it alone. Reconnect anything they might've unplugged. We'll probably need it."

"It should all be intact."

"Let's go, then," Ngo said. "We'll take my car." The three of us climbed into his waiting Yukon. Despite the roomy backseat, I felt a little cramped sharing it with Captain Sharpe. The driver took us on a longer route, but we bypassed the remnants of the morning's events, so it probably saved us a few minutes. We hopped out at the hotel and rode the elevator to the third floor.

"His room was next to mine," I said. As we approached, I pointed to the appropriate door. The forensic team must have moved on since Sharpe talked to one of them on the phone. Francis' room was a mess, and I didn't know if he was a pig or if the BPD workers pulled everything apart. A gaming rig sat under the desk connected to two monitors. I settled into the chair and snorted at the green backlit keyboard. A jiggle of the mouse brought me to the Kali Linux login screen. My own credentials would get me in but probably not let me see anything Francis did.

I tried the last password I knew for the root user account. It failed.

I looked under the keyboard. Nothing. Same on the computer itself. "I thought you were supposed to be some expert," Ngo said.

"His password isn't going to be one-two-three-four-five," I said. "I hope yours isn't, either." I lifted the mouse pad. No dice. Francis turned the desk so it faced the window rather than the bed. I remembered the various setups we went through squatting in abandoned home offices. He never offered the team a clear line of sight to the front or backs of his monitors unless showing us something. I stood and looked at the displays. A slim pink sticky note hung on the underside of the left one. I held it up. "Sometimes, expertise comes in being smart enough to know where to look."

"I don't like you very much," the commissioner said.

"Once you've signed my check, you can go back to not caring about who I am." I entered the user ID and password on the paper. The Kali desktop greeted me.

"I do care. No law enforcement background." I didn't say anything. There were bigger fish to fry than Ngo airing some list of grievances against private investigators. "You weren't in the military. I'm not sure how you even got your license."

"Won it in a claw machine at the state fair," I said. I connected the small flash drive to a USB port on the front panel of Francis' desktop. The operating system recognized the device and mounted it automatically.

"You had to put in work somewhere," he said.

"Hong Kong." Ngo frowned. "I helped Americans and political dissidents avoid getting mistreated by the Chinese government.' Sparing myself the same fate would have been nice, but Ngo didn't need to know everything. I only wanted him to shut up. "I can have my secretary type up a CV and send it to you later. For now, I'd like to work on getting all this shit turned back on. Unless you'd rather continue to rehash my background . . . ?"

"It's fine." Ngo waved a hand. "I just like to know who I'm working with. If the state signed off, then I'm sure you're good. Captain Sharpe seems to trust you."

"I do," he confirmed, "and I've vouched for C.T. on more than one occasion."

"Great," I said. "Let's all do a mojito brunch one Sunday. *After* I've finished here." I poked around the contents of Francis' flash drive. No wonder he wanted to entrust it to someone else. It held all the information for the command and control suite, plus decryption keys, plans, next steps, and even a dossier on Vincent Davenport. I considered sending it to myself in case I needed it later. Hopefully, rescuing the city here would give me a pass from the mayor.

I brought up T@kedown and authenticated with Francis' account—something else he put on the small drive. His distributed denial of service attack was brilliant. Besides the usual botnet of infected computers, Francis farmed the work out to providers offering the service over the cloud. If the city —or its Internet providers—managed to block a source, others would be ready to take over. The traffic showed me this happened twice already. I turned off everything. "The major attack should be stopped," I said. "I want to see what else this prick got his hands into."

Enciphering data formed the bulk of Francis' other activities. These were projects he never mentioned to the team.

Maybe he took his orders directly from Dale Willett. "Looks like a lot of city data is useless." I entered the decryption keys into the ransomware suite, put in a made-up Bitcoin value when it asked, and pressed Enter. Within seconds, Baltimore's information returned to its prior state. "Should be cleared up now. I think the IR firm was in on it, too, at least in the form of not doing much. The mayor knows." I checked for other systems held hostage and found the street lights off again. Turning them back on was a simple fix.

"We're looking into them," Sharpe said. "Us, the state police, and our counterparts in Pennsylvania."

"I hope to see some action there later today," Ngo added. "My understanding is things are moving quickly. Willett never expected anything to blow back on him, but he didn't do the best job keeping himself out of the whole process."

"Good," I said. "In the meantime, I think everything is back up and running like it should be."

"Thanks, C.T.," Sharpe said. "I know this was my idea, and it wasn't always easy for you, but you came through."

"All things being equal, I'd prefer not to go undercover again anytime soon. For you or anyone else."

"Fair enough."

After another double-check of the city's data and systems, I dismounted the flash drive, unplugged it, and handed it to Sharpe. "You need a lift anywhere?" Ngo asked.

"I was staying here earlier, so I'm good. I'll just get my car."

I shook hands with both cops. They left. I checked my room next door. The forensics folks already processed it. I didn't leave anything behind—or if I did, they already bagged it. I took the elevator down to the garage and climbed into the Caprice. Finally, this mess was over. I put my head on the steering wheel and blew out a few deep breaths.

CHAPTER 28

I DECOMPRESSED in the car for a few minutes. With Christmas on the near horizon, this seemed like an excellent time to take a vacation. Once the check from the city cleared, I could afford some time off. I drove back to the office. T.J. stood and hugged me as I walked in. "I'm glad you're all right," she whispered.

"I'm relieved you're not secretly plotting my demise," I said.

She grinned. "Given the season, I'll wait until the new year."

"I hope Santa brings you something nice."

T.J. sat in her chair again. "Is the case over?"

"Our involvement is. I've done as much as I can. At this point, at least three law enforcement agencies are looking for people in Pennsylvania. It's only a matter of time."

"Let's flip on the local news." Before I could answer, T.J. picked up the remote and turned on the TV. "I was watching coverage of everything earlier."

"It takes a big story to get the soaps off the air," I said.

My secretary chuckled. "My grandparents used to watch

them. I'm ashamed to admit I probably still know a few characters on *All My Children*."

"You can hop down from a third-story window, and you know fictional people on a daytime show. Is there no end to your superpowers?"

She flipped her long blonde hair. "We heroines don't discuss our weaknesses."

"Probably for the best." A commercial ended, and the anchors began talking about the aftermath of today's events. Commentators went back and forth between calling them protests and riots. I knew who planned everything and why. Even with a veneer of legitimate grievances, what transpired fell into the latter category. Grenades, fires, people storming injured cops only to be shot by handsome private investigators—these things didn't happen at protests.

"We have breaking news about an ongoing investigation," the female anchor said. "Maryland and Pennsylvania State Police have found and arrested Dale Willett for his role in the ransomware attack on the city and the unrest of earlier today. Willett is being held outside Pittsburgh and will be on his way to Maryland for arraignment later."

"The Baltimore Police Department also contributed to the investigation," the male anchor said. "City IT workers are cleaning up the last of the damage. At this time, no one has offered an official comment on how or why the attacks stopped."

T.J. threw her hands in the air. "They're not giving you the credit?"

"I'm sure the police aren't eager to talk about it," I said. "They don't want to give any props to someone in the private sector, much less toss us our kudos. The mayor might snub me, too. We'll see. I know a few reporters if I need to talk up our involvement."

"Our, huh?"

"You helped a lot. Besides, your ninja skills should get at least a passing mention."

A few minutes later, the anchors took turns informing us Vincent Davenport would be making a brief speech about the events of the last few days. I didn't want to see it, but I knew T.J. yearned for us to get a plug, so I waited it out. The mayor appeared on screen standing in front of City Hall. "My fellow Baltimoreans," he said, "a few hours ago, the streets around this great building were the site of a significant amount of unrest. Our police and the Maryland National Guard made dozens of arrests. I'd like to say things ended as peacefully as they could. No significant injuries were report-ed." I know this was crap. Darrell took a bullet to the chest near his shoulder, and mine had not been the only shot I heard. It was impossible to get shot above the waist and have the wound be insignificant.

"Thanks to the incredible work of law enforcement," Davenport continued, "we now know the man behind it all was Dale Willett. If you came to an event at D and S before all this started, you know he used to work for my company, and I gave him a lot of credit for process improvements still in use today. I haven't talked to Dale in a long time, so I don't know his exact motivations here. I suspect we'll get a chance to chat soon. Pennsylvania state police arrested him a short while ago, and he'll be arraigned in Maryland tomorrow morning."

"I've seen enough," I said.

"You leaving?" T.J. asked.

"Yeah. It'll be nice to see my wife again. Remind me not to take any more undercover jobs so soon after getting married."

"How soon are we talking?"

"I don't know." I walked toward the door. "Ten years? After Frederick a few months ago and all this, I'm pretty burned out on it. Gloria has a nice fireplace. I might set my disguise ablaze."

"Sounds like the best thing to happen to it," T.J. said. "It makes you look like a failed rocker."

"I'm going to write a song." I played air guitar for a few seconds near the door. "It's called 'Take the Rest of the Day Off.' I don't have any lyrics or a riff yet, but I think it'll be a hit."

My secretary smiled. "Music to my ears."

———

Before I pulled out of the lot, I realized I couldn't drive the Caprice to Gloria's ritzy part of the county. Her neighbors would think I'd gotten lost, or perhaps I wanted to sell them some vacuum cleaners. I swung by my house, swapped to the S4, and headed north. With so much police activity concentrated downtown, I sped with reckless abandon and made it to Brooklandville in excellent time. Gloria rushed forward to hug me the instant her front door clicked shut behind me. "I was so worried about you," she said into my shoulder.

"I'm all right. No uglier than before."

She grinned. "Your face is looking better." The mirth vanished from her expression quickly, however. "It looked like chaos down there. I watched the news."

"There was your first mistake," I said.

"I'm serious!" She batted at my arm. "I know you can take care of yourself and feel you need to do your part, but thousands of people were there. The good guys were really outnumbered. We're probably fortunate things didn't get more violent."

I nodded. "We are. I think the National Guard rolling in when they did helped. The police probably would've been overwhelmed otherwise."

"Sounds like everything is back to normal."

"More or less. I take it you watched your friend's speech?"

"I did. You?"

"Unfortunately," I said. "I never much liked Davenport before, but I never would've called him a weasel. Now, I would. Something about politics changes people. One of the reasons I don't vote."

We sat on Gloria's plush living room couch. "What's going to happen to the hackers you were working with?"

I shrugged. "The leader's fancy lawyer is part of the scheme, so I don't know. None of them got a deal. We recovered a flash drive and used it to restore access to every affected service. The state's attorney is free to throw the book at them. I hope she picks a heavy one."

"Good." Gloria snuggled into me. "Sounds like it's all wrapped up."

"Not quite."

"What do you mean?"

"Brubaker," I said. "The FBI contractor who went way beyond the pale with me. He and I still have a score to settle."

"Let him go," Gloria said. "The Bureau will handle him. You ended up all right."

"I did . . . mainly because the police walked through the door before things really got crazy. The next person he handcuffs to the pipes probably won't be so lucky."

Gloria lifted her head and looked into my eyes. "You're really going to deal with him, aren't you?"

"Of course."

"This is where you tell me some macho bullshit about a man having a code, right?" she said.

"Exactly. And mine doesn't allow people to get away with what he did."

"I can't talk you out of it?"

I put my hand on her knee and slowly moved it up her leg. "You could distract me for a while. Fill my heart. Sate my spirit."

Gloria grabbed my hand, stood, and pulled me to my feet with surprising ease—even though I wasn't exactly unwilling. Her tennis workouts continued to pay dividends. "I'll take it."

———

Later, we ate dinner delivered by a new Italian place in the area. Aromas of pasta, tomato sauce, and basil filled Gloria's spacious kitchen. I arranged the containers on the table while she set out plates, utensils, and proper cloth napkins. Brooklandville would tolerate no paper ones, and I imagined the neighborhood watch peeking in people's trash cans for violations. I poured us each a glass of white wine, and as we tore into the garlic bread, Gloria flipped the TV on.

My least favorite local politician moved behind a podium again. "Thank you, and good evening, my fellow Baltimoreans." Davenport adjusted his hair in the breeze. "I didn't expect to make a second speech today. Maybe I should take the rest of the year off from talking." He smiled at his own joke. I found it a fine idea, but I also got the feeling I wasn't his target audience. "I'd like to make a few updates to what I said earlier."

"You watched his earlier speech, right?" Gloria said.

"As much as I could stomach, yes."

"We can now confirm all our systems are up and operational," the mayor continued. "I know it's been a trying week. From traffic signals to street lights to the emergency services network . . . a lot has gone wrong recently. The ransomware which hit us is now eradicated thanks to our dedicated police officers, IT staffers, and a local consultant."

Gloria patted my arm. "He just gave you a shout-out."

I pushed a few ravioli onto my plate and added some gnocchi with a serving spoon. "I thought he looked like he was in pain for a second there."

My wife grinned. I put a similar amount of food onto her plate knowing she probably wouldn't eat it all, and if she managed it, I'd be finished with dessert and coffee by then. "I'd also like to thank the governor and the Maryland National Guard for lending a hand," Davenport said. "We'd been in discussions for a couple days, and our preparation paid off. The National Guard was able to mobilize quickly and help restore order around City Hall.

"Some of you may be wondering about Dale Willett, the man behind all this. I never imagined he hated me like he did when he left the company years ago. I always liked him and thought we enjoyed a good working relationship. D and S wouldn't be the company it became without his contributions, and it's possible he thought I should've done more to celebrate him—or pay him—back then.

"Grudges don't help anyone, and sometimes, they can be very destructive. Dale Willett carried a grudge against me for almost two decades. It led him to amass enough wealth to pull off an orchestrated cyber attack on our city. I think of all the good he could have done in the world with his many millions of dollars, and I feel sad for the people who would have benefitted."

"He's not going to take any responsibility," I said.

"He sort of did," Gloria said.

"Not really. He framed it as Dale wanting more glory or money rather than his own failing."

"They're both to blame."

"I agree, but this isn't the story the mayor is telling."

Davenport talked over our dinner table conversation. " . . . Willett is now in the custody of the Maryland State Police. He'll go before a judge in the morning. I'm sure the attorney general is going to have a long night figuring out what to charge Dale with. Honestly, I hope it's a long list. We weathered the attack pretty well, but there were many points where things could've gone a lot worse. To anyone who experienced hardship or—worst of all—lost a loved one because of our degraded ability to respond, I can only offer my sincerest condolences."

"But not apologies," I said around a bite of ravioli. Like most Italian carry-out, it needed more sauce, but the flavors were excellent.

Gloria turned the TV off. "You're grumpy when he's on," she said.

"You should see me in the same room with him."

"I have." She fought a grin and lost.

"We need to hope there are no other rich former partners or rivals in his past," I said. "Whatever good he does for the city can be washed out."

My wife held up her glass of wine. "No more Vincent Davenport conversations until after Christmas."

I clinked mine to hers. "I guess Santa got my letter after all."

CHAPTER 29

"PLEASE HOLD FOR CAPTAIN SHARPE," his secretary told me after I answered the phone in the morning. I looked at the time in the upper right—7:45 AM.

"I know it's early for you," Sharpe said a few seconds later.

"Yeah." I yawned. "I guess the commissioner didn't want to call me?"

"He delegated it to me. Sends his regrets and all."

"I'm sure he does."

"He's not so bad. Probably the best we've had in a decade or more."

"I think you're damning with faint praise there, Leon."

"Probably," he said. "I want to come by your office later."

"But you decided to call at this beastly hour?" I asked.

"Wanted to make sure you'd be going in today. I wouldn't blame you if you took the day off and let your wife dote on you."

"When everything's done, I think I will."

"What do you mean?" he said. "It's wrapped up. I'm bringing you a check this morning."

"Brubaker and I have unfinished business."

Sharpe snorted. "I know the guy's a prick, but you don't need to prove anything. Let Hess take care of him."

"Unless Hess is going to give him a solid flogging, I want to let him know exactly what I think of bullies."

"Whatever. It's your time. When can I come by?"

"How about ten?"

"See you then," he said and ended the call. Thinking about kicking Brubaker's ass left me feeling amped up. I couldn't go back to sleep. Instead, I put on some running attire and hit the not-very-mean streets of Brooklandville. The sights were quite different out here than in Federal Hill. Women walked tiny dogs they could have carried in their purses and held large coffees in the other hand. Landscapers put the finishing touches on seasonal hedge carvings. Tasteful outdoor holiday lights twinkled. Inflatable Santas and Nativity scenes visible in many Baltimore neighborhoods were probably subject to popping and a stiff fine up here.

About thirty minutes later, I walked back into Gloria's house. She remained sleeping, so I showered and dressed before venturing downstairs again. Despite a kitchen I would have considered shooting Darrell in the face to use every day, Gloria didn't keep it stocked. Our leftovers from last night took up the most room in her fridge. Still, I found eggs a few days away from expiring, a slab of bacon from a local butcher, and some fresh bread.

Fifteen minutes later, coffee brewing and pork sizzling called Gloria down. She planted a minty kiss on me, waited for the caffeine to finish, and poured us each a mug. It didn't take long for everything else to be ready, and I carried two plates to the table. "Did your phone ring this morning?" my wife asked after she took a child-sized bite of scrambled eggs.

"Yeah. Sharpe is going to drop off a check at the office. It'd better be full of hazard pay."

"I'll update my wish list, then." She winked.

"I'm going to give T.J. a bonus," I said. "It's a good time of year for it, and she deserves one. She helped me a lot behind the scenes on this case."

"I'm sure she'll be thrilled," Gloria said. "I remember when you weren't so sure about her."

"Other than calling dibs on my car in the event of my grisly demise, she's been great."

I finished eating while about half of Gloria's food remained on her plate. This turned out to be pretty typical for us. She got a lot more conscious about the volume and pace of her eating a couple years ago when she still competed in local tennis tournaments. Even though working the fundraiser circuit—and the prospect of turning thirty in the coming summer—turned her into more of a casual player, she retained her eating habits. Even if I tried to slow down, I still finished way ahead of her.

A few minutes later, I kissed Gloria goodbye and drove down I-83 into Baltimore. T.J.'s Mustang waited in the lot, and the smell of fresh coffee greeted me before my secretary could. On the whole, I was fine with this arrangement. I fixed myself a cup and sat at my desk ten minutes before the witching hour. "Sharpe is coming with a check," I said, and T.J. perked up. "Make sure it has plenty of zeroes after the first digit."

"It'd better," she said. "Overtime and hazard pay."

"And whatever the experiment which gave you super-powers cost."

She grinned. "I'll be sure they pay up."

A minute before ten, two sets of footfalls climbed the metal steps. The louder one must have been Sharpe. He walked in, a slender male uniform in tow. "Needed someone else to carry the sack of money, Leon?"

The captain snorted. "We're prepared to write a check covering all your time and expenses including a little extra for when you found yourself in significant danger on the case. The city thanks you for your hard work and dedication in putting this matter behind us."

"Impressive," I said. "You didn't need to look at an index card once. Who wrote the little speech?"

"The commissioner wanted me to let you know," he said. "I figured someone put it together for him." The young uniform's amused look told me he agreed with the assessment.

"T.J. will double-check your math." Sharpe and the other cop sat at my secretary's desk. I tried not to overhear as I perused email for the first time in a few days.

"Pleasure doing business with you," the captain said. He stood and shook T.J.'s hand, which meant hers disappeared up to the wrist inside his. "C.T."

"Thanks for coming by, Leon. Merry Christmas."

"Merry Christmas."

"Omigod, omigod!" T.J. shot to her feet, danced in place, and sprinted the short distance to where I sat. "This is the biggest check I've ever seen."

I held it up and shrugged. "Looks like it's the same size as the ones we use."

She punched me in the shoulder—considering how excited she was, it hurt. "Look at the amount."

I did. "Wow." I added my signature in the box on the back side. "Use the app to deposit it before a SWAT team comes to take it back."

She grabbed her phone, authenticated to the business' bank account, and took the required photos of the front and rear. "Done."

"Great. Can you get me the checkbook, please?"

"Why?" T.J. snickered. "Are you going to balance it?"

"What am I, ninety years old?"

She handed me the book and sat back at her desk. I couldn't remember the last time I actually wrote and signed a paper check. Probably grad school, so almost ten years ago. I wrote T.J.'s name on it, made it out for three thousand dollars, and signed it. I handed it to her, and her eyes almost popped from her head when she read it. "For me?"

"You deserve a Christmas bonus," I said.

T.J. shot to her feet and gave me a huge hug. She squeezed so tightly it almost hurt. I went with a lighter embrace in the hopes she would take the hint. She didn't. "Thank you," she said, her voice cracking. "Thank you for taking a chance on me when Melinda and I didn't know if anyone would."

"You've made the most of it."

After a few more seconds of difficult breathing, T.J. released her hold. "It means a lot to me." She wiped her eyes, put the check in her purse, and sat in her chair again.

"I hope it'll allow you to continue your gymnastics training," I said.

"Shouldn't you be taking the rest of the day off?"

I looked at my watch. "It's ten-thirty. Might as well pack it in."

———

I unwound at home for a while before calling the FBI field office.

Following a vigorous round of phone tag, I eventually got connected to Hess. "I suppose congratulations are in order," he said.

"Thanks." I wondered what became of the two women he

deployed to help the city deal with the ransomware fallout. Maybe they got lumped in with the rest of law enforcement in the mayor's speeches. "I'm calling about unfinished business."

"What do you mean?"

"Brubaker," I said.

"I dealt with him. What he did was terrible, and it should never have happened. He's suspended."

"Great. When he gets back, I'm sure he will have seen the error of his ways and always be a model representative of the FBI."

"The steps I take never seem to be enough for you," Hess said, and the edge in his voice came through the connection clearly. "What the hell else would you like me to do?"

"Nothing else you can do short of terminating his contract. I don't really care. It's all administrative bullshit, anyway. I still want a piece of him. He needs to know being a bully has consequences."

"He's feeling them right now."

"Not nearly enough."

"Do you expect me to hand you his information?" Hess said.

"You do realize I could get it in about five seconds, right? As I've demonstrated repeatedly, I don't need your help. I'm calling you as a courtesy. If your man still wants to meet me, he might be reporting for duty a little banged up. Whenever his suspension is over, at least."

Hess' sigh hissed in my ear. "Look . . . I know he went way beyond the pale. I'm sure you can take care of yourself, but Brubaker is no joke."

"We'll see how tough he is without his nightstick, badge, and the backing of the Bureau," I said.

The line went silent. "I tried talking you out of it," the

FBI man said. "It's your life, so do what you want with it. Here's the thing—I don't want you to call me and gloat if you get the better of Brubaker."

"Fine." I planned to do exactly this regardless of Hess' warning. The hell with him.

"And I don't want to hear you bitch and moan if he comes out on top."

"No worries there," I said. "Even Pontius Pilate didn't use this much soap when he washed his hands, by the way."

Hess gave me Brubaker's information, and I jotted it down. "For whatever it's worth," he added, "I'm sorry for what happened to you. If you pursue this, and he beats your ass, it's on you. No sympathy."

"Wouldn't expect any," I said and ended the call. I looked at the small piece of paper. Hess had a point—I could let the whole thing go. It would even be in the spirit of the season. If Brubaker were a capable fighter, he'd hold an even chance to come out the winner, and then I would need to explain something like a broken nose to my parents over Christmas dinner.

Dropping the matter meant letting a bully get away with what he did. Maybe he would learn the lesson of a suspension. I recalled the events. Brubaker took delight in cuffing me to the overhead pipes and leaving me virtually defenseless. He ignored everything I told him, and he enjoyed beating me with his nightstick when he held every advantage.

No. This man needed to get his ass kicked.

I picked up my phone and called the number.

CHAPTER 30

"WHAT THE HELL DO YOU WANT?" Brubaker grumbled when I told him who I was.

"To beat your ass for what you did to me."

"Good luck."

"And to teach you a lesson so you don't do it again."

"You want to fight me? Fine. It's your funeral."

"Time and place," I said.

He thought for a few seconds and then named an elementary school in northeast Baltimore which closed a few years ago. "Should be pretty remote."

"Come alone. No buddies. No weapons."

"Don't need either to beat you down again," he said. "Be there at nine o'clock."

"You got it," I said and broke the connection. I walked downstairs. My basement remained unfinished, and I stood two inches taller than the height of the ceiling. A heavy bag hung from a beam, and taking a proper stance required me to bend my knees. I strapped on a pair of MMA gloves and stretched for a couple minutes.

After getting shot last year, I developed a flinch. Any time a situation turned into a confrontation, I reacted as if someone threw a haymaker. It made actual fights difficult. Eventually, I got past it, but it took some time watching boxing matches and working things out on this bag. I couldn't afford a flinch against Brubaker. Even if I outclassed him in skill, he'd come in looking to knock my head off and kick it across the parking lot as soon as he could. I warmed up with a series of jabs.

Once my body felt loose, I worked in crosses and uppercuts. From there, I moved on to elbow strikes. I needed to find the balance between preparation and burning too much energy. Having jelly arms later would be a recipe for a beatdown. I stopped after about fifteen minutes, drank some water upstairs, and texted Gloria to let her know about my evening plans.

She replied. *I don't suppose I can talk you out of this?*

What do you think?

Be careful, then. Come here when it's over and let me take care of you.

I liked her idea. The fight with Brubaker probably wouldn't be a walk in the park, and there were worse fates in this world than letting a beautiful woman dote on you. As pleasant as those thoughts were, I tried to focus on the task at hand. I checked out the old school Brubaker mentioned using the power of Google Maps. How he knew about it would remain a mystery. Regardless, he picked a good venue. Houses in the vicinity were far enough away to retain privacy. The basketball court—the likely location for our scrum—was surrounded by a chain-link fence tall enough to make climbing a challenge.

When the time came, I drove to the school. The shape of the building and the outdoor amenities gave away its former life, but otherwise, there was no indication this was once a place of learning. All signage had long since been stripped away. A playground and overgrown Little League-sized base-ball diamond sat past the near side of the building. I parked at the opposite end close to an obnoxious pickup truck which must have been Brubaker's.

I picked my way along the building. Half the lights were out, and I couldn't put it past Brubaker to have an ambush planned. Nothing happened, however, and as I approached the outdoor basketball court, I saw him standing in the center. "Didn't think you would show," he called.

I lifted the latch, opened the gate, and closed it again after walking through. The asphalt was cracked in many places, and weeds made significant inroads. The lines and markings of the court faded to the point I could barely see any. Nets were long gone, and while the hoops remained, they sat at odd angles. Lights around the fenceline still worked, at least. "How the hell did you find this place?" I asked as I approached my waiting opponent.

"Did a bust here a year ago." He sneered. "Scared?"

"Don't you wish?"

"Sometimes . . . I get a little overzealous. I don't like terrorists, foreign or domestic, and I think your little band of hacker friends fit the bill."

"First of all," I said, "they're not my friends. I was working on the inside with the police. Second, if your word salad is supposed to be an apology, it's a shitty one."

Brubaker took a fighting stance. I did the same. "I ain't trying to kill anyone," he said. "Hope you think the same." I nodded. "Good. Someone gets knocked out, it's over."

"Fine. Same for tapping out in a hold."

He shrugged. "Fine with me." Brubaker stood about as tall as me. His arms looked a touch shorter and his legs a little longer. He was also stockier, built more like a lifter while I had more of a lacrosse player's physique. I expected to be behind in power but ahead on speed. He threw a quick jab, and I stepped to the side. Another met the same result. Brubaker didn't put a lot behind the punches. I figured he was gauging me.

Time to do the same to him.

I blocked his next punch, turned my body, and gave him a side kick to the midsection. It wouldn't count as my best, but it got him to back off a couple steps. It was only one attack, but I hoped it indicated a hole in his defense. Brubaker came forward again, and this time, he threw his punches for maximum effect. I blocked two up high and then got my elbow down in time to blunt the kick which followed. I snapped off one of my own, but Brubaker avoided it.

We circled each other again. Neither of us sweated in the crisp evening air. Brubaker wasn't yet breathing hard. "A little tougher when I can fight back, isn't it?" I said.

"Keep talking," he said.

"I'll be the only one who can when this is all over."

He took the bait and rushed me again. I turned aside a volley of punches and kicks. Brubaker showed surprising speed, pivoting off a blocked kick to hit me with a solid elbow in the side of the head. It gave me a moment of brain fog, and he took advantage. A hard right to the gut bent me in half, and Brubaker moved behind me and locked in a chokehold. I tried to pull his forearm down but couldn't get it to budge.

I had enough air for several seconds still but wanted to try something. Brubaker was a bully. He'd talk a good game about ending a fight and trying to be fair, but I didn't think he actually cared about any of it. When I couldn't move his arm, I tapped my hand on it three times. He didn't let go. I repeated the gesture. If anything, he cinched his grip in tighter.

In this hold, I would normally throw my head back and

try to slam a foe in the face. With my noggin still smarting from the elbow strike, I couldn't take the risk of ringing my own bell more soundly than his. Now, air became hard to get. I reached behind me with my left and grabbed a handful of Brubaker's hair. It helped me keep him in place for the two rights I threw behind me. After the second, I swung my arm down and hit him with an elbow somewhere in his midsection.

He released the hold and staggered back a step. I drilled him in the chest with a side kick, and he stumbled back more but didn't go down. I sucked in a deep breath and followed up. Before Brubaker could raise his hands, I walloped him with a stiff right cross, and he went down. He scrambled to all fours. I threw a knee at his face, but he blocked it and yanked my plant leg hard enough to send me toppling backwards. The asphalt provided no cushion as I slammed onto it.

I'd made a rookie mistake, and I was no rookie. Brubaker wobbled a little on his feet, so he couldn't capitalize right away. He tried to stomp on my head. I caught his foot in both hands and shoved it away with as much force as I could. He stumbled a few steps, and I got back to vertical. A breeze hit the sweat on my face and neck and almost made me shiver. Brubaker's breath sounded louder than at any time before. If he were getting tired, he would also soon get desperate and try to end things quickly.

Sure enough, he came at me again. I fell into a defensive rhythm and blocked all his punches. After turning aside a right cross, I hit him in the solar plexus with one of my own. He sucked wind and tried to back away, but I stayed on him. A side kick to the gut made him retreat more. He blocked my next two punches, but I got him with an elbow in the jaw, and he spun away and toppled to the blacktop.

As he made it back to a sitting position, I drove my right

knee into his face. His head bounced off the asphalt, and he shook it a few times. "Give up," I said.

Brubaker scrabbled rearward and got onto unsteady feet. "Screw you."

"Have it your way."

"I will," he said, and despite still struggling for breath, he launched another volley. I grabbed his arm after the fourth punch and flipped him onto his back with a loud thud. I raised my foot, driving my heel into his stomach and then kicking him in the face. His eyes swam, and I cinched in a wristlock. As Brubaker grunted in pain, I said, "If you want to tap out, I'll honor it. Unlike you."

"Fuck off," he spat.

I shrugged and gave him a stiff boot under the chin. This time, his head bouncing off the blacktop turned his lights out. I rummaged through his pants pockets and found a few zip ties. Of course. For all his talk about wanting an actual fight, Brubaker was still a bully. If he could've found a way to immobilize me and pummel me to death, he would've taken it. I dragged him to the nearest basket and used two zip ties— one to bind his right arm to the pole and the other to hold his left arm tight against his leg. He'd probably be able to get out of this predicament eventually, but it would take him a while, and maybe it would lead him to think about being a bully.

Either way, I was done with him. I got back into the S4 and drove away.

————

"Ow," I said, recoiling as Gloria fingered the knot forming on the side of my head. I lay in the center of her king bed. She brought some cotton balls and a bottle of peroxide. I didn't think she'd need to use any of it.

"Sorry." She frowned. "Looks like he got you pretty good. You sure you're all right?"

"I'll be fine."

"You don't have a concussion?"

"I'm not qualified to make such a diagnosis," I said.

"Maybe I should take you to see someone who is," my wife said.

"I've gotten my bell rung before." This did not reassure Gloria, whose brows furrowed further. "I know what it's like. This isn't it. He gave me a couple good hits, but I'll be all right."

"How's the other guy?"

"He's a bully. He got what he deserved."

"He's alive, right?"

"Of course," I said. "He's got one arm tied around a steel post and the other bound to his leg. Getting free might be a challenge." I shrugged. "*Sic semper probus.*"

Gloria checked my arms. Bruises began to form where I blocked many of Brubaker's attacks. A red mark encircled my neck from when he got me in the chokehold. "I was hoping I could dote on you a little more," she said.

"I won't stop you if you want to play nurse."

"Well." She ran her hand down my chest. "I'll need to check you out thoroughly. Don't want to have an injury you didn't know about."

"Of course not," I said.

She leaned down and kissed me. "It's a thorough battery of tests," she whispered a few inches from my face. Her hand reached my stomach and maintained its slow southward travel. "Could take a couple hours." She kissed me again. "You'll also need to stay overnight for observation. Probably have to re-evaluate you in the morning."

"I'm in your capable hands," I said.

Later, I fell into a fitful sleep. The bump on my head led me to toss and turn more than normal. At some point, Gloria grabbed me and pulled me close for the promised second round of thorough evaluation. When I woke up for good, light rimmed the blackout curtains covering the windows. I rubbed my eyes and checked my watch. Almost ten. Before I could put my phone down, it buzzed with a text from T.J. *Coming in today, boss?*

Gloria remained asleep, so I tapped out a reply. *Later. Dealt with Brubaker last night. Let's keep a light workload for a while. It'll be Christmas soon.*

My secretary promised to put up more decorations. I padded downstairs to get a pot of coffee started. After a night of inconsistent sleep, I might need an extra cup or two. I then chided myself for sounding like I was sixty years old. As the java finished, T.J. texted again. *Potential client wants to come in later. Sounds like she might have a big case.*

I rolled my eyes. After the week I'd lived through, I wanted only the easiest matters to resolve. *Tell her to come in after the first of the year, then. You and I are on light duty for the rest of the year. Make up whatever excuse you need.*

She told me she would. I poured myself a mug of coffee, and Gloria came downstairs. I fixed one for her, too. "You going to the office?" she asked after a few swigs.

"I'm not in any rush," I said. "It's been a long week."

"It has."

"Am I out of medical protocol?"

Gloria grinned. "Now that you're over thirty, I think you need another exam later."

"I might as well take the afternoon off, then."

END of Novel #13

C.T. Ferguson will return with a new adventure in 2023.

The corpse of a priest found in a Baltimore church courtyard sends C.T. down a dark path to find an unholy killer.
Preorder Concrete Angels today: https://books2read.com/concreteangels

THE END

AFTERWORD

Thanks for checking out this novel! I hope you enjoyed reading the book as much as I enjoyed writing it.

I write mysteries and thrillers with action, snark, and flawed heroes. If this sounds like something you like, you can check out my catalog below.

The C.T. Ferguson Crime Novels:

1. The Reluctant Detective
2. The Unknown Devil
3. The Workers of Iniquity
4. Already Guilty
5. Daughters and Sons
6. A March from Innocence
7. Inside Cut
8. The Next Girl
9. In the Blood
10. Right as Rain
11. Dead Cat Bounce
12. Don't Say Her Name

The John Tyler Action Thrillers

I release 3-4 new novels per year. For the most current list of books, please visit:

- www.tomfowlerwrites.com
- https://books2read.com/tomfowler

(**Note**: C.T. Ferguson appears in *White Lines*. John Tyler appears in *Don't Say Her Name*.)

While these are the suggested reading sequences, each novel is a standalone mystery or thriller, and the books can be enjoyed in whatever order you happen upon them.

Connect with me:

For the many ways of finding and reaching me online, please visit https://tomfowlerwrites.com/contact. I'm always happy to talk to readers.

This is a work of fiction. Characters and places are either fictitious or used in a fictitious manner.

"Self-publishing" is something of a misnomer. This book

would not have been possible without the contributions of many people.

- The great cover design team at 100 Covers.
- My editor extraordinaire, Chase Nottingham.
- David Smith, who helped make sure all my tech talk wasn't just a bunch of babble.
- My wonderful advance reader team, the Fell Street Irregulars.

www.ingramcontent.com/pod-product-compliance
Lightning Source LLC
Chambersburg PA
CBHW070900250626
47159CB00003B/1135